"Speaking of d
any more thou

Zack didn't answer immediately. "I had a short phone consultation with a family lawyer today. She didn't hold out a lot of hope for my custody suit, until I asked if a girlfriend would make a difference. Then she said it was a shame I didn't have a nice nurturing wife with a sterling reputation."

Rowan gave a wry smile. "Does a broken engagement damage my sterling reputation?"

"I doubt it. Although it happened so recently—"

"You and I have known each other since we were sixteen. If anyone questions our sudden decision, we can say that when we met again, that friendship caught fire and we fell in love."

"And we got married so quickly—"

"Because I love you and I love Becca, and you need me now."

He thought that over. "It almost sounds plausible."

Plausible. Right.

For a moment there Rowan had almost gotten carried away and believed her own story...

Dear Reader,

Have you ever had a well-meaning friend or relative who is always trying to push you in the direction they think you should go? Rowan's mother is like that. Rowan has always been a go-with-the-flow sort of person, but somehow not making waves has gotten her accidentally engaged to a man she doesn't want to marry. Rowan finds an excuse to run off to Alaska, but it still takes extreme action on her part before her mother will back off.

While I've never had a steamroller mom, I can identify with Rowan about avoiding conflict. As I've gotten older, though, I've learned when to go along and when to take a stand. Rowan's starting to learn that, too.

I hope you enjoy this latest visit to my home state of Alaska. If you like this story, please check out the other books in this Northern Lights series. You can find them all at bethcarpenterbooks.blogspot.com. While you're there, you can find my social media links and/or sign up for my newsletter, with book news, giveaways and recipes. I'd love to hear from you!

Happy reading!

Beth Carpenter

HEARTWARMING

An Alaskan Homecoming

—

Beth Carpenter

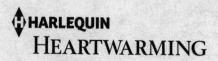

HEARTWARMING

HARLEQUIN®
HEARTWARMING™

PLEASE RECYCLE
THIS PRODUCT IS RECYCLABLE

Recycling programs
for this product may
not exist in your area.

ISBN-13: 978-1-335-17987-6

An Alaskan Homecoming

Copyright © 2021 by Lisa Deckert

This edition published by arrangement with Harlequin Books S.A.

For questions and comments about the quality of this book, please contact us at CustomerService@Harlequin.com.

Harlequin Enterprises ULC
22 Adelaide St. West, 40th Floor
Toronto, Ontario M5H 4E3, Canada
www.Harlequin.com

Printed in U.S.A.

Beth Carpenter is thankful for good books, a good dog, a good man and a dream job creating happily-ever-afters. She and her husband now split their time between Alaska and Arizona, where she occasionally encounters a moose in the yard or a scorpion in the basement. She prefers the moose.

Books by Beth Carpenter

Harlequin Heartwarming

A Northern Lights Novel

The Alaskan Catch
A Gift for Santa
Alaskan Hideaway
An Alaskan Proposal
Sweet Home Alaska
Alaskan Dreams
An Alaskan Family Christmas

Visit the Author Profile page
at Harlequin.com for more titles.

Dedicated to my neighbors, who make my world a better place.

Special thanks to my editor, Kathryn Lye, my agent, Barbara Rosenberg, and the art team at Harlequin for helping me share my love of Alaska with Harlequin Heartwarming readers.

CHAPTER ONE

"THE ONLY WAY to beat jet lag is to power through the first day." The voice belonged to Rowan's brother, Patrick, but the words were their mother's, quoted after every long-haul flight. Sadly, they'd proved true.

Rowan forced her eyes open to see Patrick and his wife, Lauren, peering in through the bedroom door. The door Rowan had left opened because when she lay down to rest for just a second, she'd never intended to fall asleep. "I'm awake."

Patrick immediately came to her bedside and passed her a yellow sticky note. "Call Mom."

"What's this?" Rowan squinted at the paper in her hand, which seemed to be a mishmash of numbers and letters.

"That's our Wi-Fi code. We don't get decent cell service on the farm, but if you'll put that code into your phone, it will work over the internet."

"I don't—"

"Call Mom," Patrick repeated. "She's already

called me, Lauren and Gran, and if you don't return her call immediately, the state troopers might be next."

Rowan sat up. "Sorry, I didn't mean to fall asleep. I'll help Gran unpack." After all, that's why she was here, in Alaska: to take care of Gran after her surgery Monday. Part of the reason, anyway.

"Bonnie's fine," Lauren told her. "She's already unpacked and right now she's beating all the contestants on a quiz show. You're the one who's been traveling for the last twenty-four hours."

Rowan yawned and picked up her phone. "What's the time difference for Tokyo?"

"Six hours earlier." Patrick gave a sympathetic smile. "But it's tomorrow."

"Right." You'd think, after growing up all over the world, Rowan would have mastered time zones, but her brain could never seem to wrap itself around the concept of flying east over the international date line and going back in time to yesterday. She did the math. "It's only six forty-five in the morning there. Mom's already called three times?"

Patrick's phone rang, and he glanced at the ID. "Four." He pocketed his phone. "She'll just keep calling, you know."

"I know."

"Once you're done, come on downstairs for lunch." Lauren took Patrick's hand and led him from the room.

Rowan opened the settings on her phone and punched in the code. How tempting it would be to stay unconnected and plead technical difficulties, but she wouldn't. The code did the trick, and two missed calls popped up on her screen. That made six. If it were anyone else, Rowan would be worried. For her mother, it was standard operating procedure.

She padded over to the window and pulled back the curtains, new since last autumn, when she came for Patrick and Lauren's wedding. She'd noticed several little updates to the old farmhouse on her way in. She wasn't sure how her new sister-in-law had found time for home decorating on top of supervising the building of a new milking barn, commercial cheese-making kitchen and tasting room, as well as managing a herd of milking goats and hiring employees, but somehow Lauren had managed to get Now and Forever Farms up and operating in less than a year.

The familiar view from the bedroom window overlooked green pastures and patches of cool forests. When Rowan was a child, the pastures had been dotted with black-and-white Holsteins. Now Lauren's beloved dairy goats grazed there, and the farm was once again alive with activity. Alaska had always been a special place for Rowan, a sanctuary away from the stress and expectations of the nomad life her family lived. And Gran and Grandy were always there, as solid as the mountains.

As Rowan watched, a trio of baby goats initiated a game of tag, running and ducking through the herd. One jumped onto his mother's back and gazed down at his pursuer. Rowan imagined he was chanting the goat equivalent of "nah, nah, nah, nah, nah."

Her phone chimed, signaling a text from Mom. Rowan sighed and dialed. Mom picked up on the second ring. "You said you'd call."

"My flight was delayed, and I missed my connection in Seattle, so I had to layover for several hours before I could catch another flight." Rowan put the phone on speaker and set it on the desk, leaving her hands free to unpack.

"You could have let me know you made it to Anchorage."

"It was the middle of the night. I didn't want to wake you." Rowan hung two shirts in the closet.

"You should have texted, then. I was worried."

"I'm fine. The phone wasn't working at the farm until Patrick gave me the Wi-Fi code just now. He brought me home from the airport. Didn't he tell you I'd arrived?"

"Yes, but I need to talk with you. Venues book up fast. We'll need to coordinate with the Tanakas to get an idea of the size of the guest list. I'll set up a lunch with Coralie." Sutton's mother had been Mom's sorority sister at William & Mary. "Did you and Sutton set a date before you left?"

"No." Rowan licked her lips and twisted the unfamiliar diamond ring back and forth on her finger. "He's so busy. He'll be in Palo Alto for another two weeks at least."

"Well, you need to get with his assistant to go over his calendar and carve out some time. We'll need at least nine months for planning. More if you don't get a move on. How do you feel about harps?"

"I don't—"

"Never mind. We can talk about music once we've chosen a venue. In the meantime, I've made a list of wedding gown designers, ranked by—"

"Mom, can we do this later? I need to finish unpacking and check on Gran." Rowan put some socks in a drawer and shut it with a little more force than necessary.

"I spoke with Bonnie fifteen minutes ago. Her surgery isn't until Monday. I wish she'd taken my advice to go to that top surgeon in Seattle, but she assures me it's a simple outpatient procedure. I don't understand why you felt the need to be there with her when you have so much you should be doing here. She has Patrick and Lauren."

"Patrick and Lauren have the farm to take care of, and Gran will need someone to take her to doctor's appointments and physical therapy."

"But your job—"

"I took a leave of absence. I need to go, Mom. I'll let you know once Sutton and I have had a chance to talk."

"Well, don't leave it too long. I'll email you this list of designers, although it would help if I knew the season—"

"As soon as I know, so will you. Bye, Mom." Rowan ended the call. How did she get herself into this situation? She twisted the diamond ring again, and then, with a decisive motion, pulled it from her finger and tucked it into the night-stand drawer.

The unmistakable scent of grilled cheese sandwiches drifted up the stairs, and Rowan's stomach reminded her she hadn't eaten much of the prefab dinner on the plane yesterday evening. The rest of the unpacking could wait.

She found everyone gathered in the kitchen. Gran ladled tomato soup into bowls, Patrick flipped a sandwich in a skillet and Lauren poured from a pitcher of iced tea. "Well?" Patrick scooped up a sandwich and slid it onto a plate.

"Done." Rowan smiled at Gran. "How are you feeling?"

"Fine and dandy. Looking forward to getting this scar tissue fixed. Did you have a nice nap?"

"Yes. Thanks." Once everyone had been served, Rowan bit into her sandwich. "So good. Is this the new white cheddar you told me about?" she asked Lauren.

"Yes. I'm really pleased with the texture. We've just finished our first experimental batch of feta, too. You'll have to try it later."

"I love feta. Patrick, remember those salads we got when we lived in Greece, with the big hunks of feta in the middle?"

"Do I. We ate them every chance we got. What's your go-to in Japan?"

"Yaki imo," Rowan answered without hesitation. "Stone-roasted sweet potatoes. In the fall and winter, there are these woodstove sweet potato trucks that drive around like ice cream trucks in the US. Delicious."

"Food trucks are getting to be a thing here, too," Lauren said. "They're all over in Anchorage, but not many in Palmer yet." Lauren looked at her watch. "Sorry to eat and run, but someone called in sick, and I need to fill in at the tasting room."

"Let me do it." Rowan finished the last bite of her sandwich and pushed back from the table. Thanks to her grandmother's generous gift, Rowan was officially a one-third owner of Now and Forever Farms dairy, but since she lived in Japan, she hadn't been able to contribute as much as she'd have liked.

"You're exhausted from flying all night."

"I'm fine, and Patrick's right. The only way to get through jet lag is to tough your way through the first day. Work will help keep me awake." She turned to Gran. "Unless you need me to stay with you."

"Of course not. My surgery isn't even until Monday, and it's minor." Gran gave her an appraising look. "In fact, up until now I was wondering why you decided to come all this way."

"Until now? What do you mean?"

Gran patted her hand. "Never mind. You go ahead and help Lauren in the tasting room. We'll talk later, and you can tell me all about that diamond ring you were wearing when you came in that isn't on your finger anymore."

"Let's try this once more." Moving slowly, Zack approached the downy yellow moose calf and waved a bottle of formula in front of his face. "Yummy stuff."

The calf butted his head against the bottle, almost knocking it from Zack's hand. He shifted his grip and tried again. "Come on, buddy. I know it's not as good as Mama's, but your mama isn't feeling up to nursing right now. Give it a try." He squirted a little formula onto his fingers and slid them into the calf's mouth.

Instinctively, the calf began to suck. Zack eased the nipple of the bottle in beside his fingers. Tasting the milk, the hungry calf sucked harder. Slowly, without disturbing the calf's rhythm, Zack retrieved his fingers.

"You got him to eat." Maggie poked her head around the corner of the stall. The calf eyed her but didn't stop sucking.

"Yeah. He wasn't too sure about this rubber nipple at first, but he's getting the hang of it. We'll just need to feed him formula until all the drugs are out of Mom's system."

Maggie watched in silence for a few seconds, but a worry line had formed between her eyebrows. "Speaking of formula, the feed bill is due."

Zack groaned. "I suppose the kitty is empty?"

"Jessie says the next grant check won't arrive until next Friday."

"Hmm." Zack mentally tallied up payments due on his mortgage, his portion of the vet clinic, his student loans and his truck, comparing that with the balance in his account. It would be close. "I'll write a check to the feed store."

"You have to stop doing that. You should be drawing a salary, not funding the wildlife rehab out of your own pocket."

"Says the woman working six days a week for free."

"I have the time. I'm retired, but you're not. WildER needs more sponsors. You know our grant is contingent on matching funds. If we don't raise more money by September, they'll reduce it next year."

Zack grimaced as he adjusted his grip on the bottle. He loved helping injured animals recover and return to the wild, but fundraising was not his strength. "Got any ideas?"

She eyed the calf. "Baby animals are always great human-interest stories for the news."

"Couldn't we just send out a newsletter or something?"

"Our mailing list isn't that big. We need new donors. And to get them, we need publicity."

Zack frowned. "I don't suppose you'd be willing to do the interview."

"Tom will want to hear it from the medical expert." She grinned. "Besides, your pretty face will bring in more money than mine."

"You're the former Miss Valley Potato Queen."

Maggie laughed. "That was fifty years and many pounds ago. No, you have to talk to him."

"Fine. Give him a call."

She smirked. "I already did. He can make it this afternoon, after the clinic closes."

Zack shook his head. "Why do I even bother to argue with you?"

"Apparently, you're a slow learner. I'll go check on Mama moose, make sure she's not waking up yet."

"Good. We'll want to get this fellow into the pen beside her before she does."

The shed door to the barn flew open with a bang and Ripley, Zack's Australian shepherd, galloped inside, two little girls right behind him. The moose calf dropped the nipple and cowered behind Zack.

"Becks, take the dog outside." Zack spoke more sharply than he intended. Becca's eyes widened, and he softened his voice. "He's frightening the moose."

"I'll get him." Maggie called Ripley to the door and smiled at the girls on her way out. "Hi, Becca. Hi, Charlotte. Go on in."

"Hi, Maggie." Becca waited until the door closed before she approached the stall, her head hanging low. "Sorry, Zack." Becca's lip trembled. "I didn't mean to scare him."

"I know. I'm not mad at you," Zack reassured

her. His eight-year-old half sister was a sensitive child. It was understandable, considering she'd recently lost her father, and never had much of a mother. He offered her a warm smile. "Moose smell dogs and think they're wolves, so it's better for everyone if we keep them apart." He held up the bottle again, and the moose latched on immediately. "See, he's fine now."

Becca's mouth relaxed, and then stretched into a full-fledged grin as she and her friend watched milk dribble from the sides of the calf's mouth as he suckled.

"He's so cute!" Charlotte gushed.

"He sure is. How was day camp today?"

"Fun. We hiked around the lake," Charlotte told him.

"Did you have fun, too, Becks?"

His sister only nodded, but she looked happy. Maybe he could pry some words from her at home, later.

Maggie returned, accompanied by Charlotte's mother, Jessie. "So, this is the adorable baby moose I've been hearing about."

Maggie shut the door behind her. "Mama moose is still out, but she's showing signs of waking soon."

"What's the baby's name?" Charlotte asked.

"We don't name animals we're not keeping,"

Becca told her. "Because they're not pets, they're wild."

A surge of pride filled Zack. Becca had been paying attention. And he liked the way she said "we." He'd been working hard to show her she had a place here with him. When his father was dying, Zack had promised him he'd care for Becca. The fact that Dad had been unconscious at the time made the promise no less important. The moose emptied the bottle and turned to bat long eyelashes at the girls. They cooed at him.

"You know," Maggie said slowly, giving Zack a little smirk, "a 'name the baby moose' contest could generate some extra buzz."

"I love it!" Jessie said. "I could set it up on the website, right next to a big donations button."

Zack quirked an eyebrow. "Really? After what Becca just said?"

Jessie laughed. "It's just for the website. You wouldn't have to tell the moose his name. As far as you're concerned, it can be a 'name the picture of the moose' contest."

Maggie rubbed her thumb and fingers together, reminding him of their funding shortage.

"Fine." Zack looked pointedly at Maggie. "But you have to explain it to the reporter."

"No prob."

"What reporter?" Jessie asked.

"My friend Tom Hackman said he'd do a story

about WildER," Maggie told her. "He's coming out to film late this afternoon."

"That's fantastic. In that case, I'd better get the contest up on the website right away. I'll get a picture to post." Jessie pulled out her phone and snapped a couple.

"Be sure to crop me out of it," Zack said.

"I know, I know." Jessie took another from a different angle and pocketed her phone. "Girls, we'd better let Zack and Maggie get back to work."

Zack glanced at his watch. "Yeah, I need to get this guy to his mother before she misses him, and then I have a date with a pug with blocked anal glands." Which would still be more fun to deal with than the interview. He walked everyone outside. Ripley waited beside the door and Zack ruffled his ears. "Becca, I'll pick you up at five thirty-five at Charlotte's." He'd learned that if he wasn't there specifically when he said he'd be, Becca worried.

She nodded, her eyes serious. "Bye, Zack."

"Bye, Becks. Thanks, Jessie. Oh, and could you drop Ripley in his yard on your way?"

"Sure. Come on, boy."

Once the girls and Jessie were out of sight, Zack carried the moose calf to the holding pen where his mother rested. Zack had used long poles to separate the calf from his mother so he wouldn't pester her to nurse. The moose's eyes twitched, and one of her legs moved. Zack and Maggie stepped upwind to wait. Soon the mother moose raised her head, looked around in confusion and pulled herself to her feet. Her first decision was to limp closer to the barrier and reach across to lick her calf.

Only when she'd reassured herself the calf was safe did she turn to sniff the rows of sutures that closed the wounds on her back leg. To Zack's relief, she didn't seem inclined to start tearing them out immediately. She went back to the baby and nuzzled him.

Zack smiled. "She looks good. Give her a few hours, and we can remove the poles and let the calf nurse. In a couple weeks, they should be good to go."

"Great. I'll call Tom and confirm that he still plans to bring out a crew to film you and the moose this evening." She looked him over. "You might want to change your shirt."

Zack looked down at the milk and moose drool staining his gray T-shirt. "I'll do that. Leave the feed bill with the receptionist at the clinic and I'll send in the check later."

"Thanks. And thank you for agreeing to the

news segment, Zack. I know how much you hate the limelight."

She was thanking him? Without Maggie's untold hours of volunteer work, WildER couldn't exist. Zack grinned at her. "I wouldn't do it for anyone but you."

CHAPTER TWO

"LET'S GET A shot here with the mountain in the background." Tom Hackman pointed to where he wanted the cameraman to stand while an assistant pinned a microphone to Zack's shirt.

Zack swallowed, mentally preparing for the interview. He'd worked with Tom before and knew he could count on Maggie's friend to make the experience as painless as possible, but he still dreaded the moment when the camera began rolling and he was expected to be articulate—or at least coherent—while he begged for money.

"We'll establish background for the rehab center, then we'll talk about the moose's story and what will happen to her. At the end, I'll ask how people can help support the center. Sound good?" Tom asked Zack.

"Yeah, thanks. We need to make it clear, though, that it's not a zoo. We're rehabilitating wild animals, and we can't have people wandering around."

"Of course."

"Maggie, where did we land on that name thing?" Zack asked.

"We're having a 'name the baby moose' contest on our website," Maggie told Tom. "It's all set up."

"Maggie can explain it better than I can. Maybe she should just do the whole interview," Zack suggested.

Tom grinned. "Nice try. Stand here. I want to get the interviews in the can, and then we'll get some video of the moose calf and some of the other animals. Yes, we'll use a long lens," he added when Zack started to object.

"Zack?" Becca's voice called from the direction of the clinic. Jessie had volunteered to drop Becca off at the wildlife center. "Where are you?"

"Over here, by Yeil's enclosure," he answered.

Upon hearing his name, the raven gave a loud "hello." Maybe this wasn't the best place for the interview.

"Jessie's coming in a minute, but Charlotte had to go to the bathroom—" Becca came trotting around the corner, but she jerked to a stop when she spotted the camera and strangers.

"Hello." Tom gave her a welcoming smile. "I'm Tom Hackman."

Becca circled around to stand close to Zack. Zack put an arm around her shoulders. "This is my sister, Becca. Becks, Tom and the camera people are going to take some pictures of the animals and show them on television."

"Cool." Her eyes grew wide.

"She's a cutie," Tom said and turned to Maggie. "Why don't we—"

"Becca won't be on camera," Zack stated. Immediately both Becca and Maggie turned to him, frowning.

"She's very knowledgeable about the animals," Maggie said. "She could show them Puddin and give her story."

Becca's expression turned pleading. "I could give Puddin a carrot and talk about how porcupines don't really shoot barbs and stuff."

"It's not a good idea." When it came to parenting, Zack was still getting his feet wet. He couldn't afford to make mistakes, especially public ones. If it came down to a custody battle, he couldn't have Becca's mother, Clarissa, saying he was exploiting Becca to further his own interests.

"Pleeeeease?"

"I'm sorry, but no."

Becca's lip trembled and he braced himself for tears. He hated when Becca cried. It made him want to bribe her with ice cream or ponies or whatever it took to put a smile on her face, but he knew he had to stand strong on this.

Maggie stepped in before the dam broke. "We can still help, Becca. You can give Puddin a carrot and get her set up for her shot. Like an animal trainer."

"Okay." Becca looked pleased at the idea. Zack flashed Maggie a thank-you.

"All right, then." Tom clapped his hands together. "Let's get this interview started."

"I LOVE THAT you chose traditional barn-red for all the new buildings," Rowan told Lauren as they walked toward the tasting room. "It really captures the pastoral feel you're going for. Very on-brand."

Lauren laughed. "I don't know much about brands. I just like red."

"The picnic pavilion out front is a great idea, too. Alaskans love to be outside in the summer."

"I just thought they'd want to see the goats."

Rowan smiled to herself. Lauren didn't need an advanced degree in marketing to sell her cheese. She loved her goats and loved making cheese, and her choices reflected her passion. She was exactly where she belonged.

Rowan wished she could find the same fulfillment in her own life. She'd studied international business because her parents had steered her in that direction, and their connections had led to her current job. She'd even met Sutton at a diplomatic function her parents had hosted. And there was nothing wrong, exactly, with any of those decisions. It was just when she saw how much Lauren loved the farm, or even how much Patrick enjoyed his job as an electrician on the North Slope, that she wondered why she didn't feel that same passion.

As they passed the corner of the tasting room, Rowan saw a dozen or so people milling around the pavilion. She checked her watch. "Looks like you already have some customers, and you don't even open for another fifteen minutes. I knew the tasting room would be a hit. Have many people signed up for goat yoga yet?"

"Both sessions filled within four days. We're still in kidding season, but I have a dozen or so early babies that are big enough to play with the yoga crowd." Lauren stopped in front of a side door and pulled out her keys.

Beside the entryway, a few daffodils were starting to open their yellow blooms, while the green tops of tulips and perennial flowers pushed their way through the mulch. Swelling buds on the rugosa roses and lilacs planted along a wire-lined split rail fence promised a lavish floral display in another month or so.

Snow still clung stubbornly in a few shady spots, but abundant sunshine had already coaxed the green from the grass in the open pasture nearby. Four goats pushed against the fence where the customers waited. One woman reached over to scratch a goat's forehead, and the goat closed her eyes in bliss.

Rowan followed Lauren inside, to find two women already in the kitchen area, slicing cheese and fruit. One, an athletic-looking blonde, appeared to be around college age, while the other woman was closer to Gran's.

"Everybody, this is Rowan. She's offered to fill in today."

"Hi," the older woman said. "I'm Violet Olson, and this is my granddaughter Amber. We usually work with Amber's mom, Gina, but her allergies are acting up this weekend, and nobody wants a sneezing waitress."

"I suppose not," Rowan agreed. "Just tell me what to do."

"You can wash up there." Violet nodded toward a sink. "And then get the dining area ready."

"Call me if you need me," Lauren said as she pushed through a door into the main cheese kitchen.

"Will do," Violet assured her. "Rowan, honey, can you make coffee? The supplies are under the counter in the dining room."

"Sure," Rowan pushed through the swinging doors into a dining room with wide-plank wooden floors, round tables and large windows overlooking the pavilion garden and the pasture beyond. A row of round stools lined a bar that separated the main area from a pass-through window.

As Rowan measured coffee into a filter, she could hear Amber whispering to her grandmother. "Rowan? Isn't she one of the bosses? Her name's on the business cards."

"She's Patrick's sister," Violet whispered back. "The one who lives in Japan. I heard she was coming to take care of Bonnie after her surgery."

"Isn't she, like, an ambassador or something?"

"No, that's her father, but Bonnie says she has an important job. 'Facilitating international business relations' or something like that."

Rowan smiled to herself as she filled a thermal pot with boiling water and set it beside a basket of tea bags. Dad did work at the embassy, although he wasn't an ambassador, and her job was far from important, but if she said anything, Violet and Amber might be embarrassed. It was easier just to go along. "Coffee's made," she called. "What else?"

Violet set a plate of sliced oranges on the shelf of the pass-through. "These go in the water dispenser."

"Thanks." Rowan lined the clear glass dispenser with orange slices and then filled it with ice and filtered glacial water from the tap behind the counter. Using the corner of her apron, she wiped a tiny smudge from the glass deli case displaying wheels of cheese to sell by the pound. Near the door, shelves of prepacked gift baskets and boxes filled the area around a cash register.

"It's time," Violet called. "You can open the doors."

As soon as Lauren turned the sign and lock, most of the guests outside surged in to inspect the menu on the chalkboard above the pass-through. "You have to try their cheese and apple plate," one woman was telling her friends. "Oh, look, they've got brie with honey and figs now. Ooh, which do I want?"

While they decided, Rowan took other orders, grateful for her experience waiting tables during college. "Three number ones, one four, one six," she called through the window.

"Are all these cheeses goat cheese?" a mom with two children asked as Rowan passed with a plate. "I thought goat cheese was soft."

"Now and Forever Farms does produce a soft goat cheese, but according to how the cheese is prepared and aged, goat milk can be made into most types of cheese. Lauren—she's the cheese-making genius around here—says goat cheeses tend to be a little softer and creamier than the corresponding cow cheese, so it's not good for, say, mozzarella, but it makes a wonderful Gouda. Sampler number five has the most different types of cheese."

"We'll share that, then."

More people pushed through the door, soon filling every table. Amber came out of the kitchen to help deliver orders to the picnic tables outside. At least half of the tasters stopped to buy bulk cheese to take home. A youngish woman frowned at the cheeses in the deli case.

"What can I help you with?" Rowan asked.

"My book club is meeting at my house this month, and they always have these impressive appetizers. I don't cook, like, at all. Is there something I can serve that's really easy but looks hard?"

"Absolutely." Rowan surveyed the cheeses. "You could do a fruit and cheese board. Or a log of soft cheese rolled in chopped figs, honey and toasted pecans. But if you really want to impress them with minimal work—"

"I do."

"Take one of these wheels of double-cream brie. The rind is edible, but for this recipe, cut the top rind off to expose the cheese underneath. Put it in a pretty baking dish or pie plate and spread a cup of jam on top. Bake it at three fifty for about thirty minutes. Serve it with a basket of crackers."

"What kind of jam?"

"That's the beauty of this recipe—anything works. If you like spicy, you could go with jalapeño jelly. Anything with berries is good, or you could do an Alaska theme with fireweed or rose hip jelly. We have some locally made jams in the gift section."

With Rowan's help, the customer chose raspberry jam and a box of multigrain crackers. "Can you write down the recipe for me?"

"Absolutely." Rowan scribbled down the instructions, added a business card and tucked both pieces of paper into the bag with the purchases. "Our email address is on there. Let us know how your book club likes the cheese."

"I will. Thanks!"

Another customer pressed forward. "I want some of that brie, too."

The rest of the afternoon passed with a steady stream of customers. By five o'clock, when Amber turned the sign and locked the door, all the brie wheels and a good portion of the other cheeses in the glass case had sold.

Rowan wiped down the tables and mopped the dining area while Amber and Violet set the kitchen to rights. Lauren came in from the main operation and asked, "How did it go?"

"Busy," Violet told her. "I'd guess almost

twice as many people as last week. Rowan was giving recipes for brie, and we sold out."

"Good, because we have a big stock, and it's aging quite nicely. I just started an experimental batch of Caprino Romano." Lauren grinned. "Of course, I won't know if it's a success until it's aged for a year."

"I don't know where you get the patience," Rowan answered. "I'm just glad people like you make the cheese, so people like me can use it in recipes."

Lauren checked her watch. "Oops, I'd better get to the milking barn. Thanks, everyone. Amber, please tell Gina I hope she feels better soon. See you next week."

Once they'd restocked and closed the tasting room, Rowan said goodbye to the Olsons and made her way to the farmhouse. When she checked her phone, she found an email from Mom with the list of wedding dress designers. Rowan sighed. How was she going to handle this?

She found Gran and Patrick in the living room, surrounded by boxes of photos. Gran moved a box to the coffee table to make room on the couch. "Paddy and I were looking for the pictures from that time we took your mother fishing. You remember?"

"I do." Rowan grinned. Gran and Grandy had

taken her and Patrick fishing many times, but only once had they convinced their mom to come along. She'd actually been a good sport about the mud, mosquitoes and mess in general, but the final trauma was more than she could bear. "It wasn't entirely her fault. Grandy did walk behind her unexpectedly."

Patrick chuckled. "Still, you'd think that the person with the fishhook stuck in his ear would be the one to faint, not the person who put it there."

"It wasn't the first time your grandfather ever got hooked, and I doubt it was the last." Gran had been the one to push the hook on through the ear and snip off the barb. "Come to think of it, he was ahead of his time. I saw a man the other day with five earrings in one ear. Maybe Tim should have left the fly there as a fashion statement."

Patrick laughed and stood. "I'd better start dinner."

"I'll help," Rowan said, returning the photo to a box.

Patrick and Gran exchanged a look that could only mean Rowan had been a topic of discussion between them. "I can handle it," Patrick said. "You and Gran talk."

Once he'd gone, Gran picked up a picture of seven-year-old Rowan, beaming ear to ear over a tray of chocolate chip cookies. "Remember how much fun we used to have in the kitchen together? We'd chop and measure, and you'd tell me everything that was going on in your life."

"I remember." The invitation was clear, but Rowan wasn't ready to share.

"We haven't had a good visit since you were here for Patrick and Lauren's wedding last fall."

"Sorry I haven't called more often."

"I'm sure your job keeps you busy. I feel bad taking you away from it."

"Don't. We've been slow lately, and they didn't mind giving me time off."

"If work isn't keeping you busy, then what? Socializing?"

"Some of that. Between rounding out numbers at the embassy for Mom and Dad, favors for friends and work connections, it seems like I'm constantly attending fancy parties." Including the large cocktail party where Sutton had unexpectedly called for everyone's attention, dropped to one knee and proposed marriage. "It's nice to be in Alaska. I didn't even pack any high heels."

"Well, I'm always glad of an excuse to have you here with me. Could you hand me the TV remote? I want to catch the weather forecast. See if we need to take our umbrellas Monday."

The newscast was in the middle of reporting the standings in the high school baseball tournament and then segued into weather, which looked to be clear through Monday with rain possible Monday night. Gran was about to turn it off when Rowan heard a familiar name mentioned.

"Wait. Let me watch that."

Gran backed up to the beginning of the segment, about a wildlife rehabilitation center not far away. It started out with a shot of a tawny moose calf cavorting around his mother inside a pen while the voiceover introduced the director, veterinarian Zack Vogel. Could it be the same boy Rowan remembered from years ago? After a moment, they cut to an interview, with the reporter standing next to a tall man with dark blond hair staring at the camera as though it might bite. The shot zoomed in.

Yes, she knew those eyes, hazel but with such a dark brown center it was hard to tell where the iris ended and the pupil began, that serious-looking mouth that occasionally would break into a devastating smile. But now Zack's face had more character, the angles sharper, the lines in his forehead deeper.

"You know Zack?" Gran asked.

Rowan nodded, listening to the interview.

"Don't moose usually give birth to twins?" the reporter asked.

"One is more common, but this moose had been spotted several times with two. We assume the other calf was taken by the same bear that injured the mother. Fortunately, this calf wasn't injured." Zack looked off to the side as though someone was giving him direction off camera. A forced smile crossed his face briefly.

"What will ultimately happen with the moose family?"

"We'll, uh, release them as soon as the cow's leg is healed enough for her to forage on her own." Zack's expression relaxed a little, but he still looked stiff. "Our goal is to keep wild animals wild. That's why we don't allow visitors."

The screen cut to a close-up of a porcupine, grunting happily while it chewed on a carrot. "What about this happy fellow?"

"This is Puddin. She came to WildER as a baby and never learned to forage in the wild, and so she'll be a permanent resident." Zack's voice was steadier now that the camera was focused on something else.

"So, if people would like to help support Puddin and the other wildlife here, they can donate at the web address on the screen?"

"Yes. Maggie Ziegler, one of our volunteers, is here to tell you about that," Zack hurried to say, obviously relieved to be done with his part of the interview.

"Maggie was head teller at the credit union until she retired," Gran commented.

In contrast to Zack, Maggie was born to be on camera. The white hair and smile lines around her eyes and mouth would put her in her sixties at least, although her energy level made her seem much younger. "You can see more photos and wildlife stories on our website, and you can enter a 'name the baby moose' contest there. The winner will receive a coupon for a large pizza courtesy of Patty's Pizzeria in Palmer."

"Thank you, Maggie." The screen cut to the website once again, and then to commercial.

"Poor man, looked like a long-tailed cat in a room full of rockers." Gran clicked off the television. "You can tell he cares a lot about that wildlife rehab center. Dr. Zack's a good vet— brave, too. He clipped Wilson's toenails for me last week."

"Brave?" Rowan laughed as she looked at the little dachshund snuggled in Gran's lap. "What does Wilson weigh, like ten pounds?"

"Thirteen. But he still has all his teeth and he does *not* like getting his nails cut." Wilson wagged his tail, confident that Gran wouldn't hold it against him. "How do you know Zack?"

"You remember that summer I stayed with you when I was sixteen and I hung out with Scarlett Mason and her friends? Zack was Scarlett's boyfriend for a while."

"Oh, that's right. Didn't talk much then, either, as I recall."

"Zack never liked to be the center of attention." Which suited Scarlett quite well, since she most definitely did. But it hadn't lasted long. Around midsummer, Scarlett moved on to the captain of the hockey team, but Zack had still been part of the group. Rowan sometimes caught him watching her and hoped he might ask her out, but if he was interested, he was too shy to say so. Still, she'd enjoyed their time together. "I should send a donation to the wildlife center."

"Even better, you should stop by and say hello."

Before Rowan could comment on that suggestion, Patrick stepped into the room. "Lauren called. There's a problem with the milking machine, so I'm heading to the barn to help."

Rowan jumped up. "I'll make dinner."

"Thanks." Patrick grabbed the jacket he'd left draped over the arm of the sofa. "All I've done so far is defrost some chicken breasts. Feel free to use whatever you can find in the fridge and pantry. Hopefully, the problem is something minor and we'll be done in about an hour."

"Sounds good."

"I'll help." Gran shifted, preparing to stand. "And we can talk about whatever is eating you."

"Honestly, I'm not at the talking stage yet,"

Rowan insisted. "Still at the mulling stage. And I do my best thinking while I cook."

"Fine. Go do your thinking. But once you've reached the point where you need a sounding board—"

"You'll be my first choice."

CHAPTER THREE

ROWAN FOUND THE chicken breasts and various vegetables, including some fresh asparagus, in the refrigerator, along with a complete selection of all the farm's cheeses. The freezer contained the remains of last summer's garden bounty. Rowan took out a bag of peas and grabbed fresh garlic and an onion from the basket in the pantry.

She started a pan of brown rice cooking while she diced the chicken breasts and sautéed them in olive oil, adding two cloves of minced fresh garlic at the last minute. She stirred, breathing in the steam, and she could feel the tension lifting from her shoulders. Did the scent of garlic have that effect on other people? Probably not, or someone would be selling garlic-scented candles and potpourris.

Next, she grated the cheeses: cheddar, Gouda and a smooth, buttery cheese she'd never seen before. It must be an advance sample. Rowan cut a small piece to taste before she added it to the mix. Nutty, tangy and oh so smooth—Lauren truly was a master cheesemaker. All three cheeses melted beautifully into a satiny sauce.

By the time she'd prepared all the vegetables, the rice was done. She mixed the chicken, shredded carrots, celery, peas, onions and mushrooms into the rice along with a nice medley of herbs, and then folded in the cheese sauce and spread the whole mixture in a casserole dish. A sprinkling of smoked paprika for color and flavor, and into the oven it went. She'd set aside a little of the Gouda to sprinkle on top later.

She washed the pans. Cooking had given her mind a nice break, but it hadn't changed anything. She was going to have to make a decision about Sutton and their sudden engagement. To be fair to Sutton, most people wouldn't call it sudden. They'd been dating for almost two years, after all.

The relationship seemed to work. They got along well. Sutton valued her organizational abilities, and he'd commented more than once how much he appreciated Rowan's undemanding personality. And she'd liked feeling useful.

But was *useful* enough? Did she love Sutton? She liked him. He worked hard, but also gave time and money to several charities. He was generous with servers and always polite to his colleagues. He treated his parents and hers with kindness and respect. And if he focused a little too much on his job, well, that's what made him so successful. She admired that.

But was it love? Rowan had always assumed that someday, she would meet the man of her dreams and would know, without hesitation, that this was the man she wanted to spend her life with. But here she was, well past thirty, and she'd never felt that thunderbolt. She'd been attracted to men. She'd dated quite a few. But she'd never felt the sort of connection she associated with love.

Maybe this was good enough. Maybe love—the sort of love they made movies about—was a myth. But Mom and Dad had it, that instinctive connection. At parties, Mom could be across the room with her back turned, but she would somehow sense when Dad needed rescuing from a conversation. When Mom would work herself into a tizzy over something, it took just a gentle squeeze on the shoulder from Dad to make her laugh at herself.

Patrick and Lauren seemed to have it, too, that almost magical connection. Maybe the problem was Rowan. Could it be that the same cautious amiability that allowed her to get along with all sorts of people also separated her from them? Commitment was a risk, and Rowan seldom took risks. Maybe this was as close to love as Rowan was capable of.

The timer chimed, driving away more unwelcome thoughts. Rowan removed the casserole dish just as she heard the back door open. Lauren's voice, laughing at something Patrick was saying. His answer was drowned out by the sound of running water as they washed up in the mudroom. There was a suspicious pause, long enough for an extended kiss, before Lauren stepped into the kitchen. "Something smells wonderful."

"You should know. It's your cheese that smells so good."

"I'll call Gran," Patrick said. "Thanks, Row."

"Did Patrick get the milking machine running?" Rowan asked Lauren as she brushed melted butter over steamed asparagus and transferred it to a serving dish.

"Yes. We'd somehow overloaded a circuit." Lauren filled water glasses.

Patrick ushered Gran into the kitchen. "I explained to your newest farmhand that he can't run an air compressor on the same circuit as the milking machines. At least not at the same time."

"Is this the teenager you hired?" Gran sat down and dished casserole and asparagus onto everyone's plates. "What was he doing with a compressor, anyway?"

"Airing up his spare tire." Lauren sighed. "He left a pitchfork lying outside and then managed to drive over it, which ruined his tire and didn't do the pitchfork any good, either. I didn't think about the outside plug being on the same circuit as the milkers."

"You know you're going to have to watch him closely," Gran advised her.

"Agreed, but today was his first day, after all." Lauren tasted the casserole. "Oh, Rowan, this is delicious. Violet said you were terrific at the tasting room today, even sharing recipes."

"I'm not sure pouring jam over brie and baking it is exactly a recipe."

"Sure, it is," Gran asserted. "You ought to make recipe cards using the different cheeses. And start with this casserole. It's the best I've ever tasted."

"That's a great idea!" Lauren said. "Bonnie's right. This is the best chicken casserole ever."

"That's because it's made with really good cheeses."

"Still, I love that mellow garlic flavor that sets off the tanginess of the cheese. You are an amazing chef."

Rowan laughed. "I'm hardly a chef. When I was a teenager, I considered culinary school, but Mom and Dad convinced me to major in business instead."

"Say, I saw something you might be interested in." Lauren reached for a magazine with a close-up of Swiss cheese on the cover. "The Cheesemakers Society is one of the sponsors of this recipe contest. The creators of the top six recipes win five thousand dollars and a chance to compete on television for the grand prize, which is a full scholarship to West Coast Culinary Institute in Portland, Oregon. You should enter this recipe."

"It's nothing special, just something I threw together. But sure, I can write it down along with a few other cheese recipes and we can make handouts for the tasting room."

Lauren took another bite and closed her eyes. "So good."

MONDAY AFTERNOON, Zack drove past the farmhouse at Now and Forever Farms to the wooden barn. According to his receptionist, Lauren needed help with a doe giving birth there.

"Lauren?" he called as he stepped into the barn, waiting for his eyes to adjust to the dim light.

An almost human bellow directed him toward the goat in labor even before Lauren answered. "Over here. I think it's a front-legs-back presentation."

Zack made his way to the stall. The goat lay against the wall, her eyes wide. She cried out again, the tip of the kid's nose visible as she strained, but as soon as her contraction eased, the kid slipped inside once again. The doe moaned. She was beginning to get that defeated look Zack dreaded.

"Let me check it out." Zack pulled on sterile overalls and gloves. Lauren stepped out of the way so he could do his examination. "Yes, the legs are back. I'll see if I can catch a hoof." The goat shifted as another contraction began. Zack waited, knowing he'd have to work fast to get the feet repositioned between contractions.

Lauren went to rub the goat's head. "I know, Fudge. It hurts. But just as soon as Dr. Zack re-arranges things, you'll be fine."

Zack hoped so. This felt like a big kid, and space was tight. If he couldn't reach the feet, he'd have to take the goat back to the clinic for an emergency C-section, and he wasn't sure Fudge had that kind of time.

The contraction tapered off, and Zack eased a finger into place. His hand slid past a tiny shoulder... And there it was, a hoof. He caught the hoof and pulled it forward next to the kid's face, which created a little more room. He'd just snagged the other leg when another contraction hit. Refusing to lose his progress, he rode it out, gritting his teeth. As soon as he could move his finger, he looped it behind the leg and worked it into position.

He stepped back, flexing his cramped hand. "That should help. It's up to you now, Fudge."

Almost as though she understood, the goat rolled to her feet and paced in a circle before she lay down again. When the next contraction hit, the head and two tiny feet appeared and then, with a groan, the doe pushed the kid out onto the clean straw.

He was big for a newborn. Between that and his position, it was no wonder the young doe had needed help. Once the first kid was out of the way, it didn't take long for a second one to come, and then, with minimal fuss, a third. Neither was as big as their troublesome brother.

"Lauren?" a female voice called from the doorway. "Patrick said one of your goats was having trouble. Is there anything I can do?"

"It's all good now. Zack worked his magic, and we have three new kids. How was Bonnie's surgery?"

"The doctor said she breezed through it and everything looks good. Her friend Molly stopped by, so she's with her at the house now. Patrick said to tell you the new hand didn't show but he's got everything covered at the milking barn."

"Oh, good. Come see the new babies. Zack, meet Patrick's sister, Rowan."

Rowan? Zack, who had been in the process of stripping off his gloves and overalls, looked up. He'd known only one Rowan, one summer when he was a teenager, and he'd never forgotten her. Her hair had been long then, almost to her waist. Brown hair, but with copper-colored threads that caught the sunlight. Blue-gray eyes, magnified by glasses, that seemed to see deeper than the surface.

He recognized the curve of her smile. It really was her. He'd spent weeks that summer working up the courage to ask her out, but before he could, she'd gone. Back to school in Europe somewhere, according to Scarlett. Now her hair brushed against her shoulders in soft waves. There wasn't enough light in the barn to tell if her eyes were still the same shade of blue, but a tentative smile revealed a familiar dimple in her left cheek. "Zack and I knew each other, a long time ago. I'm not sure if you remember?"

"Absolutely." He felt his own mouth stretching into a grin. "Rowan, it's good to see you. No more glasses?"

"Laser surgery."

"You're here visiting your family?"

"Taking care of my grandmother for a few days." She came closer to look into the stall. "Aw, the baby goats are so cute. Look at that."

Zack watched the first kid teeter on shaky legs and find his way to a teat. Lauren was rubbing the other two kids dry while Fudge watched.

The goat already looked stronger. Zack smiled. "They'll be fine now."

"I love a happy ending," Lauren said, as she guided the other two kids toward their mother.

"Me, too," Zack admitted.

Rowan tilted her head. "Speaking of happy endings, I saw your segment on the news. You run a wildlife rehabilitation center?"

"It sounds grander than it is. We have a bit of land behind the vet clinic, and my partner, Christine, agreed I could use it for wildlife rehab."

"Your moose calf is adorable. Does he have a name yet?"

"I don't know." Zack shook his head. "Jessie, the volunteer who does all our web stuff, is handling that. I don't believe in naming animals we'll be releasing in the wild, but I was overruled."

"It's a cute hook for a fundraiser. Getting attention is half the battle of marketing, you know."

"I guess. I really hate the promo part of the job."

Rowan looked amused. "The moose calf is irresistible. And the volunteer with white hair—Maggie, right? She's a natural in front of the camera."

"See, I need you to tell her that. She insists I do interviews, when she's so good and I'm just plain awful."

"You're not awful. You're just—"

"Bad?"

"Untutored. Public speaking is a skill, just like, oh I don't know, delivering baby goats."

"You do much public speaking?"

"I'm more of a background person. But I do coach public speakers."

"Is that what you do for a living?"

"It's a small part of my job. I'm with a marketing consultant firm. We facilitate partnerships and connections between overseas businesses and those in Japan. Sort of like a matchmaking service for business."

"Wow."

"It sounds grander than it is." That dimple on Rowan's cheek deepened as she repeated his words. "Do you have time to stop by the house for a cup of coffee once you're done here?"

"Sorry, I don't." He wanted to. He really, really wanted to spend some time with Rowan, to see what kind of woman the girl he knew had become. But he did have two more calls to make today. "If you like, you could stop by and I'll give you a tour of the wildlife center one evening."

"I thought the public wasn't allowed."

"You're not the public. You're a friend." Zack fished in his pockets until he found a dog-eared business card. "Here's my cell." He scribbled his personal number on the back. "Just call when you have time, and we'll set something up."

"I'll look forward to it."

"Good." Zack paused, watching the smile spread across Rowan's face until he realized he was staring. "Well, I'd better get to my next appointment."

"Thanks, Zack, for coming so quickly," Lauren said.

"Glad it all worked out." He patted the mama goat on the rump. "You take good care of those kids, now, Fudge."

Rowan walked him out. "Can't wait to see your wildlife center."

"Like I said, it's nothing grand."

"Still, I'm excited." She reached up to dust a piece of straw from his hair. "I'll call you soon."

"I look forward to it." Zack put the truck into gear and waved as he drove off, and he realized that, for once, the polite phrase he'd uttered was the absolute truth. He was looking forward to it, more than he'd looked forward to anything in a long time.

CHAPTER FOUR

"CAN I HAVE ice cream? Please?" Clearly ice cream was the only thing on earth that would make Becca's life worth living.

Zack checked her plate. "What about those peas?"

"I don't like peas."

"Sure, you do. It's beans you don't like." Or at least last week it had been.

Becca used her fork to push a few peas around her plate while she wrinkled her nose.

"At least taste them. Vegetables are good for you." When she looked askance at his plate, Zack made a show of scooping up a big forkful of peas and popping them into his mouth. "Mmm, healthy." Mushy canned peas weren't his favorite, either, but they were quick.

Becca put one pea in her mouth and made a horrible face. "Can I have carrots as my vegetable?"

"Fine." Zack pulled a couple baby carrots from the refrigerator and set them on her plate. He probably should have just done that in the first place. His mother had always maintained a hard-and-fast rule about a clean plate before dessert, but some of the advice he read online said making too big a deal of it discouraged healthy eating habits. This parenting thing seemed fraught with conflicting advice.

Becca nibbled on the first carrot. "Do I have to eat them both before I can have dessert?"

"Yes." He would at least stick to that. "So, did anything interesting happen at camp today?"

She shrugged.

"Did you get to go out on the paddleboats?" That was listed on the activity calendar the camp sent home every week.

"Yeah." Her face brightened. "We saw a beaver."

"A beaver? Tell me about it."

"Charlotte and me drove our boat over to see some ducks, and a beaver swam by with a stick in his mouth. Charlotte wanted to go closer, but I said not to scare him."

"Good for you."

"Then the counselor said we had to go back with the others, so we couldn't watch anymore." She finished the last carrot.

"That's great, though, that you saw him." Zack opened the freezer. "Peanut butter and chocolate, or caramel swirl?"

"Peanut butter." She watched him spoon ice cream into a bowl. "Is the moose better?"

"She is. We'll probably be able to release her and the calf next week."

"Jessie says Charlotte and me get to pick the name for the baby moose tomorrow, from all the ones people wrote. Can I see the baby moose again before he goes?"

"Sure. You want to come tomorrow?"

"Can I help feed?"

"Absolutely." Zack set the ice cream in front of her.

A blissful smile crossed her face. He wasn't sure if it was the ice cream or the chance to see the animals, but it was good to see her happy.

After dinner he nudged her through the bath and toothbrushing routine. She dressed Zuma, her beloved stuffed animal, in red pajamas. Dad used to find it amusing to buy Zuma outfits designed for Chihuahuas. As a result, Becca's toy probably had a bigger wardrobe than Zack did. With Zuma on one side of her and Fluff, their rescue cat, on the other, Becca snuggled into bed. They read three chapters together before she was almost asleep. He kissed her forehead. "Good night, Becca. Sweet dreams."

"Night, Zack."

Downstairs, Zack measured out Ripley's kibble and dumped Becca's uneaten peas into the dog's bowl before setting it on the floor. "You've gotten a little more variety in your diet since Becca came to stay, huh, Ripley?"

The dog wagged his tail. He might have gotten a few bits of Becca's hot dog under the table as well, but if so, he wasn't talking. Zack's cell phone rang. He frowned. He wasn't on call, unless it was an emergency at the wildlife center. If it was, he'd have to wake Becca and take her to Jessie's.

He pulled the phone from his pocket, checked caller ID and braced himself. "Hello, Clarissa. How's the weather in the Caribbean?"

"Fine, I guess." She gave a soap-opera-worthy sigh. "It's hard, you know. Being alone."

Judging from the music and laughter he could hear pulsing in the background, she wasn't exactly alone. Not like Dad would have been when he died if one of the nurses hadn't called Zack. Zack made it to Dad's bedside when he woke briefly and tried to speak, but before he could form the words, he'd slipped away. Clarissa never had explained why she'd called the ambulance but not come to the hospital. But that was water under the bridge. "I've already tucked Becca into bed, but she might not be asleep yet," Zack told Clarissa.

"Don't wake her. I need to talk to you. The hotel says there's a problem with my credit card.

I just can't deal with this right now, and with the money tied up in the estate… It's too much. Can you check it out?"

"Yeah, okay." As executor of his father's estate, Zack had the authority to do that. And as someone who cared about Becca, he had a vested interest in keeping Clarissa relatively content until he could figure out the best way to help his sister. "Which card is it?" He wrote down the information she gave him. "I'll call tomorrow."

"First thing, okay? The hotel is being difficult."

"All right, first thing. Was there anything that would have flagged the system? Unusual charges, maybe?"

"No. Well, my spa bill might have been a little higher than usual." A male voice in the background called her name. She hissed that she'd just be a sec.

"But the spa charges are legit?"

"Yeah. It's just a facial, seaweed wrap and a hot-stone massage. I've been so tense. You know how it is."

"Sure. I'll let you know what I find out tomorrow."

"Thanks. Um…" She hesitated briefly, "Any word on when the estate will be settled?"

"The lawyer says it takes time." Especially

when documents were missing. "I'll let you know what I find out about the credit card."

"Okay."

"Becca's doing fine." Not that she'd asked.

"That's good. You'll call the hotel tomorrow once you get the card straightened out?"

Well, her priorities were clear. "You didn't give me the name of the hotel."

"It's the Anguilla Transcontinental. Here's the number."

He wrote that down, as well. "Okay. I'll let you know. Good night, Clarissa."

"Bye, Zack. Thank you." She hung up, but not before he heard a soft giggle.

Just what he needed: a couple of hours of phone calls cleaning up Clarissa's financial messes. But he had been appointed executor of Dad's estate, based on a will written long before Dad married Clarissa, which, ironically, meant she was entitled to a bigger share of the estate than she would have been if Zack had been able to locate a will written after Becca was born. There should have been one in his father's office safe where he insisted on keeping all his important documents, but if it existed, it, along with the prenup Clarissa signed before the marriage, had mysteriously vanished.

Zack added the task to the calendar on his phone. It was his turn to drive Becca and Charlotte to camp tomorrow, followed by three surgeries in the morning. Which meant he'd better set his alarm two hours early so he could handle Clarissa's "difficulty." Zack rubbed his temples where a headache was beginning to take root. Maybe he should look into a hot-stone massage. Whatever that was.

"Look, Maisy, your mom is here." Zack handed over the boxer's leash. "Bring her back in ten days to have those stitches out. Karen will give you a sheet on aftercare, and you can call if you have questions."

"How long should we keep the cone on?"

"The same, ten days. Maisy will try to convince you it's not necessary, but when it comes to these matters, she is not to be trusted." As the dog moved forward, the plastic cone bumped against the receptionist's desk, knocking her off balance. She sent Zack a look of reproach as though she knew he was responsible. He laughed. "She's still a little wonky, but she'll be fine soon."

"Thanks, Dr. Vogel."

Maisy was Zack's last patient of the day. Zack yawned as he updated her chart. "Hey, Karen, is there any coffee left back there?"

She rocked back to look toward the coffee station behind her work area. "None fit to drink.

There's a half inch of road tar in the bottom of the pot."

"Desperate times." Zack pushed through the exam room door and circled around toward the coffeepot.

"Ew, don't drink that," Karen insisted. "If you're that hard up, I'll make a fresh pot."

"No time." Zack poured the dark stuff into his travel mug. "I have to pick up Becca. I'll be back in half an hour." He tried a sip, grimaced at the bitterness and started out the door.

Becca and Charlotte waited at the parent pickup area, something colorful hanging from their hands. When he reached the front of the line, a counselor helped them climb into the back seat and buckle in.

When they stopped at a traffic light, Zack looked over his shoulder to ask, "What have you got there?"

"We made—what are they called?" Charlotte asked Becca.

"Lanyards," Becca supplied. "Like necklaces with a hook on the end."

"Yeah, lanyards. Mine's blue and pink, and Becca's is red and gray."

"Nice. Crimson and gray are school colors where I went to college and vet school."

Becca held her lanyard up where he could see it. "I made it for you."

"Wow, it's beautiful. Thanks, Becks." Zack wasn't sure what he was going to do with a lanyard, but he would find a use for it.

When he pulled up in front of Charlotte's house, Jessie stepped outside to meet them. "Hi, guys. Zack, donations are up about twenty percent since you did that television appearance."

"I don't suppose it's enough to qualify for the next year's matching grant."

Jessie shook her head. "Not even close. It helps, but at the official board meeting next Saturday, we're going to have to figure out a major fundraiser."

"I figured." Their quarterly meetings consisted of Jessie, her husband, Greg, Maggie, and him meeting for breakfast at the local diner. Maybe one of them would come up with a brilliant plan between now and Saturday. "I'll tell Maggie."

"Do that. Thanks for driving today."

"No problem. See you."

Becca waved goodbye as they pulled away. Zack turned his truck toward the clinic. "I have a little more paperwork to do and then we'll go to the wildlife center, okay?"

"I'm kinda hungry."

"We can stop off at home for a snack." Zack tried to remember if they had any fresh fruit left. He should have gone shopping a couple of days ago, but he hadn't found the time. As it was, dinner would be something involving a can of tuna.

The time he'd spent on hold this morning trying to get Clarissa's mess straightened up didn't help. As he'd expected, they'd locked the card because of an unusual pattern of charges and Clarissa hadn't bothered to answer the text alert they'd sent. At least it was good to know that spa charges totaling more than twelve hundred dollars were unusual enough to merit an exception. Something about a twenty-four-carat facial? Zack didn't even want to know what that was. Dad and Clarissa had done a fair amount of traveling, but Zack was reasonably sure they hadn't traveled in the style reflected on Clarissa's credit card. Dad was a successful investor, but he hadn't been rock-star wealthy.

When they arrived home, Zack took a minute to admire Becca's lanyard crafted from colored plastic laces and beads. "Wow, you made this? I'm so impressed."

Becca beamed. "You can put your keys on it and never lose them."

"What a great idea." He transferred the wildlife center key from a peg on the wall to the clip and hung it around his neck before checking the pantry. No apples or oranges left. "How about peanut butter on…celery?" They did have celery, didn't they?

"Okay."

He spread peanut butter on slightly limp celery stalks for Becca. While he was at it, he made a couple for himself and spread peanut butter in a hollow rubber bone for Ripley.

"Can I take a carrot for Puddin?"

"Sure." Zack packed Becca's celery in a plastic dish and together they walked next door to the clinic, leaving Ripley to lick the peanut butter out of his toy. Karen and the rest of the staff had gone home. Becca ate her snack and then entertained herself with the building toy Zack had set up in his office while he made his notes on that day's patients.

As he finished, his phone rang. Not a number he recognized. "Hello?"

"Zack, hi, it's Rowan."

"Oh, hi, Rowan." It had been two days and he'd concluded Rowan wasn't going to call. He took the phone away from his mouth and whispered, "Let's get those blocks put away, Becks, and we'll go see what Puddin is up to." He walked a few steps away. "How's your grandmother?"

"She's doing well. She's back in her place in the senior apartments, and they're having a big bridge tournament tonight, so she sent me away. I was wondering if this is a good time to see the wildlife center."

"Now?" If he'd known she was coming today, he would have spruced up a little. If he'd had a moment to spruce up, that is.

"Whenever it's convenient. You said evenings, but—"

"No, no. Now's fine. I was just about to head over there, as a matter of fact. The center is just behind the vet clinic. Do you know where that is?"

"Yes, I'm in the parking lot right now."

Well, all right. "I'm inside. I'll let you in." He hung up and turned to Becca. "Wait here. I'll be just a sec." On the way to the front door, he caught sight of his reflection in the window looking into a now-darkened exam room and paused to run his fingers through his hair and straighten his T-shirt. He considered removing the plastic lanyard, but that might hurt Becca's feelings. He opened the door to see Rowan getting out of an old jeep, probably a spare car someone in the family kept around. "Hey, there."

"Hi." Rowan's hair was tied back today, but soft wisps curled around her face. Her smile was like a beam of sunshine, warming his skin. "Good to see you again. Oh, hello," she said as she looked past him. Zack turned to find Becca peering around him. "I'm Rowan."

"Rowan, this is my sister, Becca." He rested

his hand on Becca's shoulder. "Rowan and I knew each other a long time ago."

"Hello." Becca acknowledged Rowan but then frowned at Zack. "When are we going to the wildlife center?"

"Right now." Zack shepherded her out the door and led them toward the gate behind the clinic. "Rowan's coming, too."

Becca eyed Rowan suspiciously. "I thought just us and volunteers were allowed." Becca was a stickler for rules. "You said to the TV people—"

"It's okay. Rowan is considering becoming a volunteer like Jessie and Maggie, right Rowan?" He caught her eye, sending her a silent plea to play along. It was easier than explaining why Rowan was an exception.

"Sure." Rowan seemed a little surprised, but she didn't contradict him. When Zack removed his new lanyard from his neck to unlock the gate, Rowan smiled. "I remember making those at camp when I was a kid."

"I made this one," Becca told her. "I go to camp, too."

"Did you pick out the colors yourself?"

"Yes. They're Zack's favorites."

"Wow. Zack is so lucky to have a sister as thoughtful as you."

Becca beamed. As soon as Zack opened the

gate, she grabbed Rowan's hand and tugged her forward. "Do you want to see the baby moose? He's really cute."

"I do! I saw him on television."

"I have to have an adult with me to look at the moose. That's the rule. And we can't get too close, because they're wild and they shouldn't get used to people."

"I see." Rowan flashed a smile at Zack before following Becca.

He came up beside her on the trail. "As you can tell, Becca is really into rules," he said in a low voice. "That's why I told her you were thinking of volunteering. It was easier than explaining."

She nodded. "Gotcha."

Becca led them up the hill so that they could overlook the pen where the moose was convalescing. She had her head down, munching on the alfalfa Maggie had left. Zack lifted his binoculars and focused on her leg. The stitches were holding, with no sign of infection. So far, so good. He let the binoculars dangle from their strap.

The fuzzy calf also had his head down and seemed to be sniffing something. Suddenly he jumped backward. His mother stopped to look at him before going back to her hay. He tilted his head as if to get a different angle and slowly reached forward to sniff again, only to startle away.

Zack focused his binoculars and laughed. "He found a frog, and he doesn't know what to do with it."

Becca and Rowan laughed, too, as they watched the calf follow the frog until it escaped under the fence.

Rowan gave a happy sigh. "He's adorable."

"His name's Pattycake. The wild animals don't usually get names, because they're not staying, but Jessie put his picture on the website and people gave their ideas. Charlotte and me got to choose the best one. Charlotte is my best friend. We go to camp together. She made a lanyard, too, but hers is blue and pink. Do you want to see Puddin? She's a porcupine."

"Sure." Rowan kept pace as Becca tugged on her hand. "Why is she called Puddin?"

"Because she's sweet," Becca explained. "She was real sick when she was a baby, and Zack made her all better. He's an animal doctor. But she was so little when she came, Zack and Maggie had to feed her with a bottle and now she thinks people are her mother, and so she can't ever go out and be wild again." Becca raised the small gate to Puddin's pen, and the porcupine came running down the ramp, grunting happily. Becca pulled the carrot from her pocket and broke off a piece. Puddin sat up, squealing with excitement until Becca handed over the carrot.

"Look how she's holding it in her little paws," Rowan exclaimed. "That's so cute."

"You want to give her some?" Becca asked, offering Rowan the other half.

"I'd love that. Thank you. Now, what do I need to do? I know I can't get too close to her quills."

"Just hold it like this." Becca demonstrated, and then watched as Puddin took the carrot from Rowan's hand. Zack wasn't sure which of them was more delighted.

He opened the main door and stepped inside to clean the pen and check that the automatic waterer was working. According to the chart on the wall, Maggie had already fed Puddin. He'd seen her car in the parking lot, so she was still around somewhere.

"Wanna go see the otters?" Becca asked Rowan.

"Definitely." Rowan followed Becca along the trail, listening to her spiel on otters. Zack wasn't sure he'd ever heard Becca put so many sentences together at once.

Rowan looked back at the porcupine, who was following on Becca's heels. "Does Puddin need to go back in her pen first?"

"She's okay if she's with you," Zack said.

"You're not coming?"

"I'll clean out this pen. Remember, Becca, stay away from the moose and foxes."

"I know. Come on, Rowan. I hope the otters are out."

He chuckled at the sight of the three of them walking single file on the trail: his sister, the porcupine and then Rowan following along as though this was an everyday occurrence. Rowan was adaptable; he'd give her that. It probably came from all that moving she'd done as a child.

Having left the state of Alaska only a dozen or so times before he reached sixteen, Zack had been fascinated by the little bits of commentary Rowan would drop about places like Greece or Denmark. Not that she'd talked much about herself. But Scarlett, the girl he'd dated for a few weeks that summer, had been to Paris with an aunt the year before, and she liked to bring up Rowan's international background as a segue to talking about her own trip. Rowan never seemed to mind. She'd listened repeatedly to Scarlett tell the same story about almost dropping her camera from the Eiffel Tower, and she always laughed at the punch line.

It was no wonder everyone in their group liked having Rowan around. She had a smile for everyone, and she listened as though the speaker was the most fascinating person she'd ever met. She was pretty, too, with her long chestnut hair and bright eyes behind her glasses. He'd kicked himself a hundred times for never asking her out.

Could this be a second chance? He had noted that Rowan wore a dainty silver ring on her right hand and none on her left. They could go out to dinner or something. If she was interested. And if he could find the time. And a babysitter. He sighed. Or he could face reality and admit there was no room in his life for dating. Even if it was his teenage crush.

He'd just finished the pen when he heard them on their way back, laughing. Even Puddin seemed to be chortling. When Rowan spotted him, she waved. "The otters are adorable. And you didn't tell me you had a talking raven."

"I'm not sure 'hello' counts as talking."

"Sure, it does." Maggie had come up the trail from the other direction. "Hi, Becca. Who's your friend?"

"Her name's Rowan," Becca told her. "And she's going to volunteer, like you."

"Today, she's just taking the tour," Zack was quick to say. "Rowan O'Shea, this is Maggie Ziegler. She pretty much keeps this place from falling apart."

"Hello, Maggie." Rowan stepped forward to shake the older woman's hand. "I saw you on the news. Great job."

"Thank you. Are you considering—"

"Oh, and Jessie said to tell you donations are up, and to remind you of the meeting Saturday," Zack interrupted before Maggie cornered Rowan about volunteering.

"Up how much?"

"Twenty percent."

"That's good, but it's still not enough. We're going to have to do a real fundraiser this summer to raise enough by September."

"Any ideas?" Zack was resigned that they had to do it, but he had no idea how to start.

"Have you considered an auction?" Rowan asked. "You can usually get local merchants to donate prizes for good causes."

"I don't know." Would they donate more than a coupon for a free pizza? And if they did, how could the small volunteer staff handle the logistics? "Like an auction on our website?"

"You'd like that." Maggie laughed. "If we're going to raise big money, it needs to be an event, with a party atmosphere. They'll see their friends bidding and their competitive streaks will kick in. Maybe we could have a dinner or something."

"Or a food tasting," Rowan suggested. "I'll bet Now and Forever farms would donate the cheese. And there are probably other artisan bakers and food venders who would be interested, too. It would be a good marketing opportunity."

"Are you in marketing?" Maggie asked.

"Yes. I'm doing business to business now, but I've done some public relations work and fund-raising in the past."

"I don't suppose you'd be interested—" Maggie began.

Zack didn't want Maggie strong-arming Rowan into anything. "Rowan is just visiting. She's helping her grandmother after surgery."

"O'Shea. You must be Bonnie's granddaughter. Bonnie was one of my favorite customers when I worked at the credit union. She used to bring us cookies at Christmas." Maggie grinned. "She really put Palmer on the map last year. Too bad there are no historic gold nuggets on our property, Zack."

"Wouldn't that be nice?" he said. "Although it still wouldn't count as matching funds."

"Our grant will only distribute funds to match the amount we raise," Maggie explained to Rowan. "It's a shame you won't be around long enough to help with that."

"Well, if you like the idea of a food tasting and auction, maybe I could at least get the ball rolling. I can talk to Lauren—"

"We shouldn't be taking you away from your grandmother," Zack said.

"She won't mind. The only thing she needs me for is to drive her to physical therapy appointments. I'd love to help the wildlife rehab center as much as I can."

"Great!" Maggie said.

"The board would need to approve the idea," Zack cautioned.

Maggie scoffed. "We have half the board right here, and you don't seriously believe Jessie or Greg are going to turn this down. In fact, Rowan, why don't you meet us this Saturday at the Sunrise Diner and give them your ideas?"

"That would be great. If it's okay with Zack."

"Sure." He didn't want to railroad Rowan, but the idea of spending more time with her was appealing. "But before you agree, you might want to look at our website."

Rowan smiled. "I will, but I've already seen enough to know that this is the coolest place in Palmer. Right, Becca?" Rowan held out a hand.

Becca slapped her a high five and grinned. "Right."

"Sounds good, then," Maggie said. "See you Saturday, Rowan."

"I'll look forward to it."

Maggie headed off for the evening.

They passed an empty cage. "What's this for?" Rowan asked.

"Most recently, an injured marmot. We released him about three weeks ago."

Rowan tilted her head. "That must give you a

lot of satisfaction, when you've helped heal an animal and it can return to the wild."

"It does." Zack chuckled. "And that's the only reason I'm willing to do news segments and fundraisers."

"Well, I'll see how much I can get done before Saturday." Once again, that dimple flashed.

"We really do appreciate it." But Saturday was still three days away. Maybe instead of trying to figure out what to do with a can of tuna, he could take Rowan and Becca out to dinner tonight, and he wouldn't need a sitter. "Say, are you hun—"

Her phone rang. She held up a finger as she checked the ID. "Oh, sorry. I do need to take this. Excuse me a minute."

"Sure. We'll just be…" He indicated the way down the trail, toward the creek. Rowan nodded and walked a few steps away to answer her phone. "Hi, Sutton."

Sutton? Zack sincerely hoped that was Rowan's boss's name. He herded Becca along the path. "How many otters were out today?" The otters weren't technically part of the wildlife center, but a pair were raising a family on the bank of the creek that ran through it, and Becca loved watching them.

"All three babies were playing. Rowan liked them."

"I'll bet she did."

"Rowan's nice. And she has really pretty hair."

"Yes." Zack couldn't argue with either of those points.

"Sorry about that." Rowan came up the trail behind them. "We've been playing phone tag all day."

"Of course." Now, how was he going to find out if that was her boyfriend on the phone? He couldn't just come out and ask, could he?

"Who were you talking to?" Becca had no such hesitations, bless her.

"Sutton Tanaka. He's my, um…" Rowan licked her lower lip. "…my fiancé."

And poof, Zack's plans went up in smoke. No second chance for him and Rowan. At least he'd avoided the awkwardness of asking her out. "It's getting late. We'd better get home and see what we can dig up for dinner, right, Becks?"

"Thanks so much for letting me visit," Rowan told them. "It was nice to meet you, Becca."

"How long are you staying in Alaska?" Zack asked.

Rowan looked away. "I'm not sure. It depends on how things go."

"Where do you usually live?" Becca asked.

"In Japan," Rowan told her.

"Wow. Can you talk Japanese?" Becca asked.

"Yes, conversationally." Rowan smiled. "*Jaa ne*, Becca. That's like 'see you later' in Japanese."

"Jaa ne." Becca tried it and seemed to like the way it felt on her tongue. *"Jaa ne,* Rowan."

"See you Saturday." Zack held the gate for Rowan and Becca. "I'll text you the details."

"Thanks." Rowan waved as she walked to her jeep. "With luck, I'll have good news to share."

CHAPTER FIVE

"How was the bridge tournament?" Rowan held open the car door and handed Gran her cane.

"Good. Molly and I placed second." Gran pulled herself to her feet and they started toward the physical therapy center. "Alice and Ralph won, as usual, but we gave them a good run for their money this time."

"Alice." Rowan thought back to all of Gran's friends she'd met at Patrick and Lauren's wedding. "She's the former librarian?"

"No, Linda is the librarian. Alice used to work in the governor's office."

"Oh, yes, Alice is the one who set up the fishing trip for a visiting congresswoman and her new husband, only to discover at the last minute the boat captain was her first husband." Rowan chuckled. "Your friends have some great stories."

"The Mat Mates meet for yoga tomorrow. You should join us."

"Mat Mates? Cute name."

The receptionist greeted them. "Hello, Bonnie. David is just finishing up with another client. He'll be with you soon."

"Thanks, Marley." Once they'd settled into chairs in the waiting room, Bonnie continued. "It's nice having you here. How long are you staying?"

"At least two weeks, until you can drive."

"My friends could drive me around if you need to get back."

"No, no particular reason I need to."

"Not work?"

"I took a leave of absence. It's a slow period right now, anyway."

"What about your apartment?"

"My roommate has a cousin staying with her. She was happy to take over my part of the rent in exchange for using my room. As far as she's concerned, the longer I'm away, the better."

"And you don't have anyone waiting for you in Tokyo? Like whoever gave you the rather large diamond ring you were wearing when you arrived from the airport?"

"No, uh." Rowan could feel her cheeks growing warm. She'd asked her mother not to say anything, that she wanted to tell Gran and Patrick about her engagement herself, but now she almost wished she'd let Mom be the one to break the news. "Sutton is in Palo Alto on a business trip."

"Sutton?"

"Sutton Tanaka. We've been dating for a while."

"How long of a while?"

"About two years."

"Two years." Gran raised her eyebrows. "And yet I've never heard his name before. Tell me about him."

"Let's see. His father, Asao, is the founder of Tanaka Electronics in Tokyo. Sutton works in mergers and acquisitions. His mother is American. Coralie Sutton was her maiden name. She and Mom were in the same sorority at William & Mary, but Mom is three years younger, so they didn't know each other that well until they met again in Japan."

"Your fiancé didn't come with you to your brother's wedding."

"He was in Zurich. Sutton travels a lot, negotiating contracts and, um, stuff." Rowan really wasn't clear on what he did. Much of Sutton's work was confidential, and he couldn't really share the details with her. Or at least he didn't.

"And when will you see him again?"

"I'm not sure. It sounds like he'll be tied up in Palo Alto for quite a while." Rowan smiled. "So, I'm free to stay here with you. Unless you're tired of me already."

"Of course not. I'm thrilled you're here. How long have you been engaged?"

"Um…"

Gran raised an eyebrow. "It's not a hard question."

"He gave me the ring four days before I came to Alaska."

"Four days. And yet, you haven't worn the ring since you arrived. Most brides-to-be can't wait to show off their rings to everyone. What's going on?"

Rowan looked down at her bare finger. "It's just that I'm not sure."

"But you said yes?"

"Well, he proposed in front of this whole group of people, and he had the ring, and we have been dating two years. I suppose it is time to move on to the next phase."

Gran scoffed. "You don't marry because it's time. You marry because you love that person and you want to spend the rest of your life together. Do you love him?"

"I—"

"Hello, Bonnie." David, the physical therapist, stood at the door of the waiting room. "Come on back."

Gran put her hand on Rowan's shoulder. "Once I'm done here, we can go back to my place and have a nice, long talk."

"Actually, after I drive you home, I have some things I need to take care of this afternoon." Rowan had promised to work on the fundraiser, after all. "But I'll take you to yoga in the morning. We'll talk then."

Gran shot her a no-nonsense look before she followed David through the door. "Yes, we will."

"I'M HERE," ROWAN CALLED the next morning as she let herself into Gran's apartment. Rowan hadn't practiced yoga in a couple of years, but this was a class for seniors. How hard could it be?

"Molly and Linda are riding with us," Gran told her as she grabbed her cane. "The other three will meet us there."

Molly, Gran's best friend for many decades, was waiting in the lobby when they stepped off the elevator. "Rowan, good to see you. What's this I hear about you spearheading the plan to raise money for the wildlife center?"

"I'm just pitching in to get things rolling. How did you hear about it?"

"Maggie Zeigler mentioned it at church," Molly replied.

"You didn't tell me about this." Gran looked a little put out that her friend had more information than she did.

"Sorry. It's not official yet. I'm meeting with the board Saturday."

"Is this Zack Vogel's wildlife center?" A familiar woman with silver glasses pushed up on top of her head joined the group. "Rowan, I'm Linda. We met at Lauren and Patrick's wedding."

"Of course, Linda. Yes, it is. You know Zack?"

"He's my cat's vet. She's fifteen, arthritic and not particularly friendly, but she likes Zack. What are your plans for the fundraiser?"

Gran made a shooing motion. "We can talk in the car."

On the drive from the Easy Living apartments to the yoga studio, Rowan told the three women her thoughts about the auction.

"What kind of internet publicity are you planning?" Linda asked.

"Once I have some donations nailed down and a solid date, I thought I'd start a website with information and advance ticket sales."

"You should talk with Crystal, the yoga instructor," Linda advised. "A surprisingly large number of people signed up for her goat yoga mailing list. She could mention the fundraiser in her next newsletter."

"Even better, maybe she'd offer a yoga package as one of the prizes," Molly said.

"She and Lauren might be willing to do goat yoga at the event," Gran added. "Their sessions at the state fair last summer mostly sold out within minutes."

Wow, for a group of eighty-somethings, these women were on top of things. Rowan made a mental note to ask for advice later on the best vendors to approach about donating prizes. "I'll talk to Crystal," she assured them. "Thanks for the tip."

Rowan parallel parked behind a gray sedan near the studio. A woman wearing orange yoga pants and a lime green top with matching green streaks in her white hair was plugging the parking meter. She greeted Rowan. "I'm Bea and you're Bonnie's granddaughter. Sorry, I've forgotten your name."

"Rowan." People often forgot Rowan's name. That's what came of having ordinary brown hair and a tendency to listen instead of talk. She remembered Bea, but then, Bea made herself memorable.

With only minimal help from her cane, Gran followed her friends into the studio. "Rowan, do you remember Crystal, Alice and Rosemary?"

"Of course." Crystal was the instructor, a lithe woman in her fifties. Rosemary's hair fell in a silver braid down her back. At Patrick and Lauren's wedding, she'd worn a beautiful silk skirt fashioned from an Indian sari. Alice, in contrast, had dressed in a tailored navy suit. Even her yoga clothes were conservative—black pants and a gray T-shirt so simple it had to be designer. "Good to see you again."

Crystal put on some music and, in one fluid motion, sunk onto her mat. "Let's begin in comfortable pose."

All the women sat on their mats with their legs folded. Rowan settled at the back of the class and easily mimicked their pose. As it turned out, that was the last easy part to the session. Toward the end of the hour, Rowan's core muscles trembled from the effort of holding her up, while Gran, who'd walked in with a cane, made planking look effortless. But Rowan had to admit, at the end of the hour, she felt more relaxed.

When they left the studio, the Mat Mates headed toward the bakery next door. "We always have a little treat after yoga," Gran explained. "I'll grab a table. Rowan, could you get me one of those lemon scones and a cup of Earl Grey, please?"

"Sure." Rowan was last in line. Once she had Gran's order, along with tea and a poppy seed muffin for herself, she carried them to an outdoor table where the ladies had gathered.

"Sit by me." Molly pulled out a chair. Rowan sat down and took her first sip.

"So, Bonnie says you accidently got yourself

engaged," Bea stated, almost causing Rowan to choke on her tea.

She set the cup on the table and blotted her mouth with her napkin. "I—"

"How did it happen?" Bea continued. "Did he pressure you? Or did you just blurt out the wrong thing? I've done that before."

Rowan bet she had. Before she could answer, Molly laid a hand on her arm. "Rowan, what Bea is trying to say—" she flashed a warning look in Bea's direction "—is that we're here to support you. We've found that talking things out can give us perspective. How did you and Sutton meet?"

That was easy. "At an embassy dinner. Mom had asked me to fill in when someone dropped out at the last minute. We happened to be seated next to each other at dinner."

"Wasn't that convenient?" Gran murmured.

"Her mother set them up?" Alice asked.

"Renee seldom leaves anything to chance," Gran confirmed.

"Not that there's anything wrong with introducing two people you think might enjoy one another's company," Rosemary commented. "How long have you been dating?"

"Two years. That is, we started dating two years ago. But we only see each other when he's in town."

"He doesn't live in Tokyo?" Alice asked.

"His home is there, but he travels maybe three weeks out of four."

"With video phones and whatnot, I suppose you can keep in touch no matter where you are," Molly said.

"Sure. Except that when he's working, he likes to concentrate on his job. And with time zones and everything…" Rowan trailed off.

"So, you've really only dated the equivalent of six months." Alice nodded as though confirming her suspicions.

"Bonnie says he proposed at a party," Molly said. "If it had been in private, what would you have answered?"

Rowan sighed. "I would have asked for more time. But I couldn't embarrass him with everyone watching."

"Is a public proposal something you would have expected from him?"

Rowan considered. "Now that you mention it, no." Sutton was a private person, by nature and by nurture.

"That's what I thought." Linda nodded. "He must not have been too sure of your answer, so he put you on the spot."

Bea crossed her arms. "He played you."

"Now, wait," Rowan protested. "Sutton negotiates contracts as a profession. It's only natural that he would present a proposal in a way that most ensured a favorable outcome."

"Favorable for him at least," Bea grumbled.

"To be fair, he did risk a public rejection," Rosemary pointed out. "That took courage."

"Exactly," Rowan agreed. "Sutton doesn't deserve the embarrassment of a broken engagement."

Gran chuckled. "You're a sweetheart, Rowan, but you can't live your entire life not rocking the boat. Imagine it's your silver wedding anniversary. Can you see Sutton and yourself more in love than ever, looking forward to another quarter century together?"

Based on their pattern so far, the most Rowan could expect would be an extravagant bouquet of flowers and a short video call from wherever he was working. "Well, when you put it like that..."

"What did I miss?" Lauren came out of the bakery carrying a large cookie. "Sorry I didn't make the yoga class this morning. I got held up."

"Rowan is trying to figure out how to break her engagement," Alice said.

Lauren's eyes widened. "You're engaged? And you didn't tell Patrick or me?"

Oh, shoot. Now Rowan had offended Lauren. "I'm sorry. I didn't mean...it's complicated."

Alice quickly summarized the conversation for Lauren. "And now Rowan finds herself in a situation where she has to hurt someone's feelings." She gave Rowan a sympathetic smile. "I can see that's not easy for you."

"No." Rowan had spent her whole life avoiding conflict.

"When will you see Sutton again?" Rosemary asked.

"Good question," Rowan answered. "He's in California and might be there for another two or three weeks."

"Well, you can't do this by phone," Linda said. "So maybe you should put everything on hold until you're back together."

If only she could. "Mom is pushing me to make wedding plans. She says the best venues fill up fast."

"You haven't talked to your mother about this?" Gran pressed her lips together.

"Don't look at me like that. Have you ever tried talking to Mom about anything when she's in planning mode?"

"Renee can be a steamroller," Gran admitted. "But she loves you. So does your dad. They want you to be happy."

"I know, but Mom and Dad are happily married. So are Patrick and Lauren. Mom thinks it's time I was, too. I am thirty-two, and I've nothing against marriage."

"The key word being *happily*. Your boyfriend

wants to marry you. Your mother wants to plan your wedding. What do you want?"

Rowan took a deep breath and finally said aloud what she'd known all along. "I have to break up with Sutton. Not just the engagement—the whole relationship."

"Explain it to your mother now," Linda suggested, "and when you and Sutton are back in Japan, you can tell him."

Rowan shook her head. "Mom and Sutton's mother are good friends, and I don't want to risk it getting back to him before I've had a chance to talk to him."

"You can't put your mother's wedding planning off for a few weeks?" Rosemary asked.

Gran, Lauren and Rowan all laughed. "Haven't you met my mother-in-law?" Lauren asked her.

"Oh, now I remember," Rosemary said. "When that freak hailstorm ruined the peonies you'd ordered for your wedding, Renee arranged for someone to fly peonies in from Australia."

"That was so sweet of her." Lauren gave a fond smile. "Unnecessary—because I'd really only chosen peonies to support the local farmers and daisies would have been fine—but still sweet."

Gran chuckled. "Once Renee gets going, she's like a boulder rolling downhill. Best just to get out of her way."

"She means well," Lauren protested.

"Oh, yes. Renee isn't at all selfish," Gran agreed. "She's always thinking of other people. It's just that people don't always appreciate having things done 'for their own good.'"

Rowan gave a wry smile. "Like when she decided your car didn't have the latest safety features and sold it without asking you?" Gran had been spitting mad at the time.

"I've grown quite fond of the new one," Gran answered smoothly.

"In any case," Alice said, "the longer you leave it, the harder it will be to break the engagement. Rowan, you need to fly down to California and talk to him."

Rowan winced. "You really think so?" When Gran raised her eyebrows, Rowan nodded. "I suppose you're right."

Molly patted her arm. "You'll feel better once it's done."

Rowan hoped so. "I'll book a flight."

CHAPTER SIX

"WILL CHARLOTTE BE HERE?" Becca asked as she took Zack's hand in the diner's parking lot.

"Yes." Zack glanced around but didn't see Jessie's or Greg's cars.

"Can I have pancakes?" Becca asked him.

"You can have whatever you want."

"What if I want a taco?"

"They don't have tacos here."

"But you said I could have whatever I want." Becca grinned, and he realized she was teasing him. She'd never done that before. Maybe she was starting to feel more secure.

"Okay, you can order whatever you want from the menu."

"I want pancakes."

"Then you're in luck." He held the door and she skipped inside.

"Hi, Becca! Zack, we're back here," Maggie called from the big booth in the back corner. Rowan waved from the seat beside her.

Becca went dashing back. "Hi, Rowan. How do you say hi in Japanese?"

"Kommichiwa."

"Komo chihuahua."

Rowan smiled. "Close. *Kom-mi-chi-wa.* Or we could just bow." Rowan demonstrated bowing her head.

Becca bowed back and then burst into giggles. She slid into the booth and scooted up against Rowan. "I'm getting pancakes."

"That sounds delicious," Rowan answered. "Good morning, Zack."

"Kommichiwa." Zack slid into the booth. "Thanks for coming today."

"Rowan says she has good news for us," Maggie told him.

"What's that?"

"Don't tell him yet," Maggie instructed. "We have to wait for Jessie and Greg to start the board meeting."

"And Charlotte," Becca added.

"And Charlotte," Zack affirmed. He could explain to Becca that she and Charlotte weren't official members of the board, but why ruin it?

"Hey, guys." Jessie waved from the entryway with Charlotte right behind her.

"Here, you can sit by Becca." Maggie scooted toward the end of the bench but before she could stand, Charlotte ducked under the table and popped up between Maggie and Becca.

Becca bowed to her friend. "Rowan says that's how people in Japan say hi."

Charlotte bowed back, and both girls laughed.

"That's Charlotte, and I'm Jessica—call me Jessie—and that's Greg coming in the door now." Jessie waved at her husband and scooted in next to Zack. "You must be Rowan. Maggie said you were looking into holding a tasting and auction for the wildlife center."

"Nice to meet you, Jessie and Charlotte. Yes, I contacted a few local merchants—"

"If you're all here, I can take your orders," Karma, their usual waitress, interrupted as Greg sat down at the table. She set paper place mats and a cup of crayons in front of Becca and Charlotte, and then waited with her pen poised.

"I'll have the reindeer sausage skillet," Greg decided and turned to shake Rowan's hand while Karma took everyone else's orders. Rowan asked for pancakes. Zack suspected she did it just to please Becca. If so, it worked. Becca beamed.

Karma tore the order from her pad. "I'll get these in and be back in a minute with coffee and juice."

"Thanks, Karma." Once the waitress had gone, Jessie tapped her water glass with her spoon. "Okay, I'm officially calling the meeting to order." She turned to Rowan. "When Zack was setting up the nonprofit, they had to list someone as president, and I drew the short straw. Zack is VP, Maggie is secretary and Greg is officially the treasurer of WildER, although since I'm an accountant, I actually keep the books."

"And I check her numbers to make sure she's not embezzling." Greg grinned, and his wife laughed.

"We have occasional volunteers who help with big projects, but so far we haven't recruited any more board members. Anyway, we're all eager to hear about your idea. Rowan, you have the floor."

"Thank you." Rowan gave a little smile at that. "Okay, well, my brother and sister-in-law, Lauren and Patrick, love the idea and said they'd host the fundraiser outdoors at Now and Forever Farm if you want. The Salmonberry Bakery is also interested in providing food, and Pioneer Peak Sporting Goods says they will donate a new tent and pair of sleeping bags as an auction item. There will be yoga class certificates, and I'm waiting to hear back from a bookstore and a sausage-maker. They'll participate, but they haven't decided what to donate."

"That was fast," Greg said. "How many merchants did you approach?"

"Only those so far."

"If they'll let us have it at the farm for free,

that saves a fortune over renting a venue somewhere," Maggie said.

"How would it work?" Jessie asked. "You buy a ticket for the tasting and get a cheese plate to nibble on during the auction? Do we want to try to get wine, too? Although that would mean getting a special license, and I'm not sure how that works."

"We could do an elegant wine and cheese garden party," Rowan replied. "Although if I can get several venders interested in participating, I thought it might be fun to have it as more of a family event, like a street fair. You get, say, five tickets with your entry fee, and you can cash them in at different food booths. We would, of course, sell extra tickets to raise more money. I'll bet Lauren could set up a sort of petting zoo with goats, and we might have some arts and crafts activities for the kids."

"A bouncy house?" Charlotte suggested.

"I'll look into it," Rowan promised.

"One of our occasional volunteers is an amateur magician," Maggie said. "He might be available for some entertainment."

"Great idea!" Rowan said.

"I'm sold," Maggie said. "How about the rest of you?"

Before anyone could answer, Karma arrived and set up a heavy tray. "Pancakes for Miss

Becca and Miss Charlotte." It took two trips to get all their meals to the table.

There was a short pause while everyone passed syrup and jelly around the table and took their first few bites. Jessie set down her fork. "Now, where were we?"

"I can go outside while the board debates," Rowan offered.

Jessie shook her head. "Your breakfast would get cold. Besides, we all love your ideas. You're so good at this."

"Rowan is only here temporarily," Zack pointed out. "She volunteered to get things started, but if we do this, the rest of us will need to carry the ball."

"We've got to do something if we're going to raise the funds we need. Even with you donating veterinary services, we still have to pay for meds, and for your assistant. The animals have to eat," Jessie said.

"And this is the best idea for fundraising I've heard yet," Maggie said. "I move that we adopt Rowan's plan."

"Second." Greg grinned at Zack.

"I concur," Zack said. "Thanks, Rowan. We appreciate all the effort you've put in on this."

"I'll keep working and keep good handover notes," Rowan told them. "I plan to be here for at least another week or so."

"Wonderful," Jessie said. "All in favor of the tasting and auction fundraiser with Rowan as acting, um, person in charge, say aye."

The vote was unanimous, with the most enthusiastic votes coming from the two nonvoting members at the table. "Thanks, Rowan. Let us know how we can help," Zack said.

"I will. Do you want to set a date?"

"A Saturday would be good." Jessie picked up her phone and the others followed suit. "How about July?"

"The first weekend is too close to Independence Day," Maggie said.

"We'll be camping the third and fourth weekends," Greg reminded his wife.

"The second weekend, then. That's barely a month. Does that give us enough time?"

"I think so." Rowan mentally tallied up the tasks to be done. "I'll try to get most donations pledged and the tasting booths lined up before I go. You'll need to arrange for booths, pick up the prizes and verify with everyone the week before. Oh, and get an auctioneer, of course. Maggie, you'd be good."

"My friend Tom would be better."

"Tom Hackman, the reporter?" Zack asked.

"Great idea. He'll probably give us some advance publicity, too. So, we're all set." Jessie grinned. "This stuff goes a lot faster with you around, Rowan. Can't you just stay here instead of going back to Japan?"

"I wish." Rowan smiled, but something in her expression made Zack wonder if she was entirely joking.

"Anyway, we have a plan. That's good news."

"More good news. The moose is ready for release," Zack told everyone. "If any of you want to come and watch, Fish and Game said they'd be by around three on Tuesday."

"I'd love to come if that's all right," Rowan said. "Gran has therapy in the mornings, but I should be free in the afternoon."

"We'd love to have you," Maggie told her. "You can see what WildER is all about."

CHAPTER SEVEN

"One. Two…" When the Fish and Game officer called, "Three," Zack pulled open the gate and jumped back to the side of the stock trailer in case the moose inside was in a fighting mood, but she didn't immediately emerge. Instead, she poked her head out and surveyed the situation. Apparently satisfied, she jumped down from the trailer, ignoring the ramp they'd set up. A new radio collar hung on her neck. The cow trotted several yards away, turned and paused.

Zack eased over to the edge of the clearing where Maggie and Rowan watched. Maggie had a video camera rolling.

The calf stood splay-legged at the top of the ramp, eyeing it suspiciously. Mama moose returned, nuzzled her baby and trotted away, looking back to urge the calf to follow. He fidgeted but wasn't quite ready to make the leap. Mama snorted and took a few more steps into the woods. That did it. The calf galloped down the ramp and across the clearing, and they wasted no time putting distance between them and the trailer. Maggie lowered the camera as the moose disappeared into the woods.

"Perjalanan aman," Rowan whispered.

"What did you say?" Maggie asked.

"Oh, I just wished them safe travels."

"In Japanese?"

"Indonesian, actually. Sorry. That sounds pretentious."

Zack smiled at her worries. "You're never pretentious. How many languages do you speak?"

"Oh—" she ticked off on her fingers "—maybe sevenish?"

Maggie found that amusing. "You don't know how many languages you speak?"

"Well, I was a toddler when we lived in Denmark and a preschooler in Greece, so my Danish and Greek are rusty, and while I understand Spanish fairly well, my accent is atrocious." Rowan chuckled. "My Spanish teacher was from Ireland, so maybe that's why. Anyway, I'm no linguist. Most of the people I converse with speak English better than I speak their language, but I like to try."

That was Rowan. Even as a teenager, she'd always tried to make everyone around her feel comfortable. Including him. When Zack had mentioned he was considering becoming a vet, she'd wanted all the details. Their talks had helped him formulate the plan that eventually got him where he was today. He wondered if she had any idea what a difference her friendship that summer had made in his life.

"Anyway," Rowan continued, "I wanted to thank you for letting me watch. You must get such a sense of satisfaction knowing you helped those two return to the wild."

"You're helping, too," Maggie replied. "This event you're setting up may be the difference between staying open and folding. Zack doesn't talk about it, but he's been keeping us afloat with his own money." Maggie flashed him a look. "That can't go on forever."

"Nothing major," Zack protested, not wanting to put more pressure on Rowan. "Just a feed bill now and then."

"When we had those bear cubs for a month last summer, the feed bills amounted to a pretty hefty sum. Plus, you're throwing in your vet services for free."

"Well, then, we'll just have to make sure this event is a success," Rowan said. "I've found a flight-seeing service and a white-water rafting company that have promised packages for the auction."

"You're incredible!" Maggie pulled Rowan into a hug.

Zack thought so, too, but before he could say so, one of the Fish and Game officers came over.

"Looks like a successful release. Thanks for patching her up."

"Always glad to do it." Zack shook his hand.

"We'll be off, then."

"Okay. Thanks." After waving goodbye, Zack checked his watch. "We'd better head back, too. Jessie's meeting me at the clinic in forty-five minutes to drop off Becca."

They drove in silence for a few minutes until Rowan asked, "Do you think they'll be okay?"

"The moose and calf?" Zack clarified.

"Yes. I realize there are probably thousands of moose in Alaska—"

"Around two hundred thousand," Maggie volunteered.

"That's a lot. But now that I've watched this one interact with her calf, they're special to me. The mother was badly hurt. Do you think they'll make it?"

"The cow is moving well and doesn't show any signs of infection or complications," Zack said. "They're both well nourished. I'd say they have a better-than-average chance."

"Since she's collared now, Fish and Game will be tracking her movements. They'll know if anything happens," Maggie said.

"Will they share the information with you?" Rowan asked.

"If I ask nicely." Maggie grinned. "I know a guy."

Zack laughed. "Maggie always knows a guy. I swear, she's got more admirers than most Hollywood leading ladies."

"Hardly." Maggie laughed. "When you've lived as long as I have, you make connections. And speaking of connections, I have a line on two or three food service businesses who might be amenable to setting up booths at the tasting fair. I'll have them call you."

"Super. Thanks, Maggie."

When they arrived at the clinic, Jessie's Subaru waited in the parking lot with the windows rolled down. Zack went to thank her. "Hope you weren't waiting long."

"No, we just got here."

Becca got out of the car and her face lit up. "There's Rowan!" Becca dashed over. Rowan looked almost as glad to see Becca as Becca was to see her.

"I wanna say hi." Charlotte jumped out of the car and ran to join them.

Jessie got out, too, and waved. "Rowan has sure made an impression around here."

"Hmm-hmm," Zack agreed.

"Not just with the kids. Greg and I are in awe of how much she's already accomplished on the fundraiser."

"Yeah." He watched as Rowan got something out of her car and handed a small package to Maggie. Maggie hugged her before waving goodbye to everyone and driving away. Rowan gave each of the girls a package, too.

"Maggie says Rowan's an old friend of yours." Jessie smirked. "She's very pretty."

"Hmm." Zack could see where this was going. "Also engaged."

"Are you sure? I didn't see a ring."

"She mentioned a fiancé."

"Too bad. You could use a wife."

"There's a leap." Zack shook his head. "Anyway, I'm not the marrying kind. Judging from my father's track record—"

"I wouldn't," Jessie cut him off. "Judge from his track record, that is. I didn't know your dad well, but from what I've seen, you're nothing like him." She smirked. "You'd make someone a decent husband. With a little training, maybe even a good one."

Zack laughed. "Nevertheless, I'm not planning on marriage anytime in the near future." Or in the distant future for that matter. "Thanks again for picking up the girls. I'll drive tomorrow."

"Sounds good. Charlotte! Time to go."

"Okay." Charlotte ran back to the car. "Look, Mommy. Rowan gave us some special cheese from her farm." She handed over the plastic-wrapped wedge and climbed into the back seat. "Bye, Becca. Bye, everybody else," she called as her window rolled up. She waved while Jessie drove away, leaving Becca still talking with Rowan. Zack crossed to them. "We'd better head out, too, Becks, and get dinner started."

"Can Rowan come to dinner? Please? We live right next door," she explained to Rowan, pointing to their house.

"Um, sure." Zack did a mental inventory. He'd finally gone grocery shopping, but had he put the breakfast dishes in the dishwasher or left them on the counter?

"It's macaroni and cheese," Becca said.

"From a box," Zack clarified. "But we can probably find something better—"

Rowan smiled. "Sure, I'd love to if—"

Zack's phone rang. He was on call this evening. He held up a finger. "One sec. This is Zack Vogel." A milk cow with a torn udder—not what he wanted to hear right now, but that was the job. "Okay, I'll call them and get there as soon as I can." He hung up and turned to Rowan and Becca. "Sorry. I have an emergency. Becks, I'll need to drop you at Jessie's. Do you need anything from the house before we go?"

"But I want mac and cheese."

"I know. But a cow is injured. I don't think it

will take more than an hour or so. I'll make the macaroni and cheese for you when I get back."

"I could stay with Becca," Rowan offered. "Or take her to the farm with me."

"Jessie and I have an arrangement." Jessie had volunteered to take Becca whenever he was called out, and he'd insisted he would pay her when he did, although he had a suspicion that what he'd paid had gone straight into donations for the wildlife center.

"I really don't mind," Rowan said.

"I want to stay with Rowan." Becca grabbed Rowan's hand. "We can cook supper together."

"Even if you stay, you don't have to cook," Zack told Rowan.

"I like cooking. And I like Becca." Rowan winked at the girl and Becca grinned.

"Well, if you're sure."

"I'm sure. We'll have fun."

"In that case, thank you." Zack took his house key from his ring and handed it over. "Becca, be good for Rowan. Oh, and I fed the cat at lunchtime, so no matter what she might tell you, she's not starving. Fluff is notorious," Zack told Rowan. "She will swear on a stack of catnip she's never been fed in her entire life."

"Got it. Don't feed the cat."

He paused to consider if there was anything else she might need to know, but he couldn't think of anything. "Okay, then. I guess I'd better get to that cow. If it's going to be longer than an hour or so, I'll call."

"Sounds good. Becca can show me where everything is." Rowan waved over her shoulder at Zack. "Good luck."

"Thanks." Zack waited until he'd seen them unlock the door before he called the farm to let them know he was on his way. It was nice not having to worry about upsetting Jessie and Greg's evening plans. Maybe Jessie had a point about him needing a wife.

Yeah, right.

ROWAN FOLLOWED BECCA inside the two-story house with the same gray-green siding as the vet clinic. The front door opened into a tiled foyer with stairs and an archway. Beyond that was a long room with a leather couch in front of a fireplace at one end, a kitchen with a few dishes waiting beside the sink at the other and a round oak table in between. Becca set the wedge of cheese Rowan had given her on the table beside a stack of mail. Behind the table was a sliding glass door with a dog looking in, wagging his tail.

"That's Ripley," Becca announced, running over to open the door. The dog greeted her enthusiastically before running over to investigate Rowan.

Rowan offered a hand to sniff before rubbing the Australian shepherd's ears. "What a nice dog."

"He's real smart, too. Watch. Ripley, sit." The dog plopped his hindquarters on the floor. "Down." His front half dropped, as well. "Roll over." Ripley completed two complete rolls before jumping to his feet, tail wagging.

"What a good boy!" Rowan crooned, and Ripley's tail moved faster.

"I have to use the bathroom," Becca said. "Then we can make dinner, okay?"

"Sure. I'll just be in the kitchen." While she waited, Rowan moved the mail, wiped the dining table and loaded the breakfast dishes in the dishwasher. A quick inventory revealed a quarter loaf of French bread going stale, some leftover ham, carrots, onions, preshredded Parmesan and bagged salad, among other things. Definite possibilities.

"This is Fluff." Becca returned carrying a gray-and-white longhaired cat in her arms, with the dog trailing behind her. "She was asleep in the laundry hamper."

The cat jumped from her arms and ran to a porcelain bowl on the kitchen floor, mewing loudly. Rowan laughed. "Good thing Zack

warned me about you. You're very convincing."
She reached down to stroke the cat's back. Fluff
walked under her hand.

"Here's the macaroni and cheese." Becca
opened the pantry door and pointed out the blue
box tucked between a box of spaghetti and one
of elbow macaroni.

"What would you say if, instead of the boxed
mac and cheese, we make a real oven-baked
macaroni and cheese casserole with the cheese
I brought you from the goat farm?" Rowan asked
her. "We could put ham in it, as well."

"Okay!"

"Great. First, we need to wash our hands."

"I just did."

"But then we played with the animals. We
need clean hands to cook." Once they'd both
washed, Rowan opened the freezer compartment. "I wonder if you have any frozen vegetables."

"Zack always makes me eat a vegetable."
Becca frowned. "I'm tired of carrots."

"Well, maybe we can do something different
with the carrots." Rowan rummaged through the
freezer. "Here's a bag of broccoli. That would be
good in our casserole."

"I never had vegetables in mac and cheese."

"You'll love it. Trust me. Do you know if you
have a cheese grater?"

Becca didn't, but Rowan dug around in the cabinets until she'd located all the utensils they would need. "Let's get started. First, we'll put on some water to boil for the pasta, and while that's getting hot, we'll grate some breadcrumbs, carrots and cheddar." Rowan set up a kitchen chair beside the counter, like Gran used to do when Rowan was Becca's age. She put her hands over Becca's and showed her how to make breadcrumbs by running the stale loaf up and down the holes of the box grater. "Don't let your knuckles get too close."

"Like this?" Becca slowly dragged the bread downward, releasing a shower of crumbs to the plate below, and a few on the floor, but Ripley took care of those.

"Exactly like that. Keep going, while I cut up the ham." Once Becca had produced a sufficient pile of breadcrumbs, Rowan started her grating a carrot. Meanwhile, she sautéed the ham to bring out the flavor, added pasta to the boiling water and set the timer for eight minutes.

"The mac and cheese package says seven minutes."

"You and Zack must make a lot of mac and cheese." With a full-time job, a second volunteer job and a child to care for, it was no wonder Zack would go for boxed mixes and carrot sticks.

Becca giggled. "Zack says I eat so much mac and cheese I might turn orange."

Rowan laughed. "Well, in tonight's mac and cheese, we're using a white cheddar so it won't be orange, but the carrot shreds and broccoli will give it nice color." She swiped a piece of carrot from the pile Becca was creating and popped it in her mouth. "Yum!" Becca grinned.

By the time Becca had finished grating the carrot, she was tired of that chore. "Why don't you set the table?" Rowan suggested, as she stirred the pasta and added the frozen broccoli into the boiling water.

"I don't know how to set a table. We always eat at the bar."

"We can sit at the bar if you want to, but I think it's nice to sit together at a table where it's easier to talk while we eat. Your choice."

"What do I do?"

"Well, we'll start with plates." Rowan took three from the cabinet. "Put one in front of each chair." The timer went off. She drained the pasta and broccoli into a colander and turned the oven to preheat. "Then silverware. Do you know your right from your left?"

Becca held up her right hand. "The one with the birthmark is my right."

"Good. Knives and spoons go on the right, but we don't need them tonight." Rowan handed her napkins and forks. "Forks and napkins go on the left. Fold the napkin in half and set it on the left of the plate, then put the fork beside it or on top of it."

"Why?" Becca asked.

"I asked my Gran that once, and she said it had something to do with knights holding their swords in their right hands, but I think now it's just because that's how we've always done it."

"So it's a rule." Becca nodded, satisfied. She carefully folded the napkins in half and set them to the left of the plates before setting forks on top. She turned to Rowan. "Now what?"

"Now, we make a cheese sauce." Rowan had just finished grating the white cheddar. "Come over here, and I'll show you how." Ten minutes later, they'd created a smooth creamy sauce. "You stir and I'll add the Parmesan, a little at a time." Given a choice, Rowan would have preferred to grate her cheese fresh, but it would still add a nice flavor kick.

"That cheese stinks," Becca said.

Rowan laughed. "Yes, cheese is one of the few things that can smell stinky but taste good." Together they assembled the casserole and put it in the oven. Becca peered through the glass. "How long until we eat?"

"Half an hour."

"What do we do until then?"

"Well, first we should clean the kitchen—" Rowan thought back to summers with Gran and Grandy "—and then—do you like games?"

"Like tag?"

"I was thinking more along the lines of table games. Do you have cards?"

"I think so."

"Good. Let's wash dishes first, and I'll show you a game my grandmother taught me."

Rowan filled the sink with water and detergent, but before she started washing, she scooped up a dab of the suds and wiped them onto Becca's nose.

Becca giggled. "You, too!" Rowan bent down so Becca could put suds on her nose. "We're twins."

The back door opened, and Zack walked in. "Sounds like a party in here."

"We're washing dishes," Becca told him.

He grinned. "Looks like to me you're playing in the suds. Something smells great."

"We made macaroni and cheese, but Rowan showed me how to make it with real cheese and other stuff."

"It will be ready in about twenty-five minutes," Rowan told Zack. "How is the cow?"

"All stitched up. I really appreciate you staying with Becca."

"We had fun, didn't we, Becca?"

"We're going to wash dishes and then Rowan is going to teach me a game her grandmother taught her. We have cards, right?"

"Somewhere." The look he sent Rowan's way seemed a mixture of pleasure and puzzlement. "I'll get washed up and look for the cards."

"If you have something you need to be doing instead of looking for cards, we could play something else, like tic-tac-toe."

"No, believe it or not, I don't have anything else that needs doing right now."

While he searched for the cards, Rowan washed the skillet she'd used to brown the ham and handed it to Becca, along with a dish towel.

Becca went to work, polishing every inch of the skillet. "I hope Zack likes our dinner. It's the first time I ever cooked anything."

"Did you like cooking?"

"It's fun!"

"I think so, too." Rowan smiled. "Maybe next time, we can make cookies."

CHAPTER EIGHT

NEXT TIME? ZACK was busy searching for cards, but he overheard Rowan pledging to make cookies with Becca. He hoped she understood that Becca took these things seriously. But Rowan didn't seem like the type to make idle promises.

Someone had moved the pile of junk mail and set three places at the dining table. Zack tried to think of the last time he'd eaten a sit-down meal there. Well before Becca moved in, for sure. He hadn't found much time for playing games with Becca, either, but at least they'd established a tradition of reading together before bed every night.

Now, where would he have stashed playing cards? Somewhere was a novelty set some veterinary medical supply had handed out. The drawer under the living room coffee table yielded a handful of pens, paper clips, a rubber dog toy and a spare stethoscope. He'd been wondering where he put that. No cards, though.

Rowan and Becca had their heads together in the kitchen, measuring something into an empty jar. Rowan screwed the lid on tight. "Now we mix it up." She demonstrated by shaking the jar like a maraca while dancing a salsa step. "Your turn." She handed the jar to Becca.

Becca boogied around the kitchen, shaking the jar. When Rowan was satisfied that the contents had mixed, she had Becca pour the dressing over salad greens, and together they tossed the salad using the bear-claw-shaped salad tongs Christine had given Zack as a housewarming gift.

Zack wasn't sure he'd ever seen Becca quite so carefree. Never in Clarissa's company, for sure. When she was with her mother, Becca always tiptoed around, as though by being "good," she could earn her mother's love. If she ever became the least bit noisy or demanding, Clarissa would send her off to the housekeeper, pleading a headache.

Zack finally found the cards in a box in the coat closet just as the timer chimed. "Our casserole should be ready," Rowan told Becca.

"What about our card game?"

"We can play after dinner," Zack assured her.

They all sat down at the table. The macaroni and cheese sure looked a lot better than anything Zack had ever created. When Rowan unfolded her napkin and set it in her lap, Becca immediately did the same.

Rowan picked up Becca's plate and dished up a small serving. "More?"

"Yes, please."

"You're so polite," Rowan commented as she added more.

Becca sat a little taller in her chair. "Just a little of the vegetables, though."

Rowan laughed as she added salad and set the plate in front of Becca. "Zack?"

He handed over his plate and Rowan served up generous portions before serving herself.

Becca took a bite. "This is really good. I even like the green stuff."

"Broccoli," Rowan said.

"It's great," Zack agreed. It really was. Bits of ham flavored the cheesy pasta, along with broccoli and carrot. Far better than anything that had ever come out of this kitchen. "Thanks so much, Rowan."

"Thank Becca. This dinner is mostly her doing."

"Well, thank you both. May I have more of that macaroni and cheese, please?"

Rowan winked at Becca while she dished up another serving. "Zack likes your cooking."

When they'd finished dinner, Rowan started to load the dishwasher. "Leave it," Zack told her, as he put foil over the leftovers and set them in the fridge. "You've put in enough work. Let's play."

"All right." Rowan dealt the cards and explained the rules.

Becca caught on quickly. "Zack, do you have any threes?"

"Go fish."

She drew a card off the top of the pile, looked at it and gasped. "I got a three!"

"That means you get to go again," Rowan told her.

"Rowan, do you have any threes?"

"I do." Rowan grinned. "Two of them."

"Yeah, I got a book!" Rowan laid the four cards together on the table in front of her. "I'm winning!"

"You sure are," Zack agreed. In more ways than one.

They played two more games, but eventually Zack announced, "It's past your bedtime."

"I'm not sleepy," Becca protested.

"You'll be sleepy at camp tomorrow if you don't get to bed. Brush your teeth, and I'll be up to read you a story." He wanted a moment alone with Rowan to let her know how much he appreciated the time she'd spent with Becca.

"I want Rowan to read to me tonight and meet Zuma."

"Zuma is Rowan's stuffed mountain lion," Zack explained.

"Oh, Zuma the Puma." Rowan looked delighted. "I would love that, if Zack doesn't mind."

"I suppose you can have a turn just for one night," Zack said.

"Goody. Today was fun," Becca said. "Rowan, can we cook dinner again tomorrow?"

Rowan's smile faded. "Sorry, sweetie. I'll be on a plane tomorrow."

"You're leaving already?" After she'd promised Becca she would make cookies? And Maggie that she'd get more donations for the fundraiser?

"Just for two days. I'll be back Thursday night."

Zack relaxed. "Better get those teeth brushed if you want to have time for a story," he told Becca and waited for her to disappear up the stairs before turning to Rowan. "Thank you."

"For what?"

"For what? For everything. For watching Becca while I worked, and for cooking, and most of all for making Becca smile."

"Doesn't she smile often?"

"Not as often as she should."

"Rowan, I'm ready," Becca called from the top of the stairs.

"I'll be right up." Rowan turned to Zack. "Thank you for sharing your little sister with me tonight. She gave me a reason to smile, too, and I really needed that."

ZACK HAD LOADED the dishwasher and thrown in a load of laundry by the time Rowan came downstairs again. "All tucked in." Rowan shuffled the cards they'd left lying on the table. "We took turns reading. Becca said that's how you always do it. She's an excellent reader. How old is she?"

"She just turned eight."

"She's such a great kid."

"She is," Zack agreed.

"I was surprised when you said she didn't smile often." Rowan slipped the cards into the box. "She seems so eager to please."

"Yeah. Sometimes I think she worries that if she does something wrong, I'll send her away."

Rowan looked concerned. "Did something happen to your parents? Is that why your sister lives with you?"

"My dad—our dad—died recently. Becca's mom…" He blew out a breath of frustration. "She's somewhere in the Caribbean. I think."

"What do you mean, you think? You're taking care of her child and you don't know where she is?"

"Not exactly," he admitted. "She was staying at a resort there, but when I tried to leave a message with the front desk, they said she'd checked out. I imagine she'll call soon." Or at least the next time she had a problem with a credit card.

"I don't understand. Why is Becca's mother in the Caribbean when she's here?"

How to explain? "Clarissa has never exactly taken to motherhood. Dad was the parent. Clarissa treats Becca like—well, not a pet, because my clients are all better parents to their pets than Clarissa is to Becca. More like a neighbor's kid she speaks to occasionally but doesn't take any responsibility for."

"I see." Rowan shook her head. "No, I don't see."

"I don't, either," Zack admitted. "But that's the way it's always been. Right after Becca was born, Clarissa left her and went off to some resort for a couple months to 'shed the baby weight.' After Dad's funeral, she asked if I'd keep Becca for a little while. That was two months ago."

"What happens when she comes back?"

"I've been thinking a lot about that lately." Zack hadn't confided to anyone, but somehow Rowan felt like the right person. "I want custody. Becca doesn't deserve to trail around after her mother, pawned off on housekeepers or nannies. She needs a stable life. And I intend to give it to her."

"That's wonderful!" Rowan came around the table and hugged him.

He chuckled. "What's this all about?"

"Sorry." She drew back. "I'm just so glad that Becca has you as a big brother."

"Don't be sorry. It was nice. You really care what happens to Becca, don't you?"

"Of course. She deserves a wonderful life. And you're the one who can make it happen."

"I hope so. Between my job and the wildlife center, I feel like Becca's getting short-changed."

"Every parent I've ever talked to feels that way sometimes. You're doing a terrific job."

"You don't know about all the instant mac and cheese dinners."

"Oh yes, I do, and I also know Becca loves them. Don't beat yourself up." Her face grew more serious. "Will Becca's mother fight you over custody?"

"She might. Clarissa can be touchy."

"She sounds like a joy to have around."

He shrugged. "I've always gotten along with Clarissa, mostly for Dad and Becca's sake. But now that I'm the executor of my father's estate, that might change."

"Oh?"

"Clarissa's pulling something. She was my father's fourth wife. She signed a prenup but now there's no sign of it. She says he tore it up when Becca was born."

"And you don't think that's true?"

"We also can't find a will written after his

marriage to Clarissa or after Becca's birth. The most recent one we found was written during his third marriage. It mentions that wife and me, and appoints me executor. But, according to state law, the divorce means wife number three doesn't inherit. And if a current wife is not mentioned in a will that predates the marriage, the wife gets one hundred thousand, plus half of the remaining estate."

"I gather that would add up to more than the amount in the prenup?"

"Quite a bit more."

"What about Becca?"

"Since she wasn't born when the will was made, she's automatically assigned a share equal to mine. Roughly, one-fourth of the estate."

Rowan thought for a moment before she answered. "It does seem unlikely that someone would have taken the trouble to draft a prenup but not update his will. Is there any reason he would have destroyed the prenup and the will when Becca was born?"

"A little over three years ago, Dad had a minor heart attack. Afterward, he mentioned he planned to leave everything above the prenup to Becca and appoint me her trustee. But I never saw the papers, and we can't find them or any lawyer who says they drafted them. The estate lawyer I hired, named Teagarden Jones if you can believe it, says without the paperwork, it's just hearsay."

"It all sounds pretty complicated. If Clarissa were going to destroy documents, why would she have left the former will around? Would she know the third wife would be out and she would be in?"

"It took me about five minutes to find the information on the internet, so I would say yes. Contrary to the impression she tries to create, Clarissa is no airhead."

"Wouldn't it have been safer to go—what do you call it when there's no will?"

"Intestate."

"Right. Wouldn't that have been a surer option? Or would her share have been less that way?"

"No, it would have been the same amount. Maybe she left the old will to avert suspicion."

Rowan raised an eyebrow. "Apparently it didn't work, since we're both suspicious."

"You, too? You've never even met Clarissa."

"I've met you. You usually give people the benefit of a doubt. So, if you think she's up to something, I believe you. What are you going to do about it?"

"I'm not sure there's anything I can do. If the documents are gone, and there's nothing to indicate his wishes, as executor, I have to fall back to the will we found."

"Could the new will simply be misplaced? Maybe in a safe-deposit box nobody knows about?"

"Dad had two safes, one at home and one in his business office, and I've gone through them both. Also, all his filing cabinets. Dad used a local lawyer for business, but they don't do wills, and the one who wrote the old will died years ago. If Dad wrote another will, he must have used a different lawyer, but I can't find any record of it, and he kept everything. He liked to organize his paperwork so that he could put his hands on any document instantly, and I can't imagine he'd have tucked a will away in a safe deposit box or left it with a lawyer, especially without keeping a copy at home."

"Hmm. Is there anything I can do to help you get custody? If you need a character witness to testify that you're a great parent—"

"Not yet anyway, but it means a lot that you think so."

She reached for her bag. "I suppose I should be getting home. I am flying out tomorrow."

"Visiting your fiancé in Japan?" It was none of his business, but he was curious about this fiancé. And about why she never wore a ring.

"Yes—no—that is, not Japan. Sutton is in California right now on business, and I'm, uh—" she licked her lip. "—I'm flying down to return his ring."

Zack blinked. "I'm not sure how to respond to that. I'm sorry? Congratulations?"

"I'm a little confused myself. I—well, it's complicated. But I can't break up over the phone, and I don't want to wait until we're both back in Japan. By that time, our mothers might have picked bridesmaids and hired a harpist."

Zack was a little lost. Frankly, he'd lost concentration about the time she said she was returning the ring. His heart was beating faster, and it was all he could do not to grin. "Well, when you get back, you're invited to dinner again, and this time, I'll cook." He considered his skills. "Or possibly get takeout."

She laughed. "It's a date. I told Becca we'd make cookies sometime, too. I hope that's okay."

"That's more than okay. She was happier with you than I've seen her in months."

"It was a pleasure. Truly. And now, I really do need to go. Thanks for letting me tag along on the moose release today."

"Anytime. You're part of the team, now."

She smiled. "I like that. See you soon."

"Goodbye, Rowan." He stood at the door and watched her walk to her car. "Good luck," he called, "with…everything."

CHAPTER NINE

"Sure I can't get you anything?" the waiter asked in a concerned voice.

Rowan set down the menu of the veggie-forward farm-to-table restaurant. Normally, she would have been making mental notes of things to try in her own kitchen, but not today. "A glass of iced tea?"

"Sure." He looked relieved to have something to do. Rowan checked her phone. No messages. Sutton was twenty-five minutes late, but she couldn't really blame him. When she'd called to say, surprise, she was in town, he'd been apologetic. He'd already scheduled meetings for the whole afternoon, but he would cancel his dinner plans and meet her instead. His last meeting must have run long. They often did. He'd told her many times that patience was the key to successful negotiations.

The waiter returned with a mint-garnished glass. "Just wave if you want to order appetizers or anything."

She glanced around. The restaurant was filling up. "I'm sure he'll be here soon. Let's get the sampler platter for when he arrives."

"Excellent choice."

Finally, she saw Sutton making his way to her table. He looked good in his tailored suit, the neck of his shirt open and tieless in deference to casual California culture. He kissed her cheek and took the chair across from her. "Well, this is a pleasant surprise."

Rowan managed a smile, although it felt forced. Should she dive right in? Let him enjoy his dinner first? His eyes looked tired. The waiter appeared. "Can I get you a drink, sir?"

"Whiskey and soda, please." As soon as the waiter left, Sutton smiled at Rowan. "I apologize for my tardiness. The meeting ran long."

"I assumed. How are negotiations going?"

"They were moving well, but today we hit a sticking point." He sighed. "I'm afraid I'm not going to be able to stay for dinner, after all. I agreed to go over the numbers with their finance man before we take up negotiations again tomorrow, and it will probably be a late night." He gave her a chiding look. "If you'd told me you were coming, I might have been able to rearrange my schedule. How long are you staying?"

So much for waiting until after dinner. "Just until tomorrow. I—"

"Whisky and soda, sir." The waiter set the drink in front of him.

Sutton raised his glass. *"Kanpai."*

Rowan clinked hers against his and watched as he drank. "Sutton—"

"Where is your ring?" he asked suddenly.

Well, there was her opening. "It's here." She reached into her bag for the silk-covered ring box and slid it across the table toward him.

"What—"

Time to bite the bullet. "Sutton, I'm sorry, but I can't marry you."

He frowned. "I don't understand."

"It feels rushed. We haven't been together that long, and—"

"We've been dating for two years." He pressed his lips together. "What is it, Rowan? You've never been one for drama. You accepted my proposal. Publicly. And now you want to back out?"

"It's just—I'm not sure we're on the same page about where we are in our relationship."

"After two years, an engagement would seem the next logical step. My proposal can't have come as a complete surprise."

"But it was. I—"

He finished his drink in one gulp. "Unfortunately, I don't have time to talk this through right now." He covered her hand with his. "If you need more time to think about this, I can wait. We can put the wedding on hold for a little while." He opened the box as if to assure himself it was the same diamond ring he'd given her and then slipped it into his pocket as he stood. "I'll keep this for now, until you're ready to wear it."

He patted her on the head. "Everything will be fine. I'll call you in the morning. Perhaps we can breakfast together." And he was gone.

He patted me on the head. A sudden and unaccustomed fury rose in her chest. Is this what he thought of her? That she was a stubborn child who could be cajoled into behaving the way he expected? At breakfast tomorrow, she had to make it clear. The wedding wasn't postponed. She was calling it off. All of it.

"Hi, me again." The waiter was back, giving her a sympathetic smile. "The gentleman said he had to go, but he's prepaid for your dinner."

"That's okay, I—" She started to get up, but she paused. "You know what? Yes. Go ahead and bring that appetizer platter." It was too much food for one person, but so what. She was tempted to order the pink lettuce salad with truffle-crusted swordfish, as well, just to say she'd tasted pink lettuce.

"Right away." He started off but turned back. "Would you like company? There is a couple over there waiting for a table. They come in here all the time, and—"

She glanced over at the pair around her parents' age talking to the hostess. "I'd love some company." A distraction would be much preferable than sitting and stewing, and they looked like pleasant people.

"Great. I'll bring them over." She watched him go talk to the couple. Hopefully, he wasn't telling them she was some pathetic woman whose date had deserted her.

Their smiles when they came to the table reassured her. "It's so nice of you to share your table. We decided to just drop by and see if we might get lucky," the wife, a plump woman with a chin-length blond bob explained as she settled into the chair the waiter was holding. "I'm Daphne, and this is Tony."

"Glad to meet you. I'm Rowan."

"We love this restaurant," Daphne told her. "Do you come here often?"

"No. I'm from out of town. I just flew in today."

"Where from?"

Rowan decided to keep it simple. "Alaska."

"Oh, we love Alaska, don't we, Tony? We've been, what, four times?"

"Five," he corrected. "Three cruises, another time in the summer and that one winter excursion."

"That was so much fun. We saw the Iditarod

start in Anchorage, and then took the train to Fairbanks to see the World Ice Carving Championships."

The waiter arrived with a tray bearing two glasses of wine, three small plates and a huge platter overflowing with colorful vegetables and dips prepared in all sorts of ways. Rowan's eyes widened. "Please, help me eat all this."

"Well, if you insist." Tony spooned a little sauce on a plate and dipped a tempura mushroom into it. "Thank you."

"We've been to Denali National Park twice," Daphne commented as she transferred some colorful vegetable sushi pieces to her plate. "We love seeing the wildlife there. What is it you do in Alaska?"

"I was there to visit my grandmother, but as a matter of fact, right now I'm helping to organize a fundraiser for a wildlife rehabilitation center at Palmer."

"Palmer? We went to the state fair there. Remember the giant cabbage, Tony?" Daphne's laugh tinkled like a bell. "Tell me about this wildlife center."

"WildER. It's small but busy. All volunteer. A local veterinarian started it because people would bring in wild animals they'd found who needed help. Their goal is to patch them up and return them to the wild as quickly as possible.

Yesterday, I had the privilege of watching the release of a moose who had survived a bear attack along with her calf. It was so moving, seeing the two of them go off into the woods."

"Wonderful!" Daphne exclaimed.

"What sort of fundraiser are you planning?" Tony asked.

"We're calling it 'WildFair.' I'm lining up a series of food booths for tastings, activities for kids and an auction of donated prizes to follow. My brother and sister-in-law run a goat dairy farm and cheese-making operation near Palmer, and they've volunteered to host it."

"That sounds like so much fun. Tony, we should attend."

"When is it?" He finished the bite in his hand, took out his phone and waited for the information as though his wife suggesting they needed to attend an event in Alaska was an everyday occurrence.

"The second Saturday in July," Rowan told him.

"We're free," he told his wife. "Oh, do you remember watching the Mount Marathon race in Seward three years ago? They always hold it on the Fourth of July."

His wife shook her head, but she was smiling. "You're not thinking what I think you're thinking?"

Laugh lines fanned out from the edges of his eyes. "Why not?"

"He does this," Daphne told Rowan in an aside. "Runs up mountains. For fun." She sipped her wine. "Are you sure, darling? Some of those runners looked pretty raw after sliding on the rocks on the way down."

"I'd take it slow. I'm in it for the experience, not the win." He grinned. "Although, if I were to place high in my age group, it might earn me a better start position for the Hawaii race this fall."

"Oh, all right. If you really want to do this, I'll be waiting at the finish line with pom-poms."

He leaned toward his wife for a quick kiss. "She will, too," he told Rowan, and pulled up something on his phone. "This was at the finish line at a mountain race in Colorado."

Rowan looked at the photo of Tony, a race number pinned to his shirt, approaching a balloon-festooned arch and Daphne on the other side, caught midleap waving huge blue-and-white pom-poms. "Looks like a great day."

"It was." He smiled at his wife. "We've had a lot of great days together."

"Wildlife rehabilitation is such a good cause," Daphne said to Tony. "We should donate something."

"How about the Acapulco timeshare?" Tony suggested. "We won't be using it because of that

January trip to Chile, and Alaskans might enjoy a winter getaway."

"Yes, let's." She smiled at Rowan. "Does that work for you?"

Rowan blinked. "Um, yes. Absolutely. That's incredibly generous."

"Not at all. As Tony said, we won't be using it and we just love Alaskan wildlife. Here, give me your email address and I'll make all the arrangements for the transfer."

Rowan wrote down her contact information and the WildER website. "Thank you so much."

"You're welcome. Now, tell us more about this goat farm where you're holding the event."

They talked their way through a delicious dinner. Daphne, it seemed, had come up with the concept of a set of video games that allowed players to become characters in classic science fiction novels, and when she was looking for someone to help with development, Tony's name kept coming up. He'd been intrigued, by both the idea and the woman. They married, and together they founded a company that succeeded beyond all expectations. Ten years ago, they'd sold the business and now spent their time however they wished.

Rowan found them fascinating. She'd traveled quite a lot, but they'd gone everywhere. Tiny villages in China, ancient pyramids in Peru, even

Antarctica, and they seemed to have enjoyed every minute of their life together. She would bet Tony never patted Daphne on the head.

They were planning a trip to Japan in the late fall, and she made a few suggestions that were warmly received. At the end of the evening, Tony and Daphne gave her a ride to her hotel. "I'll be in touch with the details about that timeshare," Daphne promised. "I can't wait to see you again in Alaska in July."

"I won't—" Rowan started to explain that she would be back in Japan by then, but upon reflection, there was no reason she couldn't come to Palmer for the fundraiser. "I'll see you then."

She made her way to the elevator and pushed the button for her floor. What an amazing couple, and incredibly generous. She couldn't wait to get back to Alaska and tell Zack and Maggie.

In her room, a light blinked on the hotel phone, indicating a waiting message. Who would have called here instead of her cell? Only someone who didn't want to have to deal with her immediate response.

Sure enough, it was a message from Sutton, canceling breakfast. "I apologize, but this looks like an all-nighter. Right now, I need to concentrate on this deal. When I get back to Tokyo, we can talk. I'm sure you understand."

Of course she understood. Rowan always understood. She was always the one who volunteered to wait for the next elevator when the first was too full. The one who filled in if someone canceled at an embassy dinner. The one who did all the legwork in setting up events, leaving her supervisor to take the credit when things went smoothly.

The fact that her gut reaction to Sutton canceling breakfast was more relief than disappointment confirmed what she should have recognized a long time ago. Sutton was a good man. But he wasn't the right man for Rowan.

CHAPTER TEN

ZACK TIED OFF the last stitch. "How's the blood pressure?" he asked his veterinary assistant.

"Good. Pulse and breathing are fine."

Zack gave the unconscious black Labrador a pat. "You're going to feel a whole lot better, buddy."

Christine poked her head into the operating room. "Was it socks?"

Zack gestured toward the objects laid out on a rack next to the operating table. "Seventeen of them."

"Darn, I had sixteen in the office pool."

"There was a pool?" the assistant asked.

"She's kidding." Zack exchanged smiles with Christine before she withdrew to go on to her next patient. "I'm pretty sure seventeen is a clinic record, though. Let's get him to recovery and I'll go talk to his people."

Zack picked up his phone to snap a photo of the unfortunate collection of hosiery and noticed a text from Rowan. Back in town. I have news for you and Maggie. Meet at the wildlife center later?

He mentally reviewed his schedule. Five clinic appointments this afternoon, then a meeting with the estate lawyer and one scheduled stop to vaccinate a pet bison. Assuming the bison wasn't too difficult, he should be done by his usual quitting time. Jessie was driving today. He texted his reply. Good news I hope. 5:30? Dinner at my place after? I'll grill.

Yum. I'll bring a side. See you then.

Perfect. Good thing he'd picked up a package of T-bones, speculating this might happen. He'd thought of Rowan often in the last couple of days. She said she was returning her fiancé's ring, but what did that mean? Was she breaking up with him, or simply not ready to be married? Was she single now?

Did it matter? Rowan was only visiting Alaska. Zack had no time for dating. Better to stay in the friend zone. Becca would be thrilled she was back. In the three days since Rowan and Becca cooked dinner, Becca had reminded him at least ten times to invite Rowan over again.

Was he setting Becca up for disappointment later, letting her get attached to Rowan? But they both knew she lived in Japan. They might as well enjoy her company while they could. They would have plenty of time to miss her after she was gone.

"THAT'S FANTASTIC. Thanks so much." Rowan ended the call with the head of public relations from the airline and pumped her fist. The donation of round-trip airfare from Anchorage to Mexico was a go.

She pulled up the details Daphne had forwarded from the timeshare management team and paged through some promotional photos. This alone could draw a crowd for the fundraiser and help convince other businesses that a donation would result in great exposure. She made a note of several she wanted to approach tomorrow. Maybe she could even drop by one or two this afternoon. It was hard to wait.

She made careful notes for the WildER board. Gran was expected to be cleared to drive at her doctor's appointment next Monday, after which Rowan would have no excuse to stay in Alaska, and she'd have to hand the project over. It had been a long time since Rowan had worked on anything that got her this excited, though. She hated to abandon it.

Maybe she didn't have to. Work had been slow when she left. She dialed her boss. "Hi. Do you have a minute?"

"Rowan. How is your grandmother?"

"She's healing well, but she needs me to stay a little longer until she can drive. Is that a problem?"

"No. Your grandmother's health is most important." He sounded, if anything, relieved. "Yui is handling the camera merger and we have just finished the frozen vegetables. Stay where you are needed."

Ah. What he was saying was that her unpaid leave was making his life easier. Summers tended to be slow for their company. She decided to feel him out. "I've been volunteering on a fundraiser for a nonprofit here in Alaska. If you don't need me, I might extend my leave to help with that."

"Take a few weeks if you like. They are fortunate to have your expertise."

She thanked him and after inquiring about the health of his family, said her goodbyes. Feeling suddenly lighter, she realized how much she had been dreading her return to Japan. To her apartment, where she would annoy her roommate by displacing her cousin to the couch. To a job that had grown monotonous. And worst, to the endless questions her mother would throw at her once she learned the engagement was off. A week or three to fortify herself before facing her mother sounded like an excellent idea.

Unfortunately, she hadn't accounted for phone calls. Rowan had just returned to her car after a successful meeting with the owner of a new ice cream shop when the distinctive ring signaled a call from her mother. She cleared her throat, reminding herself to sound upbeat and normal. "Hi, Mom."

"Sutton called his mother, and she called me."

Oops. Rowan had counted on Sutton keeping the news to himself until he returned to Tokyo. "Oh?"

"Oh? Is that all you have to say? Go to video calling. I want to see your face."

"That's not neces—"

Mom hung up and called back on the video app. Her disapproval beamed from the tiny screen. "What's this about returning Sutton's ring?"

It seemed self-explanatory. "I, uh, returned his ring."

"But why? Even a spring wedding might be out of the question if you won't set a date. You might have to move it to autumn." Mom tilted her head and looked up. "Although autumn colors would be lovely."

"No, Mom—"

"Honey, I know this is a big step." Mom had lost most of her Virginia drawl over the years, but it tended to pop up in times of stress. Today it was front and center. "But you two are so well suited. Coralie told me Sutton is willing to give you time, but the man won't wait forever. I know once you've thought it through, you'll want to move forward."

"Mom. I don't—"

"Shh. Don't say anything else right now. I won't push you about wedding plans anymore, until you've had a chance to get comfortable with the idea of marriage. Come on home, so we can talk it out."

Bad idea. "Gran—"

"Is doing much better, I understand. I called her earlier and she said she expects the all clear for driving on Monday. I'll have someone book you a flight for Tuesday."

"No, don't. I'm not ready to come yet. There's a wildlife rehabilitation center here, and I've volunteered to help them plan a fundraiser."

"A fundraiser? That's admirable, but one doesn't need a master's in international business in order to plan a bake sale. What about your job?"

"As you know, I've taken a leave of absence. They're fine without me for a while."

"Rowan, you need to come home. I insist."

"No." This time Rowan said it a little louder. "Not until I'm ready. I have to go, Mom. I'm meeting someone." Never mind that it wasn't for two more hours. "Thanks for the call. Goodbye." She hung up before her mother could say more.

She felt like screaming but settled for huffing out a long breath. First Sutton and now her own mother. It was like being in a *Twilight Zone* episode. She kept saying no, and they kept hearing "soon." One would think that after a lifetime of being agreeable, her *no* would carry a little weight, but that didn't seem to be the case.

At least she had made it clear that she was not going back to Japan right away, despite her mother's insistence. Come to think of it, that may have been the first time she'd ever stood her ground when Mom insisted. A small victory, but she'd take it.

JESSIE'S SUV TURNED into the clinic parking lot just as Zack stepped outside. He spotted Rowan and Maggie already talking by Rowan's jeep. The second Jessie's car came to a stop, Becca was out and running toward Rowan. "You're back! Can you come over to eat today? Zack will say okay." She threw her arms around Rowan's waist.

Rowan laughed and hugged her back. "Zack already invited me."

"Can we make cookies?" Becca asked.

Before Rowan could answer, Charlotte and

Jessie joined the group. "I want to make cookies," Charlotte said. "Can I come, too?"

"We're watching Daddy's softball game," her mother reminded her.

"If you have just a second, I want to show you our latest auction item." Rowan pulled a stack of papers from her bag and passed them out. It showed photos of a nicely furnished condo with a balcony overlooking someplace with beaches and palm trees.

"Wow," Maggie said. "A week in a luxury timeshare and you got the airline to pitch in airfare, as well?"

"That should raise a tidy sum." Jessie said. "Who donated the timeshare?"

"A couple I met in California day before yesterday. They're crazy about Alaska wildlife, and when I told them about the auction, they wanted to help. They're even flying up to go to the event."

Jessie's eyes widened. "You just met these people?"

"I was shocked, as well."

"What were you doing in California?" Maggie asked.

Zack noticed Rowan's smile slip just a little. "Personal business. But I'm glad to be back in Alaska."

"We're glad you're back, too," Jessie said. "We

really do have to go, but I'll pass this on to Greg. This is awesome, Rowan."

"Me, too. But wow." Maggie waved the paper. "Nice work, Rowan."

Becca didn't care about timeshares. "What about cookies?" she asked Rowan.

"I have all the ingredients in the car." Rowan took out a well-used cookbook, opened it to a bookmarked page and pointed something out to Becca.

Knowing he was leaving Becca in good hands, Zack handed over his house key and left them to bake while he did his rounds at the wildlife center. As always, Maggie had left everything shipshape. Zack continually thanked his lucky stars that Maggie had happened to bring her cat for an office visit the same day he'd put up a sign looking for a volunteer to help feed and care for an injured wolf pup, his first on-premises wildlife patient. She'd pitched in the very first day and never looked back.

It took less than an hour for Zack to check up on all the animals and make his way home. He followed his nose to the kitchen, where Becca, her face drawn in concentration, was rolling dough into balls. A frilly apron with printed cherries covered her clothes. An unfamiliar slow cooker sat in an out-of-the-way corner. Rowan took a sheet of cookies from the oven. When she turned, Zack realized her apron matched the one Becca wore. Both were so involved with their tasks, they didn't notice him.

Rowan paused to inspect the cookies. "Perfect," she told Becca. "We'll let them cool for just a few minutes before we transfer them to the wire rack to finish cooling. How are you coming with the next tray?"

"Almost done," Becca answered as she added another round ball of dough in a neat row. "Do you think Zack will like the cookies?"

"Zack will love them. I once saw him eat a whole plate of cookies."

Zack chuckled. "It was a small plate, and that was after a day of skiing at Big Lake."

Becca looked up, grinning. "Hi, Zack. We made chocolate chip cookies because Rowan says they're your favorite. And look, we're twins!"

"Nice. Where did those aprons come from?"

"My grandmother made them when I was Becca's age. I'd forgotten all about them, but when I mentioned we were going to make cookies, Gran gave them to me. Aren't they cute?"

"Very cute." He pulled out his phone. "I need a picture."

"Let's pose, Becca." Rowan came to stand beside Becca and flared out her hand like a model gesturing to the cookies. Becca managed a fair imitation. The photo captured them both smiling.

Zack could almost feel the warmth of that smile, melting away the sharp corners that kept Becca on edge. Becca was such a great kid. If only her mother appreciated her even half as much as Rowan seemed to, he wouldn't be in the dilemma he found himself. "I'll get the grill started," he told Rowan.

"I'll get the steaks out of the fridge." Rowan waved toward the slow cooker. "I brought roasted sweet potatoes with feta to go with them."

"Oh, thanks." Odd combination, but it wouldn't kill Becca or him to try something new.

It didn't take long to grill the steaks and heat the rolls he'd bought at the bakery. Rowan and Becca set the table on the covered deck and they all sat down to eat.

Becca tried a tiny bite of the sweet potato Rowan put on her plate. To his surprise, she took a bigger bite. "This is good!"

Zack tried it. It was good. He'd never been a huge fan of sweet potatoes, but the tangy feta took the flavor to a new level.

"This is an experimental batch of feta. From goat's milk."

"Baby goats are called kids, just like people are," Becca told Rowan, between bites. "Isn't that funny?"

"It is funny. We have a bunch of kids on the farm. Maybe you can come out to see them sometime."

"Can I, Zack?" Becca asked eagerly.

"How about Saturday?" Rowan suggested.

"Sure. I guess that means you'll be in Alaska a while longer?" Zack asked Rowan.

"For a couple of weeks, anyhow." A cloud passed over Rowan's face, but it was gone almost before he could be sure he'd seen it.

During dinner, Rowan asked all about Becca's camp and what had been going on at the wildlife sanctuary while she was out of town. Zack told them about the Labrador sock surgery. It was hard to tell who laughed harder, Rowan or Becca.

"Seventeen socks." Rowan shook her head and chuckled. "Just out of curiosity, were they mostly pairs of socks, or did he eat seventeen different socks and leave their mates behind?"

"Honestly, I didn't pay that close of attention. His owners have assured me they are going to store their clothes hamper behind closed doors from now on."

After dinner, Becca insisted on another evening of Go Fish. She protested when Zack announced it was time for bath and bed, agreeing only when she'd extracted a promise from Rowan not to leave until she'd joined Becca and Zack in reading time.

Zack ran a bubble bath, added a small flotilla of rubber ducks and set a clean towel beside the tub. "Is that everything you need?"

Becca took the toothbrush from her mouth. "Why does Rowan have to go back to Japan? I want her to stay here."

"Rowan has a job in Japan," Zack said gently. And possibly a fiancé. He'd been waiting all evening to find out how that went.

"She could get a job here. She could work at the clinic with you and Christine."

"That's not the kind of work Rowan does. She's not a vet."

"Maybe she could help Maggie at the wild-life center."

"I'm sorry, Becks, but I don't think that's going to happen."

"But I like cooking with her, and telling stories while we eat, and playing games."

"We can still do those things even after Rowan goes home." He didn't know how he was going to fit it all in, but now that he knew how important it was to Becca, he would find a way. "Right now, you need to take your bath."

She rinsed her toothbrush as Zack opened the bathroom door. Just before he shut it behind him, Becca said, almost in a whisper, "Zack?"

He stopped. "Yes?"

"Is Mommy ever coming back to Alaska?"

Was being with Rowan causing Becca to miss her mother? "I'm sure she will, eventually."

She paused. "I like living with you better."

He turned around, removed the toothbrush from her hand and wrapped her in a hug. "I like having you live with me better, too." He wanted to tell her he was trying to make it permanent, but he didn't want to get her hopes up. "Take your bath before the water gets cold. I love you, Becks."

When he returned downstairs, Rowan had put away the cards and swept the kitchen. A red-checkered cookie tin set on the counter-top. Her expression changed to one of concern when she spotted his face. "Everything okay with Becca?"

"For now." He sank into a kitchen chair and rested his forehead on his hands. "This situation with her mother has me worried."

"How, exactly?" Rowan took the chair next to him and touched his arm.

"It's the same old thing. I—" He shook his head and sat up straight. "Never mind about that right now. I want to know what happened in California. Did you break off your engagement?"

"I returned the ring and I told Sutton I couldn't marry him."

"How did he take it?"

Rowan gave a wry smile. "He didn't, exactly. He said he understood that I needed more time."

"Did you ask for more time?"

"No!" Rowan huffed out her frustration. "That's what's so bizarre. He just wouldn't hear me. Before I could say more, he left. And then, today, he tells his mother he's giving me time to get comfortable with the idea of marriage. His mother calls my mother, and she calls me to say I need to hurry up or it will be too late to plan a wedding for next spring. I tell her no. She translates that as *soon*. It's like words are coming out of my mouth, but nobody is hearing them."

He considered offering advice on speaking forcefully, but wasn't that exactly what Rowan was complaining about? That no one listened? Instead, he asked, "What are you going to do?"

"Once we're both back in Japan, I'll meet with Sutton again and make him listen. I don't want to marry him. I don't want to date him. We're through."

Zack tried to hide the flash of joy he felt when she said that, but he couldn't help but grin. "That seems perfectly clear to me."

"Thank you." She sucked in a breath and blew it out. "Now, tell me what has you worried about Becca."

"I told you I want permanent custody."

She nodded.

"But I met with a family lawyer today, and she tells me that unless Clarissa agrees, it's going to be difficult. Clarissa isn't exactly mother of the year, but a single man with what amounts to two jobs isn't exactly the court's picture of the ideal guardian, either."

Rowan tilted her head. "You know what? We should get married."

He laughed. "Yeah, right."

"No, really. A wife would help your chances for custody, and it would get my mother and Sutton off my back."

He examined her face, looking for the telltale dimple that appeared when she was about to laugh, but he didn't see it. "You're serious."

"Yes. See? You can tell when I'm being serious. Why can't anyone else?"

"I—we—" Zack couldn't seem to form a sentence, but fortunately, he was saved when Becca came bounding down the stairs, her bare feet slapping against the steps.

"I picked out a really good book. Come tuck me in!"

"We're coming." Rowan met her at the bottom of the stairs and draped an arm over her shoulders in an easy hug. "I like the strawberries on your pajamas."

Still in a daze from Rowan's proposal, Zack

followed behind them. Outside Becca's room, Rowan whispered, "Think about it. We'll talk later."

Zack could only nod.

CHAPTER ELEVEN

ROWAN LISTENED TO Zack's voice as he read the last page. Calm, soothing, his full attention on Becca and the story. You'd never know he was tired and worried. The room he'd created for Becca was the same, serene and comfortable. With a simple green comforter on the bed, lots of shelves for books and a checked cushion on the window seat, it wasn't a typical little girl's room, but it was perfect for Becca.

Was that reassuring presence something Zack had developed as a veterinarian, or was it instinctive? Either way, he was exactly the person Becca needed. Could Rowan help make that happen?

"The end." Zack closed the book and set it on the nightstand. "Good story, Becks." He tugged the covers up and kissed her forehead. "Good night."

"Good night, Zack. Good night, Rowan." Becca's voice blurred with sleepiness. "I like when you're here."

"Me, too." Rowan planted another kiss on top of Zack's. "Pleasant dreams, sweet girl."

She followed Zack down the stairs, waiting to see what he would say, but instead of speaking, he went to the window and stared out toward the wooded area that surrounded the wildlife rehab center. The tension showed in his shoulders. Rowan's first urge was to wrap her arms around him and tell him everything would be okay. But would it? Did her idea help solve his problems, or had she added another worry on top of the pile he already carried?

"Zack?" She took a step closer but stopped before she touched him. "I'm sorry if I was out of line—"

He chuckled, and slowly his chuckle grew into a full laugh. He turned to her. She smiled back at him even though she wasn't sure about the joke. "What?"

"You're always apologizing. Rowan, you are the nicest person I know. You have nothing to be sorry about."

"I thought you might be struggling with how you were going to turn me down without hurting my feelings. The last thing I want is to add to your problems."

"There you go again, worrying about other people."

"Well, what about you? You're the one taking

care of your little sister and trying to win custody because you want a better life for her than she would get with her mother. Not many young, single professionals would feel that way."

"Becca means a lot to me."

"And you mean a lot to her. That's why I think we should get married. And I'm not being entirely altruistic. I've somehow gotten myself wedged into a life I never wanted. This way, I could start over."

Zack shook his head. "I spent my life watching my father's marriages and the chaos he left behind. I decided a long time ago that marriage isn't for me."

"I'm not talking about a real marriage. Just an arrangement between friends. You need a wife to help you get custody of Becca, and I need a fresh start. Once you have custody and I've had a chance to figure out what I want to do with my life, we could get an annulment."

"So, you're proposing—"

"Marriage in name only. You have a guest room, right?"

"Yes."

"Well, then, I could live here and take care of grocery shopping, cooking and chauffeuring Becca, and it would give me a home base to work on organizing the fundraiser."

"But you have an important job in Tokyo."

"I have a job in Tokyo. I'd hardly call it important. Honestly, my boss would probably be thrilled if I quit. Of course, that means I wouldn't have a paycheck, but thanks to my grandmother, I am part owner of Now and Forever Farms, and we've reached the point of paying out a small quarterly dividend. It's not making us rich, but it is enough for me to pitch in for my share of household expenses."

"I'm not worried about household expenses—"

"Maybe you should be, at least until this fundraiser happens. Maggie told me about you covering the wildlife center's bills with your own money."

"Rowan, it means the world to me that you've offered, but I can't let you do this. You'd be giving up too much."

"What would I be giving up? A job I don't like? Having my mother looking over my shoulder all the time?"

"What if you met a man you want to marry for real?"

"I'm thirty-two, and it hasn't happened yet. I need to get myself together before I think about marriage."

"And how, exactly, would taking on my problems help you get yourself together?"

"I've lived my whole life in my mother's shadow. Don't get me wrong, she's a great mom and she loves me. But she's never allowed me to…*struggle*, I guess would be the word. She smooths the path in front of me and steers me the way she thinks I should go. It's time to start making my own decisions."

He raised an eyebrow. "And your first decision is a fake marriage?"

"I know it sounds strange. But I really do care about you and Becca. Look at it this way. A lot of people take a gap year between high school and college, or between college and starting a career. We could commit to a year, where I help with Becca and you give me time to figure out what I want to do with the rest of my life."

"Becca already adores you. What happens when you leave in a year?"

"It will be hard, for both of us. But when you hire a nanny, they're not committed to staying forever, right? It's kind of the same thing." She touched his arm. "I'll leave you now. Thank you for a wonderful dinner. Think about what I've said."

How could he think about anything else?

"Ready, Becks?" Zack called up the stairs the next morning. They needed to be out in ten minutes if she and Charlotte were going to arrive at camp on time. He took the final swig of coffee from his third cup. He hadn't gotten much sleep last night, turning over Rowan's proposal in his mind. Not that he could take her up on it. Could he?

"I want a ponytail," Becca called.

"Then hurry. Come down once you're dressed and I'll fix it." His phone rang. Clarissa. Great. He had neither time nor patience to deal with her, but he answered anyway. "Good morning."

"I need another advance." Well, no one could say she wasted his time.

"Did you see the deposit I put in your account a couple of weeks ago?"

"I need more. I'm entitled to it."

"Fine, how much?"

The figure she mentioned would buy a lot of animal feed. His father had been a wealthy man, but at the rate Clarissa was spending, she'd run out of money in—Zack did a rough calculation in his head—ten years or so. He considered mentioning that she was burning through her money at an unsustainable rate, but what would that accomplish? "I'll take care of it."

"What's the delay with settling the estate, anyway? It's my money, according to the law. I shouldn't have to beg you for it."

"Legal stuff always takes time." Especially when the only will to turn up was completely out of date. "You should have the advance in your account within a week or so."

"Good."

"I want a braid, instead, okay, Zack?" Becca called as she trotted down the stairs. "Oh, who are you talking to?"

"Your mother. Here." He took the brush and hair tie from Becca's hands and handed her his cell phone. He'd let Becca believe Clarissa had called to talk to her.

"Mommy?" Becca listened while Zack brushed her hair smooth and separated it into three sections. He'd become surprisingly good at braiding hair in the last couple of months.

"Uh-huh… Oh…" He couldn't help but notice Becca wasn't answering any questions. She squirmed as though she was eager to get away from the phone, which made the braid come out crooked, but he didn't have time to do it again. Zack was just twisting the elastic onto the end when Becca said, "Bye, Mommy."

He took the phone from her hand and held it to his ear. "We need to go, Clarissa. Was there anything else?"

"Just the money. Thank you for taking care of Becca for me. Cheers." She ended the call.

Was it Zack's imagination, or did she put emphasis on the "for me" part of that last sentence? But he didn't have time to think about it right now. He fed the cat, gathered his phone and keys and stuffed the lunch he'd assembled last night into Becca's backpack.

"Ready?" he asked Becca, who was still standing where he'd left her, staring at the wall.

She looked up. "What?"

"I asked if you're ready to go." He handed her the backpack. "You okay, Becks?"

She nodded and followed him to the garage, but her mind still seemed far away. He opened the door of the truck and herded Becca and Ripley into the back seat. "What did your mom have to say?"

"She said I'd like swimming in the ocean. But I don't know how to swim."

He wasn't sure if she was upset because she couldn't swim, or if she'd picked up on the hint that Clarissa might be considering taking her there. He tried not to react. "Next week your age group at camp is supposed to start swim lessons at the high school. I'll bet you'll be a good swimmer."

"I don't have a swimsuit."

"Do you have one at the house?" Meaning Dad and Clarissa's house. Zack had brought most of Becca's clothes over, but she might have left things like sandals and swimsuits behind.

"I don't know."

"You know, you've grown so much since last

summer, you'll probably need a new one, anyway. I'll take you shopping on Saturday."

"On Saturday, I'm going with Rowan to see the baby goats." Her voice brightened. "Maybe Rowan can take me shopping. She'd be better. She has pretty clothes."

He glanced at his work pants and T-shirt and laughed. "Are you saying I don't have pretty clothes?"

"You're with animals all the time. You're not supposed to have pretty clothes."

"Good point. Well, I can ask Rowan if she has time."

"I'll bet she will. She's really nice."

"Yes." If she only knew. Rowan was the most selfless person he'd ever been around, and that concerned him. She needed to realize that her own needs and wants were just as important as anyone else's. Including his and Becca's.

Just before they reached Jessie and Greg's house to pick up Charlotte, Becca spoke again. "Zack?"

"Yes?"

"I don't want to go swimming in an ocean with Mommy. I want to stay with you."

Zack didn't want to make promises he couldn't keep, but he couldn't let Becca continue to live with this hanging over her head. "I want you to stay with me, too." He pulled into the driveway, stopped the truck and turned to look Becca in the eye. "I'll figure out a way, Becks. Just leave it to me. Okay?"

"Okay." He could see the tension melting from her shoulders. She trusted him, trusted that he would take care of her. Now he had to find a way to make it happen. Whatever it took, he wasn't going to let Becca down.

CHAPTER TWELVE

"We'll play with the goats and then eat at the tasting room before we go shopping," Rowan said, while Zack strapped Becca's booster seat into the back of Patrick's old jeep.

"Sounds good. I got a call that someone is bringing in a lynx kitten. It doesn't sound too serious. If it goes well, I can pick Becca up in two hours or so. Will that work?"

"Can we have a little longer? It's not easy to find the perfect swimsuit. We'll probably need to go to Wasilla. I can bring her home when we're done."

He laid a hand on Becca's shoulder. "Are you okay with that?" For a moment Rowan wondered about his serious tone, but then she remembered he'd said Becca liked to know exactly when things would happen.

But today Becca's mood seemed carefree. "Yes! I want to play with the goats and go shopping with Rowan."

"Okay, then. I'll probably be in the wildlife center, so call when you're on your way back."

"We will." Rowan was already helping Becca buckle up. "Good luck with the lynx."

On the drive to the farm, Becca chattered about Charlotte and the hikes they had been doing at camp. "We saw baby ducks. Did you know you're not supposed to feed ducks bread? That's what my counselor says."

"I've heard that."

"Next week is our turn to go to the swimming pool at the high school for lessons. That's why I need to get a swimsuit. I've been to the pool before, but I had to stay in the shallow part, because I can't swim. Charlotte's daddy taught her to swim already, so she'll be in a different class than me. Charlotte's swimsuit has a unicorn on it."

"Do you like unicorns?"

"I like real animals better. Maybe I could find one with a moose. Moose like to swim. They have hollow hair that helps them float. And they can close their noses while they eat plants underwater."

"I didn't know that."

"Zack told me. He knows a whole lot about animals. He's the best brother in the whole world."

"I'll have to tell him you said that. I've got a pretty good brother, too. His name is Patrick."

"Does he know all about moose?"

"I don't know, but he's learned an awful lot

about goats since he met Lauren, his wife. He's also an electrician and he's working on the North Slope this week, so you won't get to meet him, but you'll meet Lauren today." Rowan pulled up in the parking area. "In fact, there she is."

Lauren led a mother goat with a bell on her collar toward the enclosed area where they did goat yoga. Three kids followed along, prancing and dodging as they went. Becca giggled. "They're so cute. That one has a black circle around one eye."

"Yes," Rowan said. "Oh, there's Gran and her dog, Wilson. Let me introduce you."

Everyone was delighted to meet Becca, especially Wilson, who wiggled his long body in delight when Becca petted him. "My friends are meeting me later at the tasting room," Gran told Becca. "I hope you'll join us for some of Lauren's yummy cheese."

"That's the plan," Rowan said. "But first Becca wants to meet the goats."

"Then come right over here." Lauren let Becca and Rowan into the pen. "This is Spritz," she told Becca. "She's very good at escaping, so we put a bell on her to help us find her."

Spritz was a character. The goat had served as ring bearer at Patrick and Lauren's outdoor wedding, although the way she was clinging to

Patrick that day, Rowan had wondered if Spritz thought she was the bride.

"And these are Spritz's three kids," Lauren continued. "Lemon Tart, Thumbprint and Gingersnap."

Becca stroked her hands over the kids and giggled when one tried to suck on her finger. "I like the farm because I can pet the animals. I can't pet any of the animals at the wildlife center, because they're wild. Except Puddin, and I can't pet her because she's a porcupine."

"A sticky problem." Gran laughed at her own joke.

Becca, Lauren and Rowan played with the kids. Gran sat on a bench just outside the goats' pen and held Wilson on her lap while she and Becca had an animated conversation about farm animals.

The rest of the Mat Mates arrived early and came to see what Gran was up to. She introduced them to Becca.

"I'm glad to meet you, Becca. Do you have a library card?" Linda asked her. "Your brother used to come to the library every Saturday when he was your age." She dropped her voice to a conspiratorial whisper. "There was a limit of three books at a time, but sometimes I'd let him take an extra one or two to get him through the week."

"I like reading, too."

"What are you reading, now?"

"A book about pirates," Becca answered. She and Linda discussed books while petting the kids. It was interesting to note that, even though Linda was long retired, she still recognized many of the children's books Becca mentioned. When it was time to open the tasting room, Lauren returned the goats to their pasture while Rowan took Becca to wash her hands. They sat at a table where the Mat Mates had already set out three cheese and fruit platters.

"Have you ever done yoga?" Gran asked Becca as she passed her some cheese and grapes.

"We did it at school once," Becca said.

"The six of us come to goat yoga here on Sunday afternoons," Gran told Becca. "You'll have to try it sometime."

"Can we, Rowan?"

"I'll ask Zack."

"What are your plans for the rest of the day?" Bea asked Becca.

"Me and Rowan are going shopping, 'cause I need a swimsuit for swim lessons at camp next week."

"Good for you," Gran told her. "Rowan told me you're learning to cook, too. You're learning all sorts of important skills this summer. What kind of cookies did you end up making?"

While Becca told Gran all about the cookie making, Rosemary handed Rowan a slip of paper. "A friend of mine who owns a plant nursery in Anchorage wants to donate to the auction. Give her a call."

"That's great. Thanks!" Rowan tucked the paper in her pocket and told Rosemary and Molly about the timeshare. She had just accepted Molly's offer to create a poster for the fundraiser when Rowan was shocked to see a familiar figure walking toward the table. "Mom?"

Gran turned in her seat. "Renee! I had no idea you were coming."

"Don't get up." Mom bent to kiss Gran's cheek. "Rowan stayed away for so long, I thought I'd better come check in person. You look well."

"I am. You remember my friends." While Gran rattled off everyone's name, Rowan scrambled to her feet. "And this is Becca Vogel, Rowan's guest today." Gran finished the introductions. "Sit down. Try some cheese."

"It's good to see you ladies again. Hello, Becca. I'm glad to meet you."

"Hi." Becca looked uncertain, as though she could sense the sudden tension.

"How are you, Rowan?" Mom came around the table and opened her arms.

Rowan hugged her mother, catching a whiff of Shalimar. Her mother's signature scent usually reassured Rowan, but today the perfume seemed overwhelming. "I'm fine."

"I'm glad. I've been concerned. Let's—"

"Rowan," Gran interrupted, looking at her watch. "You and Becca had better get moving if you're going to make it on time."

Rowan hesitated momentarily before she caught on. "You're right. I hadn't realized how late it had gotten. I'm sorry, Mom, but I have another engagement. We can talk later. How long are you staying?"

"I haven't decided." Mom gave her that unblinking look that indicated she'd stay as long as it took.

"I'll be back by dinnertime, so I'll see you this evening. Come on, Becca. Let's go." She took Becca's hand and hurried her away before she could ask questions in front of Mom.

"Are we still going shopping?" Becca asked innocently as they climbed into the jeep.

"Absolutely. Shopping is the engagement I mentioned to my Mom. Are you hungry?" Rowan asked as she realized she'd dragged Becca away before she could eat her cheese. "We can have lunch before we shop. What sounds good? Pizza? Burgers? Tacos?"

"Tacos, I guess."

"Good, because I love tacos." So did Zack, or at least he used to. Rowan wondered if the taco stand they used to go to that summer was still in the same place. She turned the corner and circled the high school. The stand was gone, but a spacious restaurant now filled the lot, and according to the sign, it was still Arctic Tacos. She hoped they still tasted the same.

She and Becca ordered and filled their drinks. Rowan set the marker with a number four on a table near the window and they sat.

Becca stared out the window. After a moment, she asked, without turning her head. "Why is your Mom here? Is she going to take you away?"

Eerie how perceptive Becca was. "She's just here for a visit."

"What if she wants you to go back to Japan?"

"I'm still working on the fundraiser for the wildlife center, so I'm not going yet."

"I guess she can't make you go," Becca mused, "'cause you're a grown-up. My mom can make me go away, even if I say no."

"Did your mother say she's taking you somewhere?"

"Not exactly, but she told me I'd like swimming in the ocean where she is."

"And you don't want to go?"

Becca shook her head vigorously. "I want to stay with Zack. He likes me."

The implication being that her mother didn't. Rowan tried to soothe her fears. "Maybe your mom just meant you might want to swim in the ocean someday."

Becca shrugged and sipped her lemonade. The server brought a tray and unloaded their plates onto the table.

Rowan picked up one of the tacos on her plate and bit into it. "Mmm." The taste was exactly as she remembered. "Do you know when your brother was sixteen, I once saw him eat ten tacos?"

"Ten tacos?"

"We'd gone hiking that morning."

"You said he ate a whole plate of cookies, too!"

"Not on the same day, but I was amazed at how much food he could put away. He was probably going through a growth spurt."

"I grew. That's why I need a new swimsuit. Zack said my old one wouldn't fit anymore."

"Well, with any luck, we'll find you a good one. There's a store in Palmer that sells a few girls' suits. If we don't find anything you like, Zack says it's okay to take you to Wasilla to shop."

"Can you help me cook dinner?"

"Sorry. Not today. I promised my mom."

"But you'll come and cook with me another day?"

"Yes."

"Promise?"

"I promise."

"And you won't leave Alaska without telling me first?"

"I promise I won't leave Alaska without telling you first, and that we will cook together again. Okay?"

"Okay." Becca seemed satisfied. She finished the last bite of her first taco. "These are good. Maybe I can find a swimsuit with a taco on it."

THEY DIDN'T FIND any suits with tacos, nor were there any with moose, but in the third store they came upon a green one with a screen print of an otter. Becca pointed out it was a sea otter, not a river otter like the ones at the wildlife center, but still cute. "And green is my favorite color!" Rowan also helped her choose a yellow suit with polka dots as a spare, and a terry cloth cover-up with a front pocket and a ruffle at the bottom very much like the traditional kuspuks Rowan had seen women wearing in Alaska.

When she drove up in front of the house, Zack stepped outside. Becca waved her shopping bag. "We found a swimsuit with an otter!"

"Cool. Did you like the goats?"

"I love them! There was a baby goat called Gingersnap the same color as Pattycake." Ripley pushed his way out the screen door onto the porch and wagged his tail. Becca dropped her bag to pet him. "We had tacos for lunch," she told Zack.

"At Arctic Taco," Rowan added.

"Arctic Taco." Zack grinned. "I'd forgotten all about that place. I can't believe it's still standing."

"It's not. They took down the stand and built a restaurant. But the tacos are still wonderful."

Rowan handed the second bag to Zack. "I'd better go. My mother flew in, unexpectedly."

"Your mother's here?"

"Yep."

"Do you think she—"

"Probably." After checking that Becca was still occupied with the dog, she made a face at Zack. "Guess I'd better go face the music."

"Don't forget, you promised we could cook together again," Becca said.

"I won't forget."

"Don't you have something to tell Rowan?" Zack prodded.

"Thank you, Rowan." Becca ran back to wrap her arms around Rowan's waist. "I loved going to the farm and shopping with you."

"You're welcome, sweetie. I loved it, too. I'll see you, soon."

Rowan backed out of the driveway. When she looked, Becca was still on the porch, waving goodbye. Zack stood behind her, appropriately. He always had her back.

Rowan parked in her usual spot behind the farmhouse. Gran must have been watching out the window because she stepped outside before Rowan reached the back door.

"Renee is cooking supper. It should be ready in fifteen minutes or so."

Rowan wrinkled her nose. Her mother's cooking wasn't known for its originality. In fact, during much of their childhood, Mom had followed a weekly rotation of the exact same menu, mostly cooked ahead on the weekend before. About the time Patrick left home, Rowan had taken over. After she left for college, Dad had resurrected long-dormant cooking skills, and as far as Rowan knew, Mom hadn't cooked in years. "Thanks for helping me escape."

Gran patted her shoulder. "It will be fine. Just talk to her."

"Easy to say—"

"And not so easy to do. I know." Gran linked elbows and led her toward the house.

Together, they made their way into the kitchen, where Mom, with an apron tied over her travel-knit outfit, pushed something around in a skillet. She turned and smiled at Rowan. "I made tacos. I know they're your favorite."

Rowan suppressed a laugh. "Thanks, Mom. I do love tacos. How can I help?"

Gran set the table while Rowan chopped tomatoes and shredded lettuce. Mom transferred the taco meat into a yellow bowl and set it in the oven to keep warm. When Lauren came in from milking, the four O'Shea women sat down for dinner.

"Patrick sends his love," Lauren said as Mom passed her the refried beans. "He's sorry to miss your visit while he's working on the slope."

"I'm sorry to miss him, too, but I felt like I needed to come right away." Mom chewed her taco and was getting that look in her eyes that signaled she was about to launch into a "serious subject." Before she could, Rowan told the others, "I got a line on another possible donation for the wildlife center fundraiser. You know that boutique in Wasilla, the one with the starfish painted all over the building?"

"Star Nowak's store?" Gran asked. "Starlight?"

"Yes, that's the one. She said she'd donate gift certificates, but even better, she volunteered to entertain at the fair, making balloon animals. She made a really cute fish for Becca while we watched."

"Star has been doing that for years at picnics and children's events. She'll be great." Gran said.

"Becca is the little girl you had with you this morning, right?" Mom asked. "Why did you take her to your appointment?"

Rowan decided to come clean. "Becca was my appointment. She needed a new swimsuit for camp next week and I promised I would take her shopping."

"Who is this little girl, and why does she need you to take her shopping?"

"Becca is the little sister of a friend of mine from way back. Zack Vogel. He's Lauren's veterinarian."

"He's a very good vet," Lauren contributed.

"But not particularly good at clothes shopping, apparently, so Becca asked me if I'd take her instead," Rowan explained.

"His sister lives with him?"

"Yes. Their father died a few months ago, and Becca's mother is…" How should she word it? "…away right now."

"This is someone you know from where?"

"Here. The last summer I spent in Palmer, Zack was part of the crowd I hung out with."

"So, he's your age. And his sister is—"

"Eight. She's a half sister."

"And I gather he's not married if he needs you to take his sister shopping."

"No, he's not."

"He also runs the wildlife center that Rowan is planning the fundraiser for," Lauren said.

Mom gave a sage nod. "I'm beginning to see."

Rowan wasn't sure what it was her mother

thought she saw, but a change of topic was in order. "Thanks for making tacos for me, Mom. They're great." They were actually rather bland, compared with the ones she'd eaten for lunch, but a dash of salsa and a generous sprinkling of sharp white cheddar boosted the flavor. "What do you think of Lauren's latest cheese?"

The rest of the dinner conversation seemed casual, but an invisible band seemed to have formed around Rowan's chest, tightening as they drew closer to the end of the meal. Once they'd finished, Lauren carried her plate to the sink. "Thank you for cooking, Renee. I'll clean up."

"I'll help," Gran said. "Why don't you and Rowan take a walk? I'm sure you need to stretch your legs after the long flight."

"Good idea. I'll change my shoes and be right back." Mom set her plate on the counter near the dishwasher.

"Thanks a lot," Rowan whispered to Gran as she helped clear the table.

"You'll have to face her sometime," Gran whispered back.

Mom returned. "Let's walk toward the far pasture. I'd like to see the guardian dogs Lauren uses to protect the goats."

"All right."

To Rowan's surprise, Mom had little to say on the way to the pasture, other than a few comments about how picturesque the farm was looking these days. When they reached the end of the path, they leaned against the gate to take in the view.

In the distance, Pioneer Peak towered over the valley. When Rowan was a child, Grandy had explained that it was named in honor of the pioneers who had made up a community here during the Great Depression. This farm was one of the original homesteads. Nearby, two enormous white dogs watched as the kids did their baby goat thing, prancing, chasing and trying to push one another off a flat boulder. One of the dogs looked over and wagged a tail, but stayed where he was, protecting the herd. It felt good here, real. Rowan liked cities, too, but she never felt as light and free anywhere as she did here on the farm in Alaska.

One of the goats spotted them and decided to come say hello. Rowan reached over the gate to scratch the doe's neck. A kid jumped onto the goat's back and blinked at them.

Mom laughed. "They do have a lot of personality, don't they?"

"Not to mention they give milk that Lauren makes into wonderful cheeses. She's incredibly talented."

"Also, incredibly sweet. Bonnie inviting her

here was the luckiest thing that ever happened to Patrick."

"I agree." Patrick had always seemed content in Alaska, working on the slope, but now that he and Lauren were married and living here on the farm, he was even happier.

Another goat came over to poke her head through the gate. Mom stroked her face. "Aren't you wondering why I'm here?" she asked without turning to look at Rowan.

Rowan studied her mother's profile. This wasn't like her. Mom didn't waste time with guessing games and she always looked at the person she was addressing. "I imagine you'll tell me when you're ready."

Mom drew in a breath. "I came to tell you I'm sorry."

"Did you?" Rowan tried to remember if Mom had ever apologized before. "For what, exactly?"

"For rushing you. I should have realized you weren't ready yet, but Coralie was afraid if you waited much longer—"

"Wait a minute. What have you and Coralie got to do with anything?"

"She and Asao want grandchildren."

Rowan knew that, but how did it tie in with Mom's apology? "I'm not following."

"You know Sutton is an only child. That wasn't by choice. Coralie was thirty-two when she and Asao married. Coralie told me it took them six years and several rounds of in vitro before she got pregnant with Sutton. They tried again afterward, but no success. After their troubles, it's understandable that Coralie would worry. Fertility does begin to drop off for women at about thirty-two."

"Wait. Are you saying that the reason Sutton proposed when he did was that his mother told him to?"

"No, no. She just pointed out that sooner might be better than later. I should have realized you weren't ready yet, and told her—"

"You and Coralie orchestrated this whole relationship, didn't you? From our meeting, to dating, to the proposal." Now that she thought about it, Rowan realized that ridiculous public proposal had Coralie's fingerprints all over it. "Was Sutton in on this from the beginning? Was I the only one being manipulated?"

"You're perfect together, you and Sutton," Mom said, ignoring the question, which meant the answer was yes. "He has big plans, for his company and for a family, but he needs someone like you to support him and hold it all together. You're so good at that."

"How could you—"

"Rowan, take a breath. Date for a few more

months, or even a year. You'll know when it's time. You and Sutton—"

"No."

"No, what?"

"No, I'm not going to marry Sutton. He doesn't love me, and I don't love him."

"Of course he loves you. When he called me, he was so worried—"

"If he was worried, it's because he's losing a two-year investment."

"Rowan, this isn't Sutton's fault. He wanted to wait, but Coralie felt—"

"That I might be getting too old to guarantee those grandbabies she wants. Yes, I heard you. The fact that his mother is weighing in so heavily isn't helping his case."

Mom paused, tilting her head to study Rowan's face. "The little girl you spent the day with. Are you seeing her brother?"

"Is that relevant?"

"Yes, it is, because Sutton is—"

"Sutton and I are done. I told him so."

Mom frowned. "That's not what he says."

"That's because he wasn't listening. Nobody—" Rowan stopped before she came off sounding like a spoiled teenager. "Sutton had other things on his mind."

"Honey, decisions made under stress invariably lead to heartache. Just take a step back. Get some perspective."

"Yes. That's the main reason I'm here." *To get some distance from you.* Rowan didn't say it aloud, but judging from the sudden hurt in Mom's eyes, she heard it anyway. Rowan touched her shoulder, "Mom—"

"How long will they hold your position at work?" Mom interrupted, ignoring her gesture.

Rowan shrugged. "Through the summer anyway, while things are slow."

"You don't seem worried about the possibility of losing your job."

"I've been considering making a change, anyway." Now that she said it aloud, she realized it was true. "Don't worry. I've got savings, and a small income from the dairy. Even if I were to lose my job, I wouldn't be mooching off you and Dad."

"That wasn't what I meant. Your father and I are always—"

"I know, Mom."

"But I think—"

"The point is that I'm the one who needs to think."

Mom stared at her. "Rowan, I don't know what's gotten into you. You've never been the sort to wander off without a plan."

She'd never had the opportunity. "It will be

fine, Mom. I'm fine. You might not have noticed, but I'm all grown up now. You can go home with an easy mind. I'm sure you have a million irons in the fire."

"I do. But—"

"Really. Everything is okay."

"All right. I'll fly back tomorrow." That brisk, take-charge voice was back. Mom pulled out her phone. "I'm texting Coralie right now to set up a lunch date the next day. I'll tell her that she and Sutton need to be patient."

"Mom, that's not—"

"No use burning bridges."

"I'm not going to marry—"

"We'd better get back to the farmhouse. I'll need to make airline reservations, and I promised your grandmother a game of gin rummy."

"Mom!"

But it was no use. Renee O'Shea had created a plan of action and nothing Rowan said was going to derail that plan. It didn't matter, though. Regardless of what her mother said or did, Rowan was not going to marry Sutton. Ever. Eventually, Mom was just going to have to accept that.

CHAPTER THIRTEEN

"Hey, Zack, I want you to meet someone." Christine walked into his office carrying a bundle of fawn-colored fur. "This is Ruby. I'd say she's about four. What do you think?"

Zack took the cat and ran a gentle hand the length of her body. Thin but not malnourished. He pulled back the lip to see teeth in good shape with only a little tartar. Bright eyes. "I'd agree. Himalayan?"

"I think so. A landlord found her abandoned when tenants disappeared."

"Well, you won't have any trouble finding a family for this beautiful girl."

"No. I hear your latest volunteer is planning quite the fundraiser for WildER."

"You must have been talking to Jessie." Jessie did the clinic's accounting and was an active cat foster, so Christine ran into her often.

"Mmm-hmm. Rowan sounds awesome." Christine's smirk indicated she and Jessie weren't just talking about Rowan's organizational abilities.

Zack smiled, but didn't answer. Maybe this was good. If he were to take Rowan up on her offer, it would be more believable if there were rumors they'd been seeing each other. Not that he was seriously considering it. Was he? He stroked the cat and handed her back.

When Zack didn't rise to the bait, Christine grasped Ruby's paw between her fingers and waved it. "Bye, Dr. Zack."

He chuckled. "Bye, Ruby." His cell rang as they left his office. Teagarden Jones, the estate lawyer. Zack frowned and answered.

"Good morning, Zack. Say, I have a letter here from an attorney representing Clarissa Vogel."

"Oh?" That couldn't be good.

"They're proposing a meeting next week to discuss the timetable for the settlement of the estate. Meaning, presumably, that she's not satisfied with progress to date."

"We've given her every advance she asks for," Zack said. "What difference does it make to her when final settlement happens?"

"Exactly. Highly suspicious. I'm still hopeful the misplaced will might turn up. Anyway, a week from tomorrow?"

Zack checked his schedule. He could rearrange some appointments. "Afternoon okay?"

"Yes. My assistant will send you the time and a copy of the letter. It mentions Becca."

"What about Becca?"

"Nothing specific. Just as a topic of discussion."

Now, what did that mean? "Huh."

"Exactly. See you soon."

"Thanks, Teagarden." Well, wasn't this just a wonderful way to start a Monday?

The day kept him too busy to worry much, but at the end of the afternoon when he'd finished vaccinating all the new calves at a dairy farm, he received an email verifying the time next Tuesday. On the drive back to the clinic, his phone chimed, and a notice of a new text message popped up on the display in his truck. He pressed the button.

A mechanical voice read, "From Rowan O'Shea. 4:10 p.m. Any chance I could come over this evening? I can cook. Picked up some wonderful veggies at the farmers market this weekend."

Finally, some good news. Zack pulled into the clinic's parking lot and before going inside texted back. Sounds great. Six?

I'll be there.

"ANY THREES?" Rowan asked Becca.

"Go fish!" Becca sang out.

"Drat." Rowan drew an ace she had no use for

and glanced at her watch. As much as she enjoyed the time she'd spent cooking and playing with Becca, she needed a chance to talk with Zack alone. He'd seemed preoccupied this evening, as well. Twice, he'd had to ask Becca to repeat a question.

"Zack, do you have any sixes?" Becca asked.

"You know I do." He handed three of them over.

"I just drew it," Becca explained gleefully. "I win!"

"Good for you," Zack told her. "Now it's bath time."

Becca paused, as though considering begging for one more game, but the firm look he gave her seemed to change her mind. "You'll both read with me tonight?"

"Of course," Rowan told her. "Sooner you get your bath, the sooner we'll read together."

"Okay." Becca ran up the stairs, with Ripley at her heels.

"I'll run the bath while you brush your teeth." Zack followed them up. "Be right back," he told Rowan.

"I'll be here." Rowan returned the cards to the box and added a last glass to the dishwasher before pushing the button. While she waited, she checked her email. One from Coralie. An invitation, addressed to her and Sutton, inviting them to a dinner party in three weeks as though they were still together. Unbelievable.

The computer printer in the corner clattered and a printed paper emerged. She went to investigate. Reading upside down, she deciphered the letterhead as belonging to a law office in Anchorage.

"See anything interesting?" Zack asked, startling her.

"Sorry. I didn't mean to butt into your business."

"I was teasing. Teagarden got a letter from an attorney representing Clarissa, and he sent me a copy. I was just printing it out." He picked up the paper as it slid from the printer. "If you don't mind, I'd like you to look it over."

"You want my opinion? I'm not a lawyer."

"But you're logical and intelligent. I think I'm reading a few things between the lines, but I may be imagining it. See what you think."

Rowan leaned against the counter and read the letter. Then she read it again, more slowly. Like most legal writing, it seemed to use a lot of words without saying very much at all. "So basically, she's calling a meeting to discuss the settlement of the estate."

"Yes."

"Which, I assume, means she's either not satisfied with the job you're doing so far, or she wants to double-check your numbers."

"That was my interpretation."

"What do you think about this mention of Becca?"

Zack gave a grim smile. "What do you make of it?"

"Well, coming as it does at the end of a paragraph discussing division of property and such, I would see it as a veiled threat that if you want custody of Becca, you'd better give her everything she's asking for."

"That's one interpretation. But there may be another motive."

"What's that?"

"The way the law is written, Clarissa gets effectively half the estate, and the other half is divided between me and Becca. If she has custody of Becca, then more than likely the judge would also award her control of Becca's share."

"But that's Becca's money. Clarissa would have to save it for Becca, or at least spend it on her welfare, wouldn't she?"

"In theory. In practice, maybe Becca needs to be driven in a new BMW. Maybe Becca needs to stay in the most expensive suite in a hotel. Who makes that decision? Her guardian."

"I'm ready!" Becca called from the top of

the stairs. Fluff pricked up her ears and then bounded toward the stairs.

"Be right there," Zack answered. To Rowan, he whispered, "We'll talk more once she's asleep."

Becca, perhaps sensing that Zack had other things on his mind, wheedled for an extra chapter. When that was done, they tucked her in, kissed her good night and were tiptoeing from the room when Becca announced, "I'm thirsty."

"Do you want me to bring you a glass of water?" Zack asked.

"I want Rowan to do it."

Rowan filled a glass in the bathroom. When she returned, Becca sat up in bed, disturbing Fluff, who had curled up on her pillow. The cat jumped down and ran out the door.

"Make her come back," Becca said.

Zack laughed. "You know I can't make a cat do anything. I'm sure she'll be back once you're still and quiet."

Becca took one drink and set it on the nightstand. "Do you know the story about the *Lost Little Bunny*?" she asked Becca.

"I don't think so."

"It's right there on the shelf." Becca pointed. "Can we read it together?"

Rowan exchanged glances with Zack. Becca was clearly testing boundaries, but maybe she just needed some extra attention tonight. At

Zack's faint nod, Rowan picked up the book. "Why don't you lie back and close your eyes while I read it to you? Zack, I'll be down in just a bit."

"Okay." He kissed Becca's forehead once more. "Good night, Becks. Sweet dreams."

Rowan read the story, about a cottontail rabbit that wandered off and lost its mother but was adopted by a mother cat who cared for her along with her own kittens. As she read, Fluff glided back into the room and jumped onto the bed. By the time Rowan finished the story, Becca's eyes had drifted shut.

"Good night." Rowan kissed her cheek.

"Kitty was a good mother," Becca mumbled, without opening her eyes.

"Yes."

"Better than the mother bunny. She let him wander off and get lost."

Rowan thought about defending the mother bunny. After all, she had a whole litter of little bunnies to watch, and she had told them to stay close. But when it came down to it, the cat had been the one to care for the little lost bunny. "I'm glad the cat was there for him."

"Kitty loved him lots and lots."

"She sure did. Sleep well, sweet girl." Rowan tiptoed out of the room. The parallels weren't lost on her. A parent was the one who took care of the child, who loved them "lots and lots." Like Zack loved Becca.

When she came downstairs, Zack was assembling a sandwich. Surprising, since he'd taken second helpings of chicken enchiladas. "Didn't get enough to eat?"

"This is Becca's lunch for camp tomorrow. One less thing to do in the morning." He tucked the sandwich into a plastic container. "I meant to ask—how did it go with your mother?"

Rowan sighed. "She apologized, sort of."

"That's good, right?"

"It would be, except her apology is for 'rushing me,' and she still seems to think I'll eventually come around. She also let slip that Sutton's mother was pressuring him to propose and start a family. Our two mothers have been plotting together since day one, and I just let myself be led along."

"Sounds like an arranged marriage—well, sort of." He tucked the sandwich into an insulated lunchbox, along with a bag of baby carrots.

"Sutton's mother and my mother both grew up in Virginia, were in the same college sorority and married men they met on their own. This isn't a cultural thing. It's meddling, pure and simple." Rowan selected the ripest plum from a bowl on the counter and handed it to him for the lunch. "Anyway, I'm done. I love my mother, but she's not in charge of my life. Not anymore."

"Good for you." Zack set the lunch in the refrigerator and paused to listen. "It's starting to rain. Want to go sit on the deck?"

"You like listening to the rain?" Rowan grinned. "I thought I was the only one. Whenever I'd suggest it, my friends acted like I was trying to catch a cold. ."

"Well, as a medical professional, I can say sitting on a covered deck in a light rain does not cause colds. At least in dogs. I can only extrapolate to humans."

Rowan laughed. "I'll risk it."

They sat together on a wooden bench just outside the kitchen door. Ripley tagged along and settled on the floor, his chin resting on Zack's foot. Drops pattered lightly on the metal roof. As the rain grew heavier, two robins swooped down onto the grass and gathered worms.

"That's one of the things I've always loved about my visits to the farm," Rowan said. "Being in nature. Hearing the birds, smelling my grandmother's lilacs, seeing an eagle glide over the mountain. You know, that summer I met you was the last time I was in Alaska for more than a few days at a time. I should have made a point of coming more often." Rowan drew in a breath of fresh, cool air. "I might have made better life decisions."

"You think you make better decisions when you're outdoors?"

"Don't you?"

Zack gave a little smile. "I do, now that you mention it."

"Speaking of decisions, have you given any more thought to my proposal?"

Zack didn't answer immediately. The pattering on the roof slowed as the shower began to play out. "I've hardly thought about anything else," he admitted. "I had made up my mind it was too much to ask."

"You *had* made up your mind…?" she prompted.

"Until today. This letter has me worried. I had a short phone consultation with a family lawyer today. She didn't hold out a lot of hope for my custody suit, until I asked if a girlfriend would make a difference."

"A girlfriend helps?"

"It depends. A short-term girlfriend would be irrelevant or possibly work against us. A fiancée might be a plus. But then she said it was a shame I didn't have a nice nurturing wife with a sterling reputation."

Rowan gave a wry smile. "Does a broken engagement damage my sterling reputation?"

"I doubt it. Although it happened so recently—"

"My grandmother can attest to the fact that I had already made up my mind the engagement was a mistake as soon as it happened. You and I have known each other since we were sixteen. If anyone questions our sudden decision, we can say that when we met again, that friendship caught fire and we fell in love."

"And we got married so quickly—"

"Because I love you and I love Becca, and you need me now."

He thought that over for a moment. "It almost sounds plausible."

Plausible. Right. For a moment there Rowan had almost gotten carried away and believed her own story. She licked her lip. "I think we can sell it. I mean, I really do care about you and Becca."

"And I care about you. That's why I'm not sure this is a good idea. You'd be giving up a lot."

"What I'd be gaining is more valuable. I'd gain distance and time to think what I really want my life to be."

"It's not as though you need to marry me to change your life. You're an adult. You can quit your job and go wherever you want."

"Exactly, and where I want to go is here. Alaska has always been my sanctuary. Becca deserves a sanctuary, too, and I want to make that happen."

"You really feel that way?"

"I do."

He paused, looking toward the woods, where the fronds of a wild fern bobbed and swayed from the rain dripping through the overhead trees. "I always said I'd never marry."

"Because of your dad. I get that. I'll sign an agreement that I have no claim on any of your property when the marriage ends."

He laughed. "What, a house mortgaged to the hilt, a truck I'm still paying for and a bunch of college loans?"

"There's your inheritance. I don't want you to worry I'll try to grab any of it."

He shook his head. "Don't tell Clarissa because I don't want to give her any more incentive, but I plan to disclaim and let my share go to Becca. That's what Dad told me he was going to do, and it's only fair. He paid child support to my mom and paid for my undergraduate degree. Would have paid for vet school, too, if I'd let him."

"Why didn't you let him help you with vet school?"

"We had an argument. He was in the middle of a divorce with his third wife, and she was attempting to break the prenup after she caught him cheating. I said I didn't blame her, that it was a sleazy thing to do. He implied that if she got a big payout, he couldn't afford to be so generous with my education, so I told him to take his money and—" Zack shook his head. "Anyway, we didn't talk for several years."

"What brought you back together?"

"Becca. Just before she was born, Dad searched me out and apologized. He wanted me in Becca's life. She's the reason I came back here. Fortunately, Christine was looking for a partner in the vet clinic. She'd just married and moved out of this house, and so I bought it." He reached down to ruffle Ripley's ears. "It was clear from the beginning that Clarissa had no interest in parenting. Dad was thirty-four years older than Clarissa, and he had some health problems. I believe he knew he might not be around to raise Becca and he wanted to make sure I was."

"But he didn't say so, directly?"

"He hinted. A couple of times, when they would leave Becca with me while they traveled, he said something like she was in good hands with me. There's no way he would have failed to make a will mentioning Becca."

"But you didn't find any sign of it?"

"No. Just some old ones from before he married Clarissa, inside the fire safe in his study."

"Wouldn't he have destroyed the old wills when he made a new one?"

"Dad liked to hang on to documents. He said you never knew when you might need to go back and prove something you thought was long settled."

"What happens if you don't get custody of Becca?"

He shrugged. "Clarissa will leave her in the care of a nanny or someone while she runs and plays. At least until the money runs out. At Clarissa's current burn rate, that would happen around the time Becca turns eighteen."

"What about school?"

"Maybe she'd hire a tutor."

But there was so much more to school than lessons. Rowan had changed schools five times as a child, but she'd still benefited from the structure and interaction of a classroom. Where would a shy child like Becca find friends if she was stuck in a hotel suite with a nanny? "Becca needs to stay here, with you. We need to make a judge see that."

"Yes."

"Then let's get married. Now. Tomorrow. We could fly to Vegas."

"Tomorrow?"

"I guess you probably have work scheduled tomorrow. But soon. Before the meeting, anyway. This weekend?"

"You're absolutely sure about this?"

"I'm sure."

Zack was quiet, contemplating. Rowan was tempted to point out, once again, what was at stake. That's what her mother would have done. Instead, she waited, letting him weigh his options. The rain had stopped now, and the sun had dropped below the level of the clouds, sending a shaft of light into the woods to turn the clinging raindrops into sparkling diamonds.

"One year." He watched her face. "That's what you said, right? A gap year to figure out what you want to do."

She nodded. "A year. And then we'll get an annulment."

Zack nodded. "I'll talk with Christine and Maggie tomorrow and make arrangements to cover for me this weekend. I'll see if Becca can stay with Charlotte overnight."

"You don't think we should take her?"

"To Las Vegas?"

"I see what you mean."

In the distance, a shimmer appeared against the clouds. As they watched, the shimmer distilled into a brilliant rainbow, arching from the sky, across the mountain and into the forest.

"Wow." Rowan stared. "Did you ask for a sign?"

"Not in so many words," he answered, "but maybe we got one."

CHAPTER FOURTEEN

THE FOYER OF the wedding chapel was somehow simultaneously more elegant and more tawdry than Rowan had imagined. The thick rug had an abstract floral design, but upon closer inspection she noticed hearts, clubs, spades and diamonds in the pattern. On a baroque pedestal in the center, a stiff arrangement of silk flowers blocked her view of the main chapel, where in a few minutes she would be walking down an aisle to meet Zack. They had opted for the "traditional" package, as opposed to International Spy, Science Fiction, Southern Belle and several she couldn't recall. Rowan could only imagine the decorating touches in those chapels.

Once they'd handed over payment, a young woman in a silver dress with an impressive quantity of blond hair had introduced herself as "Demi, your wedding assistant," and swept Rowan off to choose a dress from the racks of rentals. Rowan had settled on a simple white jersey with a fitted bodice and flared knee-length skirt that flowed like cream when she moved.

Honestly, she liked it better than any of the designer gowns her mother had been pushing.

Demi returned and handed her a bouquet of pale pink baby's breath and light purple clusters of some flower that reminded Rowan of her grandmother's lilac bush. "It's almost time. The minister is just finishing up. All good?"

Rowan gave a little smile. "Sure." She sucked in a deep breath, trying to calm her agitated stomach. Was she really going to do this? Without consulting her family? Mom would come unglued. Of course, Rowan couldn't tell them it was only temporary. In a year, when the annulment came through, Rowan would have to listen to Mom's I told you so. But if it meant Becca was safely in Zack's custody, it would be worth it.

She pictured their faces, Zack and Becca, as they read together at night. Zack, changing his voice for the different characters to make the story more fun for Becca. The look of trust and adoration on Becca's face. Suddenly, the hummingbirds that had been zinging around Rowan's stomach paused, her heartbeat calmed and she knew that marrying Zack was the right thing to do. Was this what they meant by a "gut check"?

The radio Demi held crackled something intelligible. Demi answered, "All set here. Go ahead." She smiled at Rowan. "They're starting the music. I'll go first and once I'm at the front, we'll switch to the 'Wedding March' and it's your turn. Are you ready?"

"I'm ready."

While Demi made her way down the aisle, Rowan peered around the corner. Zack, incredibly handsome in a tuxedo, stood next to his assistant, whose name Rowan couldn't remember but would be on their official marriage certificate as a witness.

The music changed. Zack, the minister and the other guy turned their gazes in her direction. Rowan stepped into the chapel, glancing down to make sure she didn't trip over the threshold. When she looked up, Zack's eyes were locked on her. He gave the slightest smile of encouragement, but it was enough. She smiled back and came to meet him.

He took her hand without breaking his gaze on her face. The minister spoke their names and intention to marry, and despite the lack of observers, he intoned that, "If anyone has a reason they should not marry, let them speak now." And those hummingbirds in Rowan's stomach held their peace.

As prompted by the minister, they repeated their vows. Demi took Rowan's bouquet so that Zack could slip a gold band onto her finger. "With this ring, I thee wed."

Rowan took his ring from Demi and reached

for Zack's hand, strong and yet gentle. His gaze seemed to penetrate past the surface to her very core, and judging from his expression, he liked what he saw there. She slid the ring on his finger. "With this ring, I thee wed."

The minister checked his note cards. "Zackary and Rowan—" he looked up "—I pronounce you husband and wife. You may kiss the bride."

Zack hesitated for a split second, and then he touched her face, gently drawing a finger across her cheek to push a stray lock of hair away. He bent down, and when their lips touched, something happened. Something warm and glowing started in her center and bubbled up. Her arms reached to circle his neck, to keep this connection a little longer. Here, on their wedding day, they were having their first kiss. And, as Gran would say, it was a doozy.

The minister cleared his throat and chuckled. Zack pulled back, a sheepish smile on his face. The minister congratulated them, they all signed the marriage license, and it was done. She was Zack's wife.

It felt good.

"Wow, THAT'S BRIGHT." Zack lifted his hand to shade his eyes from the glare. They had stepped from an air-conditioned dream world of shadows and costumes into a searing dose of reality.

Ironically, the only part of the entire wedding experience that had seemed real was when he had kissed Rowan. Ironic because he knew she was simply acting, and yet it felt so right. It wasn't going to be easy, pretending to the world he was in love with her, while convincing her, and himself, that he wasn't.

Rowan reached into the tote she was carrying and handed him a pair of sunglasses before fishing out another pair for herself. "The taxi is supposed to meet us over there, by that bench."

They sat in the scant shade of a palm tree and waited. Although Zack had changed from a tux into shorts and a polo shirt, he started to sweat. Beside him, Rowan looked cool and easy in a sunflower-printed sundress, her hair caught up in a twist at the back of her head. The sight of her in a wedding dress had taken his breath away, but honestly, he preferred her like this. Soft, approachable, real.

The taxi arrived, and Zack helped the driver store their bags in the trunk before sliding across the sticky plastic that covered the seats to sit beside Rowan. "Airport?" the driver inquired.

"County clerk's office first, please, and then Alaska Airlines terminal," Rowan told him.

"Just married?"

"Yes."

"Congratulations. You picked a good day for it. Cooled off a bit from last week."

"It gets hotter than this?" Zack asked in amazement. How had his mother survived summers here?

"Sure. It's only ninety-nine today. Last Thursday, it got to a hundred and twelve. It's not so bad, though. It's a dry heat."

Zack had a new appreciation for Alaskan summers with highs in the sixties or seventies.

"First time in Vegas?" the driver asked.

"I was here as a child," Zack admitted. His mother had brought him, once, to visit a friend, but it only made her sad. They'd never come again.

"My first time," Rowan said brightly. "It's quite a place."

That seemed to please the driver. "It surely is." He waited while they filed their marriage certificate with the county clerk and then drove them to the airport. "You know, I see a lot of new-marrieds, and I have a little game I play. Are they gonna make it?" He gave Rowan a grin. "I'm giving you my thumbs-up."

"Why, thank you." Rowan dimpled prettily at him. Amused, Zack added to the tip he was mentally calculating and paid the man.

Once he'd driven away, Rowan laughed.

"What do you bet that's his standard line for every couple he picks up at a wedding chapel?"

"Almost certainly," Zack agreed. He pulled up the handles on their roller bags and wiped his forehead. "Let's find some air-conditioning."

While they waited in the security line, Rowan entertained him by describing some of the more outrageous dresses the wedding dress rental had offered. They reached the front of the line and the TSA agent beckoned. Zack touched the small of Rowan's back to indicate she should go first. "You can come up with your wife," the agent told him.

His wife. Zack had a wife. The agent scanned Rowan's passport and handed it back before accepting Zack's. "Oh, different name. I thought you were married."

"We are." Rowan pointed to her new ring, "As of five hours ago."

"Congratulations." He said it in the same tone as a remark about the weather, but maybe working the Vegas airport meant he heard this story multiple times a day. He scanned Zack's ID and returned it with his boarding pass. "Next."

They cleared the body scanner, collected their bags and made their way toward the gate. Rowan tucked her passport into her bag. "I guess as soon as I get back to Alaska, I should see how to go about changing my name on all my documents."

"You don't have to," Zack said. "It seems like a lot of work, and then you'd just have to do it all again in a year—"

"You don't want me to take your name?" Rowan looked hurt.

"It's not that. I just don't want to put you to any extra trouble." Even as the words left his mouth, Zack realized how silly they sounded. Extra trouble? Rowan was completely reinventing her life for him and Becca. "What I mean is that it would be an honor to have you take my name, but if you'd rather keep yours, I completely support that decision, as well."

"Ah, nice save. You say you've never done this husband thing before?"

"Never." They found a pair of unoccupied seats.

"I guess you're just a natural." She winked. Winked! Zack tried to think if a woman had ever winked at him before. "I think I'm going to enjoy being Mrs. Zackary Thomas Vogel."

"Rowan Bedelia Vogel. It does have a nice ring to it."

"Bedelia was my maternal great-grandmother, named for a Celtic goddess of fire. Heaven knows why my parents felt obligated to pass that on to me."

"Well, Goddess of Fire, I guess you fit in well here in Las Vegas, seeing as it's approximately the temperature of the sun outside."

"But it's a dry heat."

Zack laughed. Rowan's phone rang. She glanced at the screen, and her smile faded. She sat up straighter, drew in a breath and answered. "Hi, Mom."

Zack reached for her free hand. She gave him a grateful smile. "Uh-huh." She listened for several minutes. "No, I'm not going to the Tanakas' dinner party. I sent my regrets." Another pause. "No, I don't need to keep my options open. I'm not marrying Sutton. I—" Zack couldn't make out the words, but he could hear a stream of them pouring out of the phone. Rowan rolled her eyes and waited for the flood to end. "I'm already married, Mother."

"What?" He understood that one. Fortunately, Rowan had moved the phone away from her ear.

She repeated, in a calm voice, "I said I'm married. Zack and I flew to Vegas and were married this morning. He's sitting beside me right now, waiting for our flight to Anchorage." She squeezed Zack's hand. "No, don't. You'd be wasting your time. I'm married to Zack, and I intend to stay that way." A second later, she laughed and managed to make it sound almost carefree. "Of course I'll be living in Alaska.

That's where Zack has his veterinary practice. Oh, looks like we're boarding soon. I need to turn off my phone. Bye, Mom." She ended the call and gave Zack a guilty smile. "Fifty-five minutes is soon, isn't it?"

"Sure. It's all relative, right? And speaking of relatives—"

"My mom's not happy."

"Did you expect her to be?"

"No." Rowan looked at the ring on her hand. "But that's okay. It's not my job to make my mother happy. I don't need her approval."

"You don't need mine, either, but just so you know, I think you handled that very well."

"Do you?"

"You were calm, clear and firm in your decision."

"Thanks. Speaking of which, I guess I'd better call Sutton. He shouldn't hear this secondhand." She dialed and waited. "It's going to voice mail," she whispered, and in a normal voice, "Hi, Sutton. Hope the negotiations are going well. Listen, I'm sorry to leave this on your voice mail, but I couldn't reach you directly. I wanted to tell you I'm married. It's someone I knew in Alaska long before I met you, and I'm sorry for—well, I'm sorry. Goodbye, Sutton. I wish you good fortune in all you do." She ended the call and blew out a breath. "Is it bad that I'm glad he didn't answer the phone?"

Zack smiled at her. "Even strong people who don't need their mother's approval are allowed a certain amount of discretionary conflict avoidance."

"I do hate conflict."

"I know." He remembered how much it would distress her when their friends would fight. "Becca's the same way. If I sound even a little bit cross, it upsets her."

"I've never seen you cross with Becca."

"I try not to be, because she tries so hard to please. It concerns me."

Rowan raised her eyebrows. "Because your sister is too well behaved? Oh, my goodness, what are we going to do with that child?"

He laughed. "Okay, it's not such a bad problem to have. It's just that I worry she's so good because she's afraid to be bad."

"Afraid you won't love her anymore, you mean?"

He nodded.

"I see your point," Rowan said slowly, "but I've also seen the two of you together. I've seen her begging for one more story. She knows you love her. If she's insecure, it's because she's afraid her mother might sweep her away somewhere."

"She talked to you about that?"

"A little bit. She said her mom said she'd like swimming in the ocean, but she doesn't want to go. How are Becca's swimming lessons going, by the way? On Tuesday, she said she was learning to float and kick."

"She likes it. They'll be swimming every day for another two weeks."

"Am I allowed to drop in and watch?"

"Sure, she'd love that. I'll just call and add you to Becca's approved contact list."

"That means I'll be able to drop off and pick up her and Charlotte, right?"

"Yes. Of course, Jessie or Greg will have to contact the camp first, once I tell them we're married."

"You didn't tell them in advance?"

"No. Just that you and I had some out-of-town business."

"Won't Becca spill the beans?"

"I didn't tell her, either."

Rowan frowned. "I thought you'd already cleared this with Becca. What if she doesn't want me there, in your house?"

"She adores you."

"Maybe, but if I move in, she might feel like I'm coming between you."

"But you're not. Just the opposite, in fact."

"It's still a big change," Rowan fretted.

He squeezed her hand. "Becca will be happy. And even if it takes her a little while to get used to the idea, it's for the best. That's why we're doing this, after all. For Becca's sake."

"Right." Rowan nodded decisively. "For Becca's sake."

IT WAS ALMOST ten o'clock by the time they'd collected their bags, driven from the Anchorage airport and made their way to Greg and Jessie's house. But the sun still lit up the two-story A-frame with flowers spilling from a window box on the balcony. Zack came around to open Rowan's door and offered his hand. "Are you ready, Mrs. Vogel?"

Was she? This was their first test. Would Becca accept her as Zack's wife? What would Jessie and Greg say? She put her hand in his. "I'm ready."

They stepped onto the porch, but before Zack could push the doorbell, Jessie opened the door. "Come in." She glanced at their joined hands. "Did you two get your business taken care of?"

"We did," Zack said as they stepped inside. Ripley ran to greet them, and Zack reached down to rub his ears. Greg got up from his chair. Zack started to say something else, but just then Becca came running in from another room, already in her pajamas, with Zuma tucked under her arm.

"You're home!" She ran to Zack. After a solid hug, she turned and gave one to Rowan. "Hi, Rowan."

"Hi there." Rowan smoothed a hand over her hair. "Did you and Charlotte have fun?"

"We were watching a movie. With elephants."

Zack cleared his throat. "About our business in Vegas."

"Yes?" Jessie asked.

"This morning—" he reached for Rowan's hand "—Rowan and I got married."

"Married?" Jessie's mouth fell open.

"I told you," Greg whispered. "Why else Vegas?"

"B-but—" Jessie stuttered.

"You're married?" Becca looked at Rowan and then at Zack. "To each other?"

"That's right," Zack said gently.

"Rowan's going to live with us?" Rowan couldn't yet detect any emotion other than surprise.

"That's the plan." He picked Becca up in his arms. "Is that okay with you?"

Becca twisted around to look at Rowan. "Can we make cookies every day?"

Rowan laughed. "Well, maybe not every day, because too many cookies aren't good for us, but now and then."

"Will you be bringing goats?"

"No, the goats will still live at the farm."

"Will you read with me every night?"

"Yes."

"Will you teach me how to wear makeup?"

"Nope." Rowan laughed and booped Becca on the nose. "Because you're too young, and you're perfect just like you are."

"Will you paint my toenails?"

"Not tonight. It's late."

"But tomorrow after camp, you'll paint my toenails?"

Rowan exchanged looks with Zack, who grinned. "Yes," she told Becca. "I'll paint your toenails tomorrow."

"Well, congratulations!" Jessie stepped up to give Rowan a hug and Zack a kiss on the cheek. "I'll stop by in the morning to pick up." Jessie shot Zack a look that said there were many questions to come, but not in front of the kids.

Rowan told her, "If you want to add me to Charlotte's approved list, I can take over some of the driving chores."

"We'll do that," Greg said and offered Rowan a hug, as well. "Best wishes to you both."

Zack thanked them and they made their leave. Ripley jumped into the truck. Becca climbed in after and buckled her belt. "You're married, just like Charlotte's mommy and daddy."

"That's right," Zack told her.

"And we'll all live happily ever after."

Rowan and Zack exchanged glances. Ever-after wasn't the plan. But they had a year.

ROWAN WAS UP EARLY, but not early enough to beat Zack to the kitchen, judging by the scent of brewing coffee wafting up the stairs as she went down. She found him bent over, looking for something in the refrigerator. "Hope you made enough coffee for two."

He jumped and bumped his head. Rowan winced. "Sorry. I didn't mean to startle you."

"I just didn't know anyone else was awake. I was making Becca's lunch."

"Let me do that." When Zack hesitated, she laughed. "Seriously, you don't need to treat me like a guest. I know you're working today, and you probably have extra stuff to do to make up for the two days you took off, so let me handle this."

"Okay, thanks. You might throw in a few baby carrots. It's about the only vegetable I can count on Becca eating."

"I will. Do you take your lunch?"

"No, I usually drop by here to grab something and let Ripley out." He reached into the cabinet for two mugs, poured coffee and handed one to her. "Cheers."

She took a sip. "Lovely."

"Well, then, I'll just…" He waved his hand in the general direction of the stairs.

"You do that." Once he'd gone, Rowan surveyed the contents of the refrigerator. Not a lot there, other than enough milk to pour over cereal for breakfast, a bit of sliced turkey for Becca's sandwich and assorted bottles and jars. She would need to fit in some grocery shopping today, in between soliciting more donations for the fundraiser, ordering more recipe cards for the tasting room from the printers, driving her grandmother to the doctor in Anchorage for a final checkup and, oh, yeah, telling Gran, Lauren and Patrick that she was married. Yep, it was going to be a busy day.

Jessie showed up a few minutes earlier than expected, but she came inside and accepted a cup of coffee while Rowan went upstairs with Becca to find a missing shoe. Rowan located it under the bed. "Okay, put that on and brush your teeth. I'll go put your lunch in your backpack."

Charlotte stroked the cat. "I'll stay with Becca."

When Rowan reached the kitchen door, she could hear Jessie talking with Zack in a teasing voice, "When I said you needed a wife, you claimed you weren't interested." Rowan paused outside the door to listen to his answer.

"I changed my mind."

"Obviously. But what about that fiancé you told me about?"

"That turned out to be a misunderstanding."

"Huh. You know, I really like Rowan, but you've only known her—"

"I've known Rowan for years. We met when we were just sixteen."

"Really? Then, why didn't you know about her fiancé?"

Hearing the girls on the stairs, Rowan breezed into the kitchen and grabbed the lunch from the refrigerator. "They're coming. Sorry to keep you waiting." She zipped Becca's backpack closed.

"No problem. I was early."

"Well, like I said, I can drive tomorrow if you like."

"Super. So, should I drop off Becca here or at the clinic this afternoon?"

"Here," Rowan said, at the same time Zack said, "At the clinic."

They looked at each other. "I'll come over to the clinic," Rowan suggested, "and we can decide then."

"Okay. Let's go, girls." Jessie set her empty mug on the counter.

Zack poured coffee into a travel mug. "I need to head out, too. Thanks for making Becca's lunch, Rowan."

Jessie and the girls had been heading toward

the door, but Becca stopped and turned. "Aren't you going to kiss? Jessie and Greg always kiss when they say goodbye." Becca looked at Zack expectantly.

Jessie smirked. "That's true." She crossed her arms and waited.

Zack's glance moved from Becca to Rowan. He raised an eyebrow in question. Rowan set her coffee mug on the counter. She put her hands on Zack's shoulders and raised on her tiptoes, intending to just brush her lips against his to placate Becca and keep Jessie from speculating. But Zack seemed to have other ideas. When their lips made contact, he slipped an arm around her waist and pulled her closer. Despite knowing it was all for show, a tingle of excitement ran down Rowan's spine. For the briefest moment, she forgot all about Becca, Charlotte and Jessie.

But too soon, Zack pulled back from the kiss. He brushed his lips against her forehead and let her go. "I'd better get to work."

Rowan blinked, and then, to cover her confusion, busied herself loading bowls into the dishwasher. "See you later."

Jessie chuckled. "Okay, girls, we'd better go before we're late for camp. Have a nice day, Rowan."

"You, too." Rowan just hoped it turned out that way.

CHAPTER FIFTEEN

"You did what?" Patrick, usually the world's most laid-back brother, stared at her in horror.

"I got married," Rowan repeated. She felt a little sorry for her brother. He'd just finished his two-week rotation working on the North Slope and hadn't even been home for an hour when she'd driven up with Gran and dropped her bombshell. "To Zach Vogel."

Gran looked slightly less shocked, but not exactly thrilled. Lauren rubbed a soothing hand over Patrick's back. "Zack is a great guy."

"Sure he is, but he and Rowan have only known each other for, like, five minutes."

"We've known each other for years," Rowan argued, taking a page from Zack's playbook. "We were just sixteen when we met." Let it be implied that they'd kept in touch between then and now.

"But haven't you been dating some guy in Japan for a couple of years now?"

"That's over. Obviously."

"Have you told Mom and Dad about this?"

Patrick asked, and Rowan felt a lot less sorry for him.

She set her shoulders. "Yes, I have."

"Mom must have hit the roof."

Rowan shrugged. "Her opinion is irrelevant."

Patrick looked skeptical. "Oh, really?"

"Yes, really. I'm an adult. I can make my own decisions. Just like when you decided to become an electrician."

"That's different."

"How is that different?"

"It wasn't a spur-of-the-moment thing. I had a plan."

"Maybe Rowan has a plan, as well," Gran finally spoke. "Maybe she has a good reason for marrying so quickly."

"O-oh." Patrick glanced at Rowan's stomach. "Are you—"

Rowan laughed at his obvious discomfort. "No, I'm not pregnant. We decided to marry sooner rather than later because of Zack's little sister. Zack wants permanent custody of her, and his odds improve if he's married."

"I knew Zack's father died recently," Lauren said. "But what happened to her mother?"

"Apparently, she's somewhere in the Caribbean." Rowan gave a broad outline of the situation. "Becca's happy with Zack. She belongs with him. And I can help make that happen."

"What about your happiness?" Gran asked.

"Zack makes me happy," Rowan assured her. It was even sort of true. Spending time with him and Becca, working on the fundraiser, feeling useful—all those things made her happy. And then there was that kiss this morning, which made her feel—well, best not to think too deeply about that. "So," she said briskly, "Gran and I had better go if we're going to make that doctor's appointment. I just wanted to give you all the news in person. I'll still be here on Sunday afternoon to help with goat yoga, and I can fill in at the tasting room or anything else you need."

"Thanks." Lauren gave Rowan a hug. "And congratulations."

"Yes, congratulations." Patrick hugged her, too. "Sorry I was—"

"It's okay," she interrupted, ignoring her own guilty twinges at misleading them.

"Mom will probably call soon," Patrick predicted. "I'll tell her you know what you're doing."

"Thank you. Come to think of it, I'm surprised she hasn't already called you. She's known about this for—" Rowan checked her watch "—hmm, sixteen hours." This was entirely out of character. What was her mother up to?

Judging from the silence that followed, everyone else wondered, too. But then Gran grabbed her cane and got up from her chair. "Come on.

We don't want to be late for my appointment." She tucked the cane under her arm and did a little dance step. "I want to show the doctor I can cha-cha-cha."

Gran was quiet during most of the drive to Anchorage. It was only when they approached the city limits that she spoke. "I'm proud of you."

"For what?"

"For making up your mind and standing your ground. I may not necessarily agree—if I had my druthers, you'd have told us first instead of sneaking off and getting married behind our backs—but you showed gumption."

"Um, thanks?"

"You're welcome. Now, on Sunday, after goat yoga, I'm going to fry up some chicken, and I want you to bring Zack and Becca out to the farm for Sunday dinner."

"That sounds nice. I'll check with Zack, but I'm sure he'll come."

"Good." Gran sat back in her seat. "Because I've got a few questions for him."

SUNDAY AFTERNOON, Rowan decided to take Becca along to goat yoga. Zack had agreed to meet them at the farm at dinnertime, even after Rowan's confession that he would most likely be the one being grilled. As they approached the farm, Rowan spotted Patrick hard at work in the front pasture near the road, cutting back some brush. One of the goats stood close by, rubbing her head against his leg. Looked like Spritz.

At the turn-in to the farm, a woman was setting up a Goat Yoga sandwich board. All Rowan could see of her was a pair of tiger-striped yoga pants straining over her ample bottom, but it was enough. She rolled down the window. "Hi, Bea. Want a ride back?"

"Sure." Bea climbed into the passenger seat. "I hear you two couldn't wait to rush to the altar. Congratulations."

"Thank you." It felt a little awkward, receiving genuine good wishes from others for a fake marriage. But for Becca, she could do it.

"You know, my husband and I eloped," Bea continued.

"Did you?"

"We were both teachers. My parents—" she glanced toward Becca before choosing her words "—discouraged our relationship."

"Why?"

"Snobbery," Bea said in her blunt way. "They wanted a rich son-in-law, 'to support me in the manner to which I was accustomed.' As if I cared about that. When my mother heard we were married, she predicted it wouldn't last six months. Bill and I laughed about that when we celebrated our fiftieth anniversary." She twisted in her seat to look over her shoulder. "Hello, Becca. Did you find a swimsuit?"

A glance in the rearview mirror confirmed that Becca was staring, fascinated by the orange streaks in Bea's hair. "We got two of them. One with an otter, and one with dots."

"I used to have a swimsuit with polka dots." Bea cleared her throat and sang some song about a girl in a tiny yellow bikini.

Becca giggled.

"Becca is doing great in her swim class," Rowan told Bea. "Yesterday she swam all the way across the pool." When Becca had popped out of the water and saw Rowan watching, she'd grinned from ear to ear.

"Next week I get to move to Charlotte's group and jump off the diving board," Becca said.

"You go, girl!" Bea gave Becca a high five.

Rowan let Bea out near the pavilion where Gran and the other ladies had already gathered before parking the car behind the barn to leave the main parking lot open for guests.

By the time she and Becca had walked back, the whole area was abuzz with activity. Lauren was leading two goats with their kids toward a pen at the edge of the pavilion that already held several goats. Gran and two of her friends were filling paper cups with some sort of goat food,

Linda was setting up with a laptop computer and a cash box, and Crystal was rolling out her mat.

Rowan kept Becca by her side while she held the gate open for Lauren, who led the two mama goats in, with their kids close behind. They immediately started a game of tag with the kids already inside. Rowan latched the gate. "How can Becca and I help with the setup?"

"Can you tie ribbons around the kids' necks?" Lauren nodded at a basket of colorful ribbons on a table nearby. "That always goes over well."

"Sure."

"I know how to tie a bow," Becca announced.

"Great. I'll go bring the rest of the goats," Lauren said.

Rowan riffled through the ribbons in the basket before choosing a blue-and-white stripe and a bright red. Becca picked a green satin. Rowan reached for the nearest kid, white with black spots who would look adorable with a red ribbon. The goat had other ideas, though. She ducked away from her and ran to the other side of her mother, peering around her legs. "Come on, sweetie. I'm not going to hurt you. I just want to make you beautiful."

The kid seemed doubtful, but while Rowan was trying to coax her into coming closer, another kid wandered up to sniff her. She sat on the grass and the kid crawled into her lap. So that was the secret—let the goats come to her. "Here, Becca. Why don't you tie on the ribbon while I keep the goat still?" She petted the kid while Becca painstakingly tied the ribbon around his neck and formed a slightly lopsided green bow. Working together, they had soon beribboned most of the herd.

Lauren returned with two more goats and five more kids. "This should be plenty of kids to play with the guests. As soon as they're finished with the milking, two more people will be coming out to help wrangle the goats."

Becca leaned over to pick up a ribbon that had fallen on the ground, and a kid jumped onto her back. She giggled. The kid jumped off and frolicked across the pen, practically begging Becca to follow. She skipped after him.

The black-and-white kid finally came close enough for Rowan to lure into her lap so she could tie on the red ribbon.

"Good for you," Lauren told her. "Madeleine is a shy one. I only brought her today because her two siblings are so energetic and outgoing."

Rowan made a bow, fluffed the loops, and studied the effect. Madeleine tilted her head and looked up at her. Adorable. "There's nothing wrong with feeling a little shy, is there, Madeleine?" She stroked the kid's soft face. "They are so cute. I can see why you chose to be a goat farmer."

"Yeah." Lauren smiled as she scratched one goat's neck. "But they've been known to pull a few pranks."

"These innocent little angels?" Rowan asked as Madeleine bounded from her lap to chase after the other kids.

"They're no angels, believe me. But if they were, my life wouldn't be nearly as interesting. Right, Spritz?"

The goat Lauren was petting bobbed her head and her bell tinkled. Rowan blinked in surprise. "Did you teach her to do that whenever you ask a question?"

"You can blame your brother for that. Spritz adores Patrick. But then, who doesn't? Right, Spritz?"

Spritz nodded again and Rowan laughed. "You and Spritz can start a fan club. I'm not sure I've ever forgiven him for going off to Alaska to take an electrician apprenticeship instead of the college degree Mom had all laid out for him. It made her doubly determined that I would."

"He told me about that. But you're making your own choices now."

"Yes." Yesterday, Rowan had formally resigned her job. Her roommate's cousin had been eager to take over her lease and had even offered to ship her things. It was almost disconcerting, how easy it had been to cut ties with her life in Tokyo.

Rowan tied on the last ribbon and rotated it so that the bow was over the perky goat's ear. "There. All done."

"Cute. And just in time." Lauren nodded toward two cars in the parking lot. "Here come our first customers."

"Do you want me to take tickets or something?"

"No, Linda's got a system. Just go greet people as they arrive, send them to her and join in once the session is ready to start."

"Sounds good. Becca, come on. We need to go round up the customers." People trickled in. Judging from the conversations Rowan overheard, many had participated before.

At the posted starting time, Crystal put on some soothing music with nature sounds in the background. Gran and most of her friends spread their mats at the back of the group. Linda motioned to Rowan. "You and Becca go ahead and join the class. We're only expecting two more, and I'll wait for them."

"Thanks." Rowan helped Becca spread a mat next to Gran's and situated herself on Becca's other side. Gran showed Becca how to sit and cross her legs.

"Let's move to table pose," Crystal's serene voice called out, and everyone shifted to a hands-and-knees position. Lauren opened the gate, and the dozen or so eager kids bounded out. Most of them went to sniff and rub against the guests, while three immediately jumped onto a convenient back and balanced there. Little Madeleine looked around until she spotted Rowan and trotted over, positioning herself underneath and peeking out at Becca, batting her long eyelashes.

"Now let's try a birddog pose," Crystal said, demonstrating by reaching out with her right arm while straightening her left leg. A white kid jumped onto her back and walked along her outstretched leg like a balance beam. The guests laughed.

Rowan followed Crystal's instructions, running a hand over Madeleine's head before stretching her arm forward. Madeleine must have liked it, because she followed the arm and thrust her head under Rowan's hand for more petting. When Rowan lifted her hand, Madeleine shifted her attention to Becca, rubbing under her outstretched hand like a cat. Becca's smile reached almost ear to ear.

Two of the kids began to chase each other among the yoga mats until one jumped onto someone's back and the second kid followed. Then they jumped onto the next back until they'd traveled all the way across the pavilion. Some of the participants had abandoned any pretense of yoga and were just petting and laughing at the goats.

"Let's sit back and move to child pose," Crystal called.

Rowan obediently tucked her knees under her and moved her upper body into a forward stretch. A brown kid stepped onto her shoulder and walked up her back as though they'd rehearsed it. The tiny hooves on her back felt surprisingly good and the cuteness factor was off the charts. Rowan smiled. No wonder the tickets sold out so quickly.

After several more poses, Crystal brought the session to a close, with everyone sitting in comfortable position, eyes closed and breathing deeply. Some of the kids climbed into laps and curled up, but others took it as a challenge, climbing and butting against their new playmates to try to encourage more fun. Rowan had never heard so much laughter during a yoga session, and it felt great. The view of the mountains, the fresh air, the cute kids—nature made yoga so much better.

She got up, rolled her mat and helped Lauren and her helpers distribute treat cups so that everyone could feed the kids. Becca joined the others in feeding and petting them. Rowan snapped a few photos on her phone, and then offered to take photos for the other participants. After ten minutes or so of play and photo ops, Lauren rounded up the kids and returned them to their mothers in the pen to wait for the next class.

Gran tapped Rowan's arm. "The Mat Mates have a table outside the tasting room. Get Becca and join us."

"Don't I need to stay and help set up for the next class?"

"We scheduled in a one-hour break," Lauren told her, "to give everyone a chance to hit the tasting room or buy souvenir cheese. Get me an iced tea, would you please? I'll be there in a few minutes."

Becca was standing next to the goat pen, reaching through the bars to stroke Madeleine's face. Rowan went to stand beside her. "She likes you."

"I like her, too. She's so cute!"

"Gran and the ladies have a table. Want to go get a snack and something to drink?"

"Okay." Becca gave Madeleine a last pat. As they walked toward the tasting room, she reached for Rowan's hand. "I like it here."

"When I was your age, I used to come here to visit my grandparents. They had cows instead of goats. My grandmother taught me all about cooking and gardening and canning. It was fun."

"I wish I had a grandmother."

"Well, you can borrow mine. Come on. Let's get washed up."

Between Gran and her five friends, Becca received the full grandparent experience over the next half hour. Linda had brought a new book for her about buried treasure, one of Becca's favorite themes. Rosemary showed her how to create a crown from some dandelions that had sprung up in a corner of the garden. And after Becca mentioned the matching aprons she and Rowan wore when they cooked together, Gran offered to sew another set. "Get Rowan to bring you to my apartment so you can look through my fabric stash and pick out your favorite."

Rowan loved watching her. The day had grown even warmer, and it was nice sitting in the shade, sipping iced tea and chatting. Alice opened a folder and handed Rowan a sheet of paper. "We've rounded up a few more sponsors for your auction. The dance academy says they'll offer a package of lessons, but also that some of their children's classes are interested in performing if you can manage a stage of some sort. I think Hank at the lumberyard," she said and tapped on the contact information about halfway down the page, "could set you up with that."

"Wow. Excellent." Rowan skimmed the list. "This is gold. Thank you!"

As people began arriving for the second yoga session, the party broke up. Lauren took Becca with her to check on the goats while Rowan pitched in to help clear the empty tables and prepare the tasting room for the next onslaught. When she finished, she looked over to watch Becca on a mat between Gran and Rosemary, laughing when a goat tried to chew on Rosemary's braid. Madeleine hopped over and nuzzled Becca's face. She giggled and stopped to pet the goat. Madeleine and Becca were two of a kind: shy at first but brimming with love.

ZACK PARKED IN front of the big farmhouse and hopped out of his truck. He was late for dinner because he'd been called in on an emergency, but Rowan had told him not to worry, they understood. He hoped so, because he'd taken the time for a quick shower and change after finishing up at the clinic. He'd been to the farm many times in his professional capacity, of course, but today was different. He wanted to make a good impression.

The farmhouse felt welcoming. A picket fence surrounded a large lawn, with beds of flowers. Rocking chairs and a table with a checkerboard painted on top tempted passersby to sit on the front porch. He reached for the doorbell, but the door opened and Rowan's beautiful smile greeted him. "You made it! Come in!"

"Thanks." He followed her inside.

"Perfect timing. We just sat down to dinner. Becca helped Gran snap the beans." She led him through an archway to a dining room with a long dining table piled with food. An empty place waited for him next to Rowan.

Becca waved at him from her chair. "Hi, Zack. I helped cook, and I played with goats and did yoga and picked flowers and ate cheese, and I watched them milk the goats and everything."

"Cool!" Zack settled into his chair. "Hello, everyone. Sorry, I'm late."

"No problem," Patrick said. "Rowan told us you'd had an emergency."

Zack nodded. "A beagle had a disagreement with a porcupine."

"Wow, that was a tough lesson," Rowan said, passing him a bowl of mashed potatoes.

It had been. It had taken Zack almost two hours to get all the quills out of the dog's face and feet. "The sad thing is, if my other patients are anything to go by, given the chance, he'll do it again." Rowan passed him another platter. "Is that fried chicken? I haven't had homemade fried chicken in years." Probably not since his mother moved to Florida.

Rowan's grandmother beamed. "Have some green beans."

"Thank you." Noticing Becca watching him, he took a bite. "Yum. These beans are great."

Becca looked delighted. "I helped make them!"

"Wow. Between lessons from Rowan and Mrs. O'Shea, you're learning to be quite a cook."

"What's this Mrs. O'Shea business? You've always called me Bonnie, and Becca calls me Gran. We're family now."

Family. Zack wondered if Rowan had anticipated this when she'd proposed this mock marriage. Would her family be upset when she dissolved the whole thing next year?

"So, hot one today, huh?" Patrick commented, obviously fishing around for a conversation starter.

"Sure was. I heard on the radio it was seventy-seven, only two degrees off the record for the day," Zack told him. Casually, he added, "But it's a dry heat."

Rowan snorted. When Zack turned to look at her, they both burst out laughing.

"What's so funny?" Patrick asked, but Rowan's grandmother grinned.

"Never mind," Gran told Patrick, chuckling. "It's obviously an inside joke between the two of them. One of the joys of marriage."

CHAPTER SIXTEEN

THE NEXT AFTERNOON, Rowan pulled into the pickup line for camp. Even though she was ten minutes early, there were several cars ahead, so she would be waiting a while. She got out her phone to note the two food vendors she'd recruited that day, a game and fish processor and a local tapas restaurant that was just getting off the ground. She set a reminder to talk with Patrick about the best way to get power to the booths.

Her phone signaled an incoming video call. Well, it was only a matter of time. Rowan had gone more than a week without hearing from Mom, and since the silent treatment wasn't working, Mom was no doubt ready to move on to the next phase. Rowan smoothed her hair and accepted the call. But it wasn't her mom's face that appeared on the screen. "Dad!"

"Hi, Rosebud. Good to see that beautiful face." There was a reason Dad was a professional diplomat. When he smiled at you, it was easy to feel that you were the most important person in the world.

"It's good to see you, too. Did the speech at the trade assembly go well?"

"I believe so. It was a good audience. Do you have a few minutes?"

"Yes, but not too many. I'm in my car, waiting for camp to finish so I can pick up two girls and drive them home."

"Carpool duty? That's new." His mouth quirked up at the corner. "But then, I hear you've made quite a few changes lately."

"I suppose you could say that."

"Your mother is worried."

"I know. Are you?"

"Well, that depends. One of Renee's biggest concerns is that she inadvertently pushed you into a poor decision."

"What do you mean?"

"Honey, I know your mom can be…assertive."

Rowan snorted. "That's one word for it."

He smiled. "And you're the opposite. You've always been accommodating."

"Again, a kind word. Some would say I've been a doormat."

"Some might. I wouldn't." A fond smile flitted across his face. "*Doormat* implies weakness, and you've never been weak, Rowan. You simply value peace over getting your own way. Do you remember that incident with the two girls at your school in Athens?"

"Yes, of course." It was an international school with students from all over the world. When Fiona, an Irish student, had transferred in, one of the girls in Rowan's class decided to flaunt her alpha status by excluding Fiona and insisting all the other girls follow her lead. Rowan had befriended Fiona instead, which had resulted in the two of them being shunned from most social activities for the rest of the year. "But I didn't realize you knew about it."

"Of course I knew. Your mother was ready to march into the headmistress's office with a flamethrower. I told her you'd made your choice, and to let you see it through. Do you have any regrets?"

"I couldn't let them make Fiona miserable just for sport." It had been a tough year, but they'd survived. Fiona had gone on to study medicine and now worked in a clinic in Mumbai. They still exchanged the occasional email. "No. No regrets."

"I was so proud of you. You don't go along with others because you're weak, you do it because you're strong enough to know what matters. But your mother is afraid that by, shall we say, encouraging you to marry Sutton, she pushed you too far, and that you rebelled by marrying someone you thought she wouldn't approve of."

"She thinks I married Zack out of spite?"

"Well, it did happen rather suddenly, and it was right on the heels of your broken engagement. Just for the record, I'm glad about that."

"You didn't like Sutton?" She'd never guessed.

"It's not that I don't like him. I just felt you weren't the priority you should have been in his life."

"You never said."

"It wasn't my decision. But now, here you are married to someone I've never met. You didn't even let me walk you down the aisle." He still smiled, but she detected hurt in his eyes.

"Oh, Dad, I'm sorry. But you can't throw stones. I heard a rumor that you proposed to Mom on your second date."

"True, but we weren't married for another year and a half."

"That's just because Mom and Grandmother needed that long to plan the wedding details, down to the thread count of the tablecloths. Admit it—if it had been up to you, you would have eloped, as well."

Dad chuckled. "You're right about that."

"You'll like Zack. He works hard, he loves animals and he's devoted to his sister. Becca is the main reason we decided to marry so quickly."

"Your grandmother told me something about this custody situation."

"I love spending time with Becca, and she

likes having me around. In fact, she's asked me to help chaperone her day camp's end-of-summer overnight campout. Becca's doing really well with Zack. I've never met her mother, but it sounds like she's not much of a parent. Being married increases Zack's chances of gaining custody. So, you can tell Mom this isn't about her." Not entirely, anyway. "Like you said before, it's my choice. Let me see it through."

"Okay. But…" He gave her a wry smile, "I am your dad. So, let me just say that if you ever find you need help, don't let pride keep you from asking. Because I love you."

"I love you, too, Dad. No regrets."

He looked down at his desk and flipped a page in his ever-present day planner. He had never learned to trust an electronic calendar. "I have something I can't get out of on Friday, but I could carve out a few days next week. Your mother and I could come and meet your new husband."

"Oh, um…" Not a good idea. Rowan could fool her mother, but Dad had always been able to read her. If he was around her and Zack as a couple, he'd spot a fake marriage in no time. "This may sound odd, but with Becca and all, I think we need some time to ourselves as a family for a while before we have guests. Can you give me that?"

The worry lines in his forehead deepened. "Rosebud—"

"Trust me, Dad."

He hesitated, and then nodded. "Okay. But if you need me—"

"I know where to find you. Say, the car in front of me is moving, so I have to go. Love you."

"I love you, too. Goodbye, Rowan." His image shrank to nothing and disappeared.

"Bye, Dad," she whispered. "Thanks."

ZACK FINISHED UP at the clinic and made his way through the gate behind it. Rowan was picking up the girls, leaving him free to check on the animals in the wildlife center and still get home early, which would give him more time with Becca and Rowan.

Rowan. Just thinking of her made him smile. It was a different life since she'd moved in. When he walked through the door at the end of the day, he would be greeted with wagging tails, happy faces and delicious smells. When he left for work tomorrow morning, it would be with a kiss. Granted, the kiss was a sham, for Becca's sake, but that didn't mean he couldn't enjoy it.

Tomorrow afternoon was the lawyer's meeting. That's when he would announce he was married, and that Becca was thriving under their care. He'd have liked to bring up the idea of custody, too, to sound out Clarissa, but his lawyer advised him to wait until they had their arguments lined up and were ready to formally file for custody, so that he could ask for temporary guardianship at the same time. He was nervous, wondering if Clarissa's lawyers had any surprises in store, but with Rowan beside him, he felt like he could handle whatever they threw at him.

He passed the storage shed where they kept the feed, and then stopped and turned back. Was that a new coat of paint? Maggie must have done it. Usually they left maintenance jobs like this for the periodic workdays when they recruited extra volunteers. He'd have to talk to Maggie, make sure she wasn't overdoing. The last thing he wanted was to lose his primary volunteer to burnout.

Hearing voices, he veered off toward the porcupine cage. Becca was there, feeding Puddin carrots. A few feet closer, Maggie was talking to Rowan. "Be sure you wear long sleeves and gloves, and a face mask. If it gets on your skin, it can cause blisters."

He waved to Becca and joined Rowan and Maggie. "What's up?"

"Oh, hi, Zack. Your wife—" Maggie cast a smile toward Rowan "—painted the storage shed this morning and tomorrow she says she's going to tackle that patch of cow parsnip growing too close to the trail."

"You don't have to do all that," Zack protested. "We'll gather up a work crew in August to take care of things like that."

"I wanted to get it done in advance," Rowan told him, "so everything will look good for the slideshow."

"What slideshow?"

"For the fundraiser. Gran's friend Alice put me in touch with a photographer who wants to put together a presentation showing the people all the good you do at the wildlife center. His name is—" Rowan checked her phone "—Gordan Malee."

"You're kidding."

"Why do you say that?" Rowan asked.

"Gordan Malee is a famous wildlife photographer. His work is in museums all over the world. I can't believe he volunteered to help a little non-profit like us."

"Well, I met with him today, and he's quite enthusiastic. Of course, wildlife is his passion, and he loves that your focus is to get the animals you help back into the wild as quickly as possible."

"He gave a major donation after the moose segment on television," Maggie told Zack. "Didn't you look over the donor list Jessie gave us last week?"

"I guess I haven't gotten around to that."

"Well, you have been busy, what with eloping and all." Maggie grinned and put an arm around Rowan's shoulders. "Good choice there, by the way. She's a miracle worker."

"You can say that again." Zack chuckled as he watched Rowan's cheeks turn pink. The marriage might be a fake, but Rowan was genuinely one in a million.

"The question," Maggie continued with a twinkle in her eye, "is why she would agree to marry you. I'm guessing you whisked her off to Vegas before she could figure out what a hermit you really are."

"Hey, I'm not a hermit. I just don't like public speaking." He couldn't let Maggie know the real reason they'd married so quickly. If anyone let it slip that they'd married only to increase his chances of custody, it could backfire big-time. He adopted a teasing smile, "And, yes, I figured I'd get a ring on her finger before she could realize she's out of my league."

"Oh, I don't know about that. Highly educated medical professional. Founder of a successful nonprofit. Master Go Fish player." Rowan's ring winked in the light when she reached for his hand. "I think I'm the one who came out ahead on this deal."

"Hmm," Maggie hedged. "Zack's a pretty

good guy, but not everyone could rope in a world-famous photographer to take publicity photos."

"That wasn't my doing, it was my grandmother's friend." Rowan clarified. She turned to Zack. "By the way, Maggie is going to show him around later this week. Is it okay to give him your cell in case he has questions for you?"

"Absolutely."

"Great. So anyway, that's why I wanted to spruce up a little. Any other chores you can think of I should do before he comes?"

"I think you're doing more than enough already. Maggie's right. You are a miracle worker."

Becca ran over. "Puddin likes strawberries even more than she likes carrots."

"I'll bet."

"I'm on my way out," Maggie said, "but I wanted to tell you that you might want to take a look at that beaver you worked on yesterday. The incision looks a little irritated to me."

"I'll check it." Maggie seemed to have a sixth sense about which animals were doing well and which were not. She'd have made a heck of a vet.

"Other than that, everything is done. All fed, watered and cleaned."

"Thanks, Maggie. Have a great evening."

"Can we see the beaver?" Becca asked Zack.

"Sure, but let me grab some medicine from the clinic before we go."

"When did the beaver come in?" Rowan asked Zack when he returned, and they were walking along the trail.

"Yesterday. There was some internal bleeding," he said, "but fortunately, the bicycle rider who hit him brought him right in. If Maggie's correct about the infection, I'll mix antibiotic into his feed."

"What do you feed baby beavers anyway?"

Zack laughed. "They do pretty well on rodent chow."

"Rodent chow is a thing? How did I not know that?" She followed Zack and Becca inside a blind overlooking the beaver's pen.

"There he is," Becca whispered, pointing to where the little beaver huddled in the corner.

"He's tiny," Rowan whispered back. "You don't have to bottle feed him?"

"This one is about two months old. Beavers wean at just a few weeks," Zack told her. "Once he's better, we'll return him to the lake where his family lives." He picked up binoculars and zeroed in on the incision. Maggie was right. It was showing early signs of infection. "Yeah, looks like he's going to need extra antibiotics."

"I hope he feels better soon." Rowan stepped out of the blind and the three of them walked a little way down the trail. "Well, I left chicken potpie cooking in the slow cooker."

"I have a slow cooker?" Zack asked.

"You do now. I need to make a salad, but there's no hurry for dinner. The potpie just needs fifteen minutes in the oven to brown the cheddar biscuit crust, so text me when you're ready to come home. Becca, are you coming with me or staying here with Zack?" Becca looked wide-eyed between them, frozen in her dilemma. Gently, Rowan told her, "Whatever you want to do is fine. You won't hurt my feelings or Zack's."

"I'll stay with Zack," Becca said, watching Rowan carefully. Zack had seen that look on Becca's face too many times when she watched her mother, alert for any clues to her mood. Eager to please, desperate not to offend.

Rowan smiled. "Great! Have fun." She gave Becca's shoulders a casual squeeze and started to walk away.

"You forgot the kiss," Becca reminded them.

Rowan grinned. "Can't have that." She came back to brush her lips against Zack's for a regrettably short time. "See you soon."

Only a few days, and Rowan had already changed their lives from controlled chaos to joyful calm. If only—Zack caught himself. They'd agreed to a year, no more, and he'd do well to remember that. He tweaked Becca's braid. "You want to help me mix this medicine into the beaver's food so he can get better and go home to his family?"

"Yes!"

EVERYTHING WENT SMOOTHLY that evening until Becca's bedtime, when Zuma turned up missing. "When did you last see him?" Rowan asked.

"This morning, I guess, when I woke up."

Zack selected a stuffed penguin from the shelf. "How about if you sleep with Peppy tonight and we'll look for Zuma tomorrow?"

"But what if he's lost? What if I never find him?" Becca was getting close to tears.

"I'm sure he's here," Rowan said in that reassuring voice. "Let's go through the steps. You got up from bed, and went to the bathroom, right?" Rowan took her hand and led her to the bathroom. "Do you think you had Zuma with you then?" she asked as she checked behind the shower curtain and in the linen closet.

"I think so."

"Okay, then where?"

"I got dressed."

"Okay." Rowan led her back to the bedroom and opened the closet door. "You picked out a top and some jeans." Rowan pretended to pull out the clothes.

"And socks."

"Ah, socks." Rowan tried to open the second drawer of the chest, but it was stuck. She pulled harder and it opened with a jerk. "Well, look who we have here." She handed the toy to Becca.

"Zuma! Thank you!"

"You're welcome, sweetie. Now, better pop into bed. Zuma's already in his pajamas."

"Tonight, I'll just read the story," Zack said. Becca's eyes were shut before he'd finished the last page. He closed the book and watched her for a moment, peacefully hugging her stuffed puma. Her eyelashes fanned out against her round cheeks.

Fluff opened one eye and regarded him before closing it again. Rowan touched Zack's shoulder and slipped out into the hallway. He picked up a stray sock, dropped it into the hamper and followed.

"Nice work finding Zuma," he whispered, once he'd closed the door behind him.

"Nice work on the bedtime story." She held up a hand and he slapped a quiet high five. "We make a good team."

"Yeah."

Downstairs, Zack took out the kitchen trash while Rowan started the dishwasher. When he returned from the shed, she was sitting outside on the bench. "May I join you?" he asked.

"Sure." She scooted over to make room and

looked at her watch. "Alaskan summers still amaze me. It's almost ten, and we've still got another two hours before sunset."

"I love the way the grass and trees almost seem to glow when the sun is low in the northwest like this."

"Beautiful." Together, they watched as a Steller's jay flew in with a peanut from some feeder and hid it under the forest duff.

"Should I be at the meeting tomorrow?" Rowan asked, still looking toward the forest.

"You don't have to be." Legal meetings were never much fun.

"I would like to be there, but if you don't want me—"

"I want you." As the words came out of his mouth, he realized it was true. He wanted her. At the meeting. In his life. By his side. Forever. He touched her face, and she turned to look at him, those gentle eyes of hers meeting his without hesitation. He leaned closer, heard her intake of breath as she realized his intentions. But she didn't draw away. This time, when their lips met, it wasn't for show. This time, it was just for them.

Her hand came up to caress his cheek and then slid behind his neck, pulling him closer. He deepened the kiss, tasted the sweetness that was Rowan. She let out a tiny moan of pleasure, and his heart thumped in response. The jangle of tags gave a second's warning before a canine body launched itself onto the bench and tried to squeeze between them.

Rowan laughed. "Really, Ripley?"

Zack pushed the dog off their laps, but at his wagging tail, Zack gave in and scratched his ears. Maybe Ripley had done him a favor by interrupting. Maybe having Rowan around all the time was giving Zack illusions of permanence, but that wasn't the deal. This was a temporary marriage. Once he and Rowan had both gotten their lives in order, she would be moving on. That's all Rowan had promised, and all he had the right to ask for.

"Well, big day tomorrow." He leaned over for another kiss, but he landed this one on Rowan's forehead. "Guess I'd better turn in."

Was it his imagination, or did she look a little disappointed? But all she said was, "Good night, Zack. See you in the morning."

CHAPTER SEVENTEEN

THE CONFERENCE ROOM at the law office in Anchorage seemed to have too little air for the number of people jammed around the table. Or maybe it was the unfamiliar tie that was cutting off the oxygen to Zack's brain. He tugged at his collar. Under the table, Rowan reached for his free hand and gave it a squeeze. Instantly he felt calmer.

Clarissa had greeted him cordially enough when they arrived at the same time to the reception area, but now she sat across the table, carefully avoiding looking at him. He was struck as always with how young she seemed. She was thirty, only five years younger than him, but in her orange sundress, with her hair falling in blond corkscrews past tanned shoulders, she could have passed for a college student on spring break. Those twenty-four-carat facials must work.

Zack didn't know Clarissa's background, but from a few hints his dad had dropped, he gathered Clarissa's growing-up years hadn't been all birthday cake and sorority parties. Now she seemed to be making up for lost opportunities. Zack didn't begrudge her a period of carefree living, but Becca shouldn't have to suffer for it. It was in both their best interests for Zack to get custody. Could he make her see it?

The attorney beside her was shuffling through a stack of papers while they waited for Teagarden. Rowan had been in the bathroom when Clarissa arrived, so Zack hadn't introduced her yet. Clarissa probably thought Rowan was one of the legal team. She looked it today, wearing a conservative navy dress, with her hair pulled back in a silver clasp.

The estate attorney swept in and took a seat at the head of the table. "Apologies for keeping you waiting. A phone call ran long. I'm Teagarden Jones. Now, before we get down to business, I understand congratulations are in order. Zack, would you like to introduce us to your wife?"

"Your wife?" Clarissa leaned forward.

Zack reached for Rowan's hand and held it where everyone could see. "Yes, this is Rowan. We were just married this past week."

Clarissa mumbled something that could have been congratulations.

Teagarden smiled at Rowan. "Welcome, Rowan." He cleared his throat. "Now, I know you've all come for an accounting of the estate, so let's get started." He handed a stapled stack of papers to Clarissa's lawyer and an identical one to Zack. A rental cabin in Girdwood was first on the list. "I'll go over the properties, one by one. Please hold your questions for the end."

Clarissa appeared to listen closely while Teagarden explained the first two properties, their appraisal reports and the repair and refurbishing recommended in order to get top dollar, but about ten minutes into the monologue, she was looking down at her lap, probably checking messages on her phone. Zack had to wonder why she'd bothered to fly all the way to Alaska when she could have easily sent her attorney to handle this alone.

"...located an expert from Vermont who will be flying in tomorrow to appraise Thomas's collection of vintage fishing lures and equipment." Half an hour from when he'd started, Teagarden tapped his papers together on the table. "So, as you can see, while we have made considerable progress in settling the estate, there is still much to be done. Now, what questions do you have for me?"

Clarissa's attorney asked a few clarifying questions, but Zack got the feeling he knew the answers before he asked. Maybe he felt like he needed to say something in order to justify his fee. It seemed to be simply an update, until he pulled something from his briefcase. "Since you anticipate more delays in settling the estate, Mrs. Vogel will need an advance on her share." He handed the paper to Teagarden.

Another advance? What was she doing with all that cash? Zack looked at Clarissa to see if she would offer an explanation, but her eyes didn't leave her phone.

"I'm sure that won't be a problem," Teagarden answered as he accepted the paper.

"She is also requesting a release of an advance from her daughter's portion of the estate."

Teagarden looked up from the paper he'd been skimming. "Why would she need an advance for Becca, when Becca is living with Zack?"

"In order to prepare for her daughter's arrival, Mrs. Vogel will need funds to rent a villa more suitable to family life than the resort at which she's staying now, as well as to procure the services of a nanny and arrange for a suitable school."

"What? When—?" Zack couldn't seem to form a coherent question.

Teagarden interrupted. "I'm not sure a judge would agree. I'd need to look into it."

"Please do. We can schedule a hearing if necessary." Judging by the smug expression on the attorney's face, he was satisfied with the response.

Clarissa met Zack's eyes briefly, but he couldn't get a read on her before she looked away.

"Any other issues we should discuss?" Teagarden asked.

"Not at this time. We'll be in touch." Everyone stood and Clarissa's lawyer opened his briefcase on the table and began packing it.

"How long will you be in town?" Zack asked Clarissa.

"I'm flying to Belize in the morning." At a nudge from her lawyer, she added. "Give Becca my love."

He had been about to ask if she'd like to at least see her daughter before she left town again, but why bother. It would only inconvenience Clarissa and upset Becca's routine. As if reading his mind, Clarissa added, "I wish I could take her out to dinner tonight, but I promised to attend an engagement party while I'm here. Someone I know from the golf club."

"I see."

Clarissa glanced at her phone. "You know, the party isn't until seven. Maybe you could bring her by my hotel room in Anchorage for a little while before that?"

It was a forty-five-minute drive from the law office in downtown Anchorage to pick up Becca in Palmer. That meant an extra hour and a half of driving for him so that Becca and Clarissa could spend a few minutes together. He considered making an excuse, but Rowan nudged him with her knee and gave an almost undetectable nod. "I can do that."

Clarissa smiled. "I'm at the Captain Cook. Say, six thirty?"

"That's fine." If the party was at seven, that probably meant fifteen minutes with her daughter. Did she really intend to have Becca move to be with her in Belize? A thought occurred. "Becca can't leave the country. She doesn't have a passport."

"She doesn't?" Clarissa's lawyer looked up.

"Not that I'm aware of, anyway. She's always stayed with me when Dad and Clarissa traveled outside the country."

"You'll need to do that," Clarissa's lawyer told her. "You have to apply for a passport in person with her birth certificate and her father's death certificate. It can take a month or more to get it processed."

Clarissa checked her watch. It was already late afternoon. "I won't have time before I go. Can't you handle that?" she asked Zack.

"I don't think he can," Teagarden said. "I'd have to check if there are any exceptions, but I believe only the parents or legal guardians can apply for a child's passport."

Clarissa huffed out a breath of annoyance. "I'll do it next time I come up. Zack, do you know where I can find her birth certificate?"

"Not offhand." Most likely it was in his dad's office safe where the will and other papers should have been. No use antagonizing Clarissa. "I'll look for it."

"Thank you."

"It was nice meeting you, Clarissa." Rowan offered a hand, and Clarissa shook it. Rowan's smile looked genuine, but Zack knew her well enough to know it lacked her usual warmth.

"Yeah, you, too." Clarissa looked from Rowan to Zack. "How long have you—"

"We've known each other since we were teenagers." Rowan leaned closer to Zack and slipped an arm around his waist.

"Huh. Okay. See you later." Clarissa followed her lawyer from the room.

Once they were out of sight, Teagarden shut the door, and everyone sat down again. Zack started. "An advance on Becca's funds?"

"More than likely, it's an empty threat," Teagarden asserted. "Just a legal maneuver. They're hoping that if she threatens to take Becca, you'll speed up the distribution of funds."

Zack massaged his temples, trying to rub away the headache forming there.

"We should call their bluff," Teagarden continued.

"Becca is not a poker chip," Rowan asserted.

"I didn't mean—" Teagarden started to say, but Rowan interrupted.

"No, I realize that. I just mean that you can't take a chance assuming that they will back down. What if they don't?"

"Clarissa may well be serious about this plan," Zack agreed. "At the rate she's burning money, she'll run out in a decade. Becca's money would give her another five years or so."

"Can she really spend Becca's money on herself?" Rowan asked the lawyer.

"Short answer, no. But in practice…" Teagarden shrugged. "If she did, Zack could take her to court. If he could prove it."

"And if she had any of her own money left to pay it back," Zack pointed out.

"We can ask a judge to appoint you as trustee for her inheritance instead of Clarissa," Teagarden suggested. "That would remove the financial incentive to take Becca away."

"I need full custody," Zack said. "That's the only way Becca can feel secure. We need to file now."

"When you take something to court, there's always the chance of losing what you have," Teagarden hedged. "The mother certainly has precedence. It's possible that the court would not only refuse you full custody, but they might not even grant you visitation if Clarissa doesn't want it."

"Clarissa and I have always gotten along," Zack said. "She asked me to take Becca after the funeral. And up until now, she hasn't questioned my handling of the estate."

"Up until now, you've always given her whatever she asked for," Teagarden said. "If you cross her, things might be different."

No doubt he'd had experience in this sort of thing, but his wasn't the perspective Zack trusted most. He turned to Rowan. "What do you think?"

"I think you're right, that Becca will never be secure until you have full custody."

"Let's do it," Zack said. "We'll word it diplomatically, but we need to make it clear Becca stays with me."

"If Becca starts school here at the end of August, would that be a factor in deciding custody?" Rowan asked.

"It couldn't hurt," the lawyer agreed. "Overall, the longer she stays with you, the more solid your case. I'd find that birth certificate and have it ready to hand over when she asks for it. If this goes before a judge, you want to show good faith. How is Becca reacting to this marriage?" Teagarden asked Zack. "That is, if a judge asked, would Becca say she was upset at the change in her routine?"

"On the contrary," Zack replied, "she's happier than she's ever been since Rowan moved in."

"Good, good." Teagarden made a note. "I'll transfer another advance to Clarissa's account, and we'll delay their request for an advance on behalf of Becca. We'll plan to move forward with a custody hearing soon."

"All right." Zack checked his watch. "If I'm going to collect Becca and bring her back to town, we'd better get moving. Thanks, Teagarden."

Rowan was quiet as Zack navigated his truck through downtown Anchorage. Once they'd made it to the highway, he asked her, "So, what was your impression of Clarissa?"

"Honestly," Rowan replied, "I felt sorry for her."

That was unexpected. "Why?"

Rowan shook her head. "She's desperate to grab as much money as she can, because it's the only security she trusts. If I were to guess, she's spending most of it to impress other people, so they'll hang around and act like friends, because she has no real friends."

"That's a lot from just a few words."

"And I may be completely wrong, but that's the impression I get."

"I suspect you're right. I don't know any details of her background, but I've never heard her mention family or close friends. None came to my dad's funeral, or even sent a card, as far as I know."

"I wish, for her sake and for Becca's, that she could be a better parent, but it may never happen. So—" Rowan smiled at Zack "—it's good Becca has you."

And you. He almost said it before he remembered that Rowan's role was temporary. She was there only to help him get custody of Becca and smooth their path. It wasn't a real marriage. Even if he wished it was.

ROWAN TRANSFERRED A load of laundry from the washer to the dryer and returned to the kitchen. "Coffee's ready." She poured two cups and handed one to Zack as he sat down to eat his bowl of cereal.

"Thanks." Zack was never particularly communicative first thing in the morning, which suited Rowan fine. She liked a few minutes of calm to sip coffee and plan her day. Last night Zack had mentioned he needed to go in early to check on the beaver kit before his first appointment, so he and Rowan were up well before Becca this morning.

Rowan prepared Becca's lunch and poured

the remainder of the coffee into Zack's travel mug. She carefully stepped around Ripley, who had stretched out across the rectangle of sunlight streaming through the kitchen window onto the golden wood of the floor. Rowan loved this kitchen.

Zack's phone chimed as he finished his breakfast and he checked his messages. "Oh, shoot. The housekeeper at my dad's house has to take her mother to the doctor this afternoon and won't be there to let in the appraiser."

"What appraiser?"

"He's flying in from out east to value my dad's fishing collectibles. It seems like a lot of fuss to me, but Teagarden says he's the expert. I have appointments all day, so I can't do it. I'll see if Teagarden can get one of his office staff to let him in."

"I can do it."

"No, you're meeting with the Hawaiian plate lunch restaurant owners today about the fundraiser."

Rowan smiled, pleased he remembered. "We changed it to this morning at ten. I'm free in the afternoon, and Jessie is driving today. Just give me the time and the key."

"Are you sure? You might need to stay a couple of hours. At least until the housekeeper gets back."

"I don't mind. I can take my laptop and work on the fundraiser while I wait. Oh, and if you want, I can look for that birth certificate while I'm there."

"Thank you." He ran upstairs and returned with a key ring and a sticky note with a series of numbers written on it. "The combination to the safe in the study."

"Should I have this?"

"I trust you more than anyone else I know. Just tear it up when you're done." He accepted the coffee she held out. "You are a lifesaver." He checked his watch. "Gotta run." He planted a sweet kiss on her mouth before heading out the door.

Rowan pressed her fingers to her lips. To keep Becca happy, they'd been kissing goodbye every morning, but Becca was still asleep in her bed, upstairs. Maybe he'd just kissed her from habit. Or maybe it was a thank-you for handling the appraiser. Or maybe—

No. Zack had been clear he didn't want or need a romantic attachment in his life. But there was that kiss outside on the porch. That was no casual thank-you or goodbye. It felt like a kiss that meant something, that acknowledged what she felt was growing between them. If Ripley hadn't come along when he did… But he had. And Zack hadn't mentioned the kiss or made any more moves since. So maybe, as they said, a kiss was just a kiss.

Fluff padded into the kitchen, checked her bowl and meowed, demanding to know why no one had emptied the leftover dry food and replaced it, because eating yesterday's kibble was completely out of the question for royalty like her. That must mean Becca was out of bed.

Rowan had tagged along when Zack took Becca to Clarissa's hotel suite the day before, curious to see them together. Their reunion was heartbreaking in its uneventfulness. Mother and daughter had greeted each other politely. In that too-bright voice people who were uncomfortable around children used, Clarissa had asked a few questions and received mostly one-word answers. The only time she showed real interest was when Becca complimented her necklace. "It's a conch pearl," Clarissa explained, of the pink globe encased in a platinum cage. "They're very rare."

"I like the color."

"Thank you. I like it, too."

After that, Becca had relaxed a little, as though she'd completed her assigned task of making her mother smile. When Zack suggested it might be time to go, everyone seemed relieved. He'd taken Becca and Rowan to a local burger place for dinner, and Becca had suddenly remembered half-a-dozen interesting things from camp that day. They'd listened to her stories and laughed when she caught Zack sneaking onion rings from her plate. Rowan suspected Clarissa's party wasn't nearly as much fun.

The dryer buzzed. Rowan pulled out the warm clothes and breathed in the lovely scent of fresh laundry. She was halfway through folding when she heard Becca's voice calling down the stairs. "Rowan, do you know where my red shirt is?"

"I have it." She dumped the rest of the clothes in the basket and started up the stairs. Time to get this day in gear.

"COME THIS WAY." Rowan had never been inside the house before, but Zack had given her directions on where to take the appraiser. As she led him across the marble floor of the entryway and into a living room with five, no seven different couches and at least a dozen chairs, she wished she'd had Zack draw a map. The back of the living room was a two-story glass wall with a mountain view. The wall on the right had three doors.

The first door led to a half bath with a hammered copper sink raised above a granite countertop. The next door opened into an office dominated by a walnut desk. Finally, behind door number three, Rowan found a room lined with glass-fronted cabinets displaying fishing rods and other equipment. Below each case was a set of shallow drawers anchored by an ornately carved molding. In the center of the room, four leather club chairs surrounded a glass-topped square table. Twenty or thirty wooden fishing lures were displayed in a velvet-lined tray under the glass. "In here, Dr. Jennison," she called to the appraiser, who had stopped to admire the mountains.

"Splendid view," he commented as he followed her in and watched as she unlocked the cabinets. "Ah, what have we here? A Finis bamboo fly rod. I bid on one of these for a client in an auction in Wyoming a few years ago." He took a pair of white gloves from his bag and pulled them on.

"I'll leave you to it, then," Rowan said. "I'll be in the next room if you need me."

He nodded, already engrossed in his inspection. Rowan returned to the study and found the safe under the desk. Inside, she found stacks of file folders, a box and an unmarked envelope. A quick glance inside the envelope showed a motley collection of euros, pounds, pesos, yen and several other currencies. The box held jewelry, with a diamond tennis bracelet and several rings on top.

She returned the box and cash to the safe and

set the folders on the desk. Bold writing labeled each one. Auto Titles. Insurance Documents. Several folders with street addresses that seemed to contain titles, plot maps, appraisals and such. Another folder, labeled Old Wills, contained several going back to before Zack was born. Zack had told her the will they were using was fifteen years old. She had to wonder if it had come from this folder.

Toward the bottom of the stack, she found a folder with Becca's name. The official birth certificate was right on top. Rowan set it aside. Behind it was a hospital certificate with tiny footprints and a photo of newborn Becca, wrapped in a pink blanket and looking at the camera with wide blue eyes. How could anyone see that tiny baby and not immediately fall in love?

The folder held several other documents, including a record listing every immunization from birth to a tetanus shot six months ago. A paper stapled to the back of the card noted that Becca had stepped on a nail and the doctor had recommended an extra tetanus booster just in case. Another note mentioned a mild rash in response to an antibiotic she had taken for an ear infection when she was four.

Rowan shut the folder and returned it to the pile. Zack was right. A man who kept track of every shot and drug reaction for his daughter would not have neglected to update his will. Since she was going to be there a while anyhow, Rowan leafed through all the folders before returning them to the safe. She even checked the jewelry box for a false bottom or hidden compartment, but nothing came to light.

After locking everything back in the safe, she checked on the appraiser, who was happily photographing a tray of fishing flies. The rest of the afternoon she spent going through every item in the study bookshelves and every folder in the oak file cabinets. Thomas Vogel might have been a bit of a packrat, but each folder was neatly labeled in his distinctive handwriting and contained exactly what the label promised, and none of them contained any mention of a new will. He was obviously a man of organization and method. He would not have neglected to provide for his daughter. Would Clarissa really have destroyed the will? There didn't seem to be any way to prove it.

CHAPTER EIGHTEEN

ROWAN REALLY WAS a miracle worker. How else to explain that the predicted rain on the day of the fundraiser should mysteriously vanish, to be replaced by a perfect sunny day? Mouthwatering smells came from the row of food booths offering samplings of everything from smoked duck to thumbprint cookies, and an empty stage promised entertainment later. Judging by the number of people Zack saw lined up to buy tickets outside the gate, WildFair was a hit.

"Where's Becca?" Charlotte asked Zack when she and her mother located him just inside the entry to the fundraiser. "We're supposed to get our faces painted."

"She's over there with Rowan." Zack pointed toward the cheese booth.

"Becca, I'm here!" Charlotte took off, galloping across the grounds.

"Charlotte, wait. You'll need tickets…" Jessie trailed off when it became apparent Charlotte was too excited to hear her. She grinned at Zack. "This is amazing!"

"I know." Even though he and all the volunteers had been here yesterday, setting it all up, it was incredible to watch the festivities taking place. They'd cleared the goats from one of the pastures and located the fair there. A juggler, two clowns, a magician and a unicyclist roamed among the crowds. There were family activity booths, with art projects, a ring-toss game with prizes, the face-painting booth, balloon animals and many others.

"Hey, Zack." Greg joined his wife and handed over a fistful of tickets. He looked around. "Wow!"

"I can't believe all the people Rowan managed to round up," Jessie said. "How many different tasting booths did we end up with?"

"Fourteen, I think."

"We're signed up to help with the auction, but do you need us to do anything in the meantime?"

"Maggie might want you to take a shift at the WildER information tent. Other than that, you'll need to ask Rowan. Let's go check with her. I need to give Becca some tickets, anyway, so she and Charlotte can do the bouncy house and face painting."

They made their way to the cheese booth. Lauren and three other ladies were doing a brisk business giving out samples. Becca was there, too, with Charlotte by her side, accepting tickets from hungry customers.

Rowan stood to one side, consulting her clipboard and giving directions to two volunteers. "We've got dancers performing in half an hour," she was saying, "so don't set up the chairs until four. The auction starts at five."

When they left, Jessie and Greg stepped up. "Reporting for duty."

"Hi." Rowan hugged them. "I don't have you scheduled until four forty-five for the auction, but if you'd like to take Charlotte and Becca around, maybe Zack can take over Becca's ticket-taking duties."

"I'm on it," Zack agreed. He stayed busy for the next hour, taking tickets and watching the crowds. Rowan had done an amazing job. All of Palmer and half of Anchorage seemed to have decided to come out and play. She'd managed to get all the expenses, even advertising, covered by donations, so the entire gate fee was going toward the wildlife center. And that was in addition to the proceeds from the auction. Rowan had put together some incredible prize packages.

She and her clipboard seemed to be everywhere today, answering questions, organizing volunteers, even helping a crying child locate his mother. Now she stood in the open center area, calling for attention. "Hello, everybody."

Rowan's voice sounded gentle, even amplified through a portable microphone. "Welcome to the first annual WildFair for WildER. It's great to see you all here today. In ten minutes, we'll start the sack race, sponsored by Frozen Tundra Treats. The winner will receive ice cream for a month—that is thirty-one free ice cream cones—so anyone who wants to participate, come and get your sack!"

Becca hurried up to the cheese booth, sporting a ladybug on one cheek and a butterfly on the other. She carried half a tiny taco in her hand. "Zack! Me and Charlotte are going to enter. Come watch." She popped the last bite into her mouth.

"Go ahead," Lauren told Zack. "The rush has died down. We can handle things here."

He followed Becca over and helped get a couple of kids into their sacks. Rowan flashed him a grin. "Having fun?" she called.

"You bet!" Usually he hated crowds, but outdoors on the grass with kids playing and laughing, he didn't mind at all.

Rowan stood at the line. "On your mark. Get set. Go!" Thirty or so children leaped forward in their sacks. At least a fourth immediately fell and had to scramble back to their feet and into their bags before they could move on. A couple of boys bounded ahead almost to a photo finish, but Maggie, who had come to judge and offer the prize, declared one of them a winner by a nose. Charlotte and Becca finished in the middle of the pack, and all the children received a certificate for one free cone.

Zack helped Rowan reclaim the sacks. "Have you had a chance to eat yet?" he asked her.

"Not yet." She checked her watch. "I have twenty minutes before the egg-in-a-spoon race."

"Then let's try out some of this great food. Becca was eating a taco."

"It must be from The Smokery. They were going to serve dilled halibut tacos and smoked salmon mini bagels. Do they have any left?"

"Let's go see." He set the stack of sacks in their crate. "The cheese booth was popular. The kids love the cheese kabobs, and the parents were crazy for those little cheese cupcake thingies."

"Vegetable timbales with goat cheese. I thought those would be fun for a tasting."

"You made those?" He didn't know why that surprised him. "Is there anything here today you didn't personally handle?"

"Lots. Molly, Bea and Rosemary are over in the face-painting booth. Linda and Alice took tickets. Lauren's friend Marissa from the reindeer farm loaned us several animals, including two reindeer calves, and Gran is supervising the petting zoo. Patrick is troubleshooting the power supply and the sound system for the auction. And then there are all the volunteers from the wildlife center. Everyone has been so generous."

And no one more generous than Rowan, but if he said it, she would just deflect the praise to someone else. "What happens next?" Zack asked as he handed over tickets for the smoked-fish treats.

"Games every half hour with a few performers interspersed. The auction is scheduled for five. We'll do a short thank-you from the wildlife center before the bidding starts." Rowan smiled at him. "Don't worry. I got Maggie to do the presentation. I know how much you hate public speaking."

"Whew." Zack pretended to wipe his forehead. "Thank you."

Rowan laughed.

"No, really." Zack passed her a tiny taco. "Thank you. For everything."

"PLEASE SIGN YOUR name on the sheet beside a number and take the matching bidding paddle," Rowan explained. "If you'd like to receive a monthly email from the wildlife center, just check the box and add your email. That also enters you into a drawing for a two-night stay from Luxury Yurts."

"Can I skip down and take number fifty-six?"

a man asked. "That's my lucky number. It's the year my wife was born," he whispered, as though sharing a secret.

"Ah, no wonder it's lucky, then." Rowan handed him the paddle. Five other volunteers who sometimes helped at the wildlife center were also checking bidders in, so the process was going quickly. As she'd hoped, they were also enthusiastically answering questions about WildER and volunteer opportunities to anyone who asked.

Maggie hovered at the edge of the stage, talking with Zack. In full makeup and wearing a red maxi dress instead of her customary work pants, Maggie looked every inch the former beauty queen Zack said she was.

"It's even better than I thought it was going to be!" A familiar voice brought Rowan's attention back to the table.

"Daphne! Tony! You came!" Rowan came around the table to hug them. "Did you do the Mount Marathon run?"

"I did indeed," Tony said.

"Second in his age group." Daphne pretended to wave a pom-pom.

"Congratulations."

"Thanks. Sorry we were late today." Tony cast an amused glance at his wife. "Someone got carried away fishing."

"If I had known it was so exciting, I'd have been fishing for years," Daphne told Rowan. "Did you know you can fish for king salmon in Ship Creek, right there in downtown Anchorage?"

"I've heard that. Did you catch one?"

"I did! Thirty-six pounds, which they tell me isn't that big for a king but good grief, it was a monster. I was incredibly lucky."

"I'll say. Good for you!"

"So, of course we had to drop the fish off at a processer before we could drive out here to the WildFair," Tony explained.

"Fortunately, I'd seen your list of sponsors on the website, so we knew to take the fish to The Smokery, and we told them where we heard about it. They're going to smoke half our fish and freeze the rest. I just hope it comes out as good as the fish on those little bagel treats. Yum!"

While she had been talking, Tony had signed up and taken a paddle. "We'd better let Rowan get back to work." He put his hand on Daphne's back to urge her forward.

"We'll talk later," she told Rowan over her shoulder.

"I want to have you for dinner when you're free," Rowan called to her. "I'll phone."

When they were down to the last few stragglers, Rowan excused herself and went up on the stage. Patrick handed her the microphone, adjusted a few knobs and gave her the okay sign.

"Hello, everyone, and thanks for coming to the WildFair. I hope you've been looking over the great prize packages. I know you're eager to get the auction started, but before we do, Maggie Ziegler would like to say a few words about the wildlife center. Maggie?"

Maggie waved as she walked onto the stage. Rowan handed over the microphone and retreated to where Tom, Maggie's reporter friend, was waiting to step into his role as auctioneer.

Maggie smiled and scanned the crowd until the applause died down. "Is everyone having a good time?" A round of applause and whistles erupted and Maggie grinned. "That's what I like to hear. I do have a short presentation—" she crossed her heart "—very short, I promise. But first, Zack Vogel, our founder and the veterinarian who dedicates himself to the well-being of these animals on a daily basis, asked if he could say a few words."

Zack wanted to talk? He looked a little pale as he came onto the stage, but he took the mic from Maggie and laughed. "Those of you who know me know that I would take dealing with a wounded grizzly over public speaking any day of the week." Several twitters in the crowd demonstrated that his aversion was well known. "But

I couldn't let this evening go by without publicly thanking the woman who pulled this whole thing together from the very beginning." He gestured toward the side of the stage. "My incredible wife, Rowan."

Suddenly, the crowd was applauding wildly. Zack handed the microphone back to Maggie and came to take Rowan's hand and pull her up on stage. People continued to clap, and some in the first row stood up. Soon the whole crowd was standing and applauding. A bouquet appeared from somewhere and Zack handed it to her. And then, in front of everyone, Zack kissed her—a happy, joyous, spontaneous kiss. She stared in wonder.

"I think we've left her speechless." Maggie laughed. "Rowan Vogel, everyone."

A fresh round of applause sounded as Rowan waved at the crowd and she and Zack made their way off the stage. Maggie started her presentation about the wildlife center featuring Gordon Malee's photographs. Once Rowan and Zack were down the stairs and out of sight from most of the crowd, she turned to him. "I can't believe you voluntarily went on stage for me."

"After everything you've done for WildER? And for me?" He took the flowers from her and set them aside before he took her in his arms. "You give and you give and you give. You deserve some recognition." And he kissed her once again.

"Zack! Rowan!" Becca came running up.

"Hi." Rowan smoothed Becca's hair back from her face, exposing a streak of dirt and a smudged ladybug on her cheek.

"I made this for you." Becca handed over a wooden heart glued to a magnet. She'd painted a figure with long hair in the middle, holding hands with two taller figures. It must have been one of the projects from the local craft store booth. "See, it's me, and Zack, and you."

"I love it! Thank you!" Rowan held it up to better admire it. "Are you having a good day?"

Becca gave a happy sigh. "This is the best day of my whole life."

"Group hug," Zack suggested as he enveloped them both in his arms. Becca giggled.

As Rowan squeezed them both, she had to agree. This might well be the best day of her whole life, too.

CHAPTER NINETEEN

"So, I REALIZED I'd hooked the fish, and I didn't know what to do." Daphne was using her fork to demonstrate how she'd caught the king salmon. "Everyone was yelling different instructions. Tony had gone to retrieve the fishing gear we'd left farther down the bank. Then this boy about ten years old came to stand beside me and told me, step by step, exactly what to do."

"Once I got there, all I had to do was scoop it up in the net." Tony smiled at his wife. "Now that she's a confirmed fisherwoman, we've booked our fishing charter out of Seward for Thursday."

As if it weren't enough that the package based on their Mexican timeshare had brought in enough cash to pay the wildlife center's feed bill for several months, Tony's had been the winning bid for a hotly contested deep-sea fishing charter package.

"You'll have a great time." Zack took seconds on the au gratin potatoes and glazed salmon and passed them around the table. "Rowan, this salmon is excellent."

"It's part of Daphne's king," Rowan told him. "She brought us four fillets."

"Don't forget, you promised me recipes." Daphne put a little more fish on her plate and passed the platter to Tony. "Save room for dessert. I understand this wonder child—" she winked at Becca "—made a chocolate raspberry torte for us."

Becca giggled. She found Daphne fascinating. As soon as she'd arrived, Daphne had presented Becca with an Alaska yo-yo she'd picked up at a craft co-op in downtown Anchorage, and she and Becca spent a half hour taking turns trying to get the two fur balls on strings spinning in opposite directions. When Becca achieved success, Daphne had quickly produced her phone and recorded it for posterity. "Wait until I show this to my nephews. I got them each a set last time we visited Alaska, and they never were able to make them work."

"So, Zack," Tony said, as he added more potatoes to his plate. "We know the wildlife rehab center isn't open to the public, but we were wondering if it might be possible for Daphne and me to get a sneak peek. Feel free to say no. We don't want to disturb the animals."

"After all you did for the fundraiser, I'd be honored to give you the tour."

"You have to be quiet around the wild animals," Becca told them. "And you have to hide from some of them, so they don't get used to people. But you can meet Puddin and Yeil. They live there. Puddin is a porcupine, and she loves carrots and stuff."

"I don't believe I've ever met a porcupine," Daphne said. "A new experience!"

It wasn't until dessert that Rowan happened to mention the name of Daphne and Tony's company.

"You're the company that put out the video game based on Jules Verne's *From the Earth to the Moon*? I loved that game." Zack laughed. "If not for you, my undergrad grade point might have been at least half a point higher."

"Well, you got into vet school, so it must not have been too much of a distraction," Daphne said.

"I just wish our office software worked as smoothly as your products. The appointment scheduler has been giving us fits lately," Zack said.

"Show me." Tony finished his last bite of torte and set down his fork. "Maybe I can help."

"I can't ask you to do that," Zack said. "We'll call the IT guys next week."

"Seriously, I don't mind. Let's go take a look. Your office is next door, isn't it?"

"Okay, then. Say, Becks, Christine brought in

a pair of kittens that are up for adoption. Want to come socialize with them while we look at the computer?"

"Yes!" Becca jumped up and asked Daphne, "Do you want to play with the kittens, too?"

"Tempting, but I think I'll stay with Rowan. But promise you'll come and get me before you visit the porcupine."

"I promise," Becca said solemnly before skipping off with Zack and Tony.

Daphne picked up two plates to carry to the kitchen. "You and Zack are newlyweds, I take it."

"Yes. We've only been married three weeks."

"Hmm. The waiter at the restaurant in Palo Alto seemed to think you'd just broken off an engagement. I gather you reconciled."

"Uh, no. The engagement I broke wasn't with Zack."

Daphne raised her eyebrows. "Do tell."

Rowan scraped a plate and stacked it in the dishwasher before she answered. "Can you keep a secret?"

"Do you know what my natural hair color is?"

"No."

"Neither does Tony." Daphne's eyes crinkled at the corners. "In other words, yes, I can keep a secret, but don't tell me unless you want to."

Rowan walked across the room to look out

the window toward the forest. "Have you ever gone into a situation with good intentions, but you discovered you were in over your head?"

"Oh, many times, but we're talking about you. Do you regret marrying Zack so quickly?"

"Not marrying him, but—" Rowan turned to face Daphne. "It's not a real marriage, just a temporary arrangement. Zack wants full custody of his sister. Becca's mother has no interest in her, but Zack is afraid Clarissa won't give up her rights, because Becca is set to inherit a substantial sum of money."

Daphne didn't seem shocked. "And if Zack is married to someone caring and nurturing like you, it makes his case better."

"Frankly, yes."

"Okay. That explains why he married you. Why did you marry him? What did you get out of it?"

More confession. "I married Zack because I'm a square peg, and for my whole life, my mother has been lovingly molding me to fit into this perfectly round hole she thinks is best for me. She chose my college major, my job and even my fiancé. I'd had enough, but I didn't have the strength to get out of it on my own. Marrying Zack cut my ties and gave me the chance to take stock and figure out what I really want."

Daphne shook her head. "No."

"What do you mean 'no'?"

"That may be true, but it's not the reason you married Zack. Not the whole reason anyway."

"Well, there's Becca, of course. I adore that little girl, and I know she belongs with Zack."

"We're getting warmer." Daphne looked at her encouragingly.

"I don't know where you're going with this."

"Of course you do. What are your feelings toward Zack?"

"Zack." Rowan felt her lips curve at the mention of his name. "Well, we're friends. I respect and admire him, and I care about him. I uh…"

"You married Zack as a way to escape your mother, and to help him get custody of Becca, and because…" Daphne paused meaningfully.

"Because I love him." It was suddenly so clear. How could Rowan not have realized this a long time ago? "I love Zack."

"Bingo."

"But our arrangement."

"What about it?"

"This marriage isn't about love. It's about getting custody of Becca."

"Then maybe it's time to come to a new arrangement."

Was that possible? "Zack told me after watching his father go through four less-than-happy marriages, he never intended to marry."

"And yet he did."

"For Becca."

"Becca. Right." Daphne gave an amused smile. "I saw that kiss. If I were you, I would schedule some uninterrupted time alone to talk this through with your husband."

"But—"

Daphne held up her hand. "That's my advice, free of charge. You can take it or leave it." She looked past Rowan out the window. "And if I'm not mistaken, that's Becca running over to tell us it's time for that tour of WildER. She's such a sweetheart."

"Yes. She's worth whatever it takes to make sure she's secure and happy."

"So are you, darling." Daphne put an arm around Rowan's shoulders and squeezed. "So are you."

ROWAN STRAIGHTENED A napkin and set the new candle she'd picked up at the store in the center of the table. Was it too much? She wasn't trying to seduce Zack, just to make the conversation smoother. She'd been putting it off for five days, turning over in her mind how best to approach the topic. She'd promised Zack a year, but she wanted a lifetime. How do you tell your friend you're in love with him? Especially when you're already married to him?

It had been a good week. When Jessie had totaled up the proceeds from the fundraiser, it was enough to match the grant and cover the expenses for the wildlife center for a full year, plus some left over. Jessie had called an emergency meeting of the board and they'd decided to set aside the extra in a rainy-day fund for future repairs and projects. And thanks to Maggie's friend Tom Hackman, the WildFair auction had made the ten o'clock news. The news clip had included Zack thanking Rowan and the now-famous kiss. What if her confession changed everything?

A knock sounded from the back door and Charlotte ran in ahead of Jessie. "Is Becca ready? We've got movies and popcorn. Is she bringing Zuma?"

"Maybe you should run up to her room and see."

"Okay." Charlotte dashed for the stairs.

"Something smells fantastic." Jessie lifted the pot lid. "What is this?"

"Boeuf bourguignon. It's just beef stew with a French accent."

"Nice." She replaced the lid and looked at the table. "Candlelight. Ooh la la." She grinned. "Maybe next Friday, the girls can sleep here, and I'll cook a romantic dinner. I could make Greg's favorites—corn dogs and ice cream."

Rowan laughed. "Anytime. I appreciate you taking Becca tonight, but if she gets homesick, feel free to call and we'll pick her up."

"She was fine with us while you went to Vegas," Jessie pointed out. "Don't worry about Becca. Just have fun."

"Thanks. Oh, here." Rowan handed over a cookie tin. "Becca and I made dark chocolate, raspberry and goat-cheese brownies."

"That sounds amazing."

The girls came clattering down the stairs with Ripley right behind them. "Fluff is hiding under the bed, so I left the door open," Becca told Rowan. "I took three books and two outfits for Zuma. And I brought the Alaska yo-yo Daphne gave me."

"How about pajamas?" Rowan asked Becca.

"I got those, too."

"Toothbrush?"

"Yes."

"Sounds like you're all set, then. I'll pick you up in the morning. Give me a hug?" Rowan treasured the moment when Becca's arms came around her. "Be good for Jessie and Greg."

"We will," Charlotte and Becca sang in unison as they scurried out the door. With a wave, Jessie followed.

Rowan checked the clock. Time to remove the Gouda from the refrigerator to bring to room temperature. She would add it to the crisp garden salads at the last minute, just before serving.

She went upstairs to change from her jeans into a simple dress and stopped by Becca's room on the way back. "Fluff, she's gone for the night. You might as well come down and socialize with the rest of us."

"Meow!" The cat jumped onto the bed, gave Rowan a haughty look and curled up on Becca's pillow.

"Fine. But when you're hungry, you know where to find me." Rowan started down the stairs, but she'd gone only halfway when she heard Zack in the kitchen greeting Ripley. "You're home early," she called as she made her way into the kitchen.

"My last appointment canceled, so I was able to get my rounds done at the wildlife center. You look nice. What's all this?" He gestured toward the table set for two.

"Becca is spending the night with Charlotte."

"Okay."

"And I thought maybe we could talk."

"Um, sure. What did you want to talk about?" He looked nervous, but what man wouldn't when faced with the can-we-talk question?

"You know what? Let's eat first, and we can talk later."

"Are you sure?"

"I'm sure. Wash up. I remember how much you liked the coq au vin, so I thought we'd try boeuf bourguignon over garlic mashed potatoes."

"You've never steered me wrong."

Rowan served the salads. "How was your day at the clinic?"

"Good. Oh, the sock-eating Lab was back."

Rowan cringed. "More socks?"

"No, this time it was a few coins. According to the X-ray, two nickels and five pennies. We're keeping him overnight to make sure it all passes through. Christine said she'd check in on him this evening, and I'll do it in the morning. We've decided his motto is 'How do you know what's edible unless you eat it?'"

Rowan laughed. "Speaking of edible, let me get our main course."

They laughed and talked through dinner. Rowan almost hated to disturb the mood. What if Zack thought she was trying to trap him into more than the year they'd agreed on? Was telling him how she felt worth rocking the boat? It was, after all, a very pleasant boat.

And that's why she wanted more, she reminded herself. "Becca and I invented a new goat cheese dessert. Want to try it?"

Zack laughed. "Like I'm going to say no."

She drizzled raspberry syrup over glass plates as a base for the triple-layer dessert, then placed three raspberries on top of the dark chocolate ganache of each piece.

Zack took the first bite. "Wow, this is incredible. Brownies, cheesecake and chocolate on top, like a triple treat. What do you call it?"

"I was thinking something like raspberry cheesecake brownies, but I like your name better."

"It's awesome. Are you going to serve it at the tasting room?"

"No, the kitchen there isn't set up for commercial baking. We'll probably print out recipe cards, though. Lauren sometimes posts recipes on the website, too."

"I hope you already took pictures, because this isn't going to last long."

"I did. And I already sent some with Jessie." She finished her dessert and dragged her fork across the raspberry syrup on the empty plate, playing with the design while she formulated her next comment. "You know, it's been so much fun being here with you and Becca."

He stopped with a fork halfway to his mouth. "I hope that's not a prelude to saying you're leaving."

"No, no. Not at all."

"Good. You scared me there for a second." Zack finished the last bite and set down his fork.

"I, uh…" Rowan picked up their dessert plates

and carried them to the sink. She could hear Zack pushing back his chair. Without turning, she blurted it out. "I love you, Zack."

Silence. Slowly she turned her head to see him staring at her. Other than shock, she couldn't read the emotion on his face.

"This doesn't have to change anything," she hurried to assure him. "I know you said you never intend to marry anyone, and I know the plan is just for one year. I just—I felt like you should know—"

With three steps he closed the distance between them and took her in his arms. She pressed a hand against his chest and then, as he captured her mouth with his, she slid her arms around him, pulling him closer as the heat of the kiss spread through her body and down to her toes. She heard distant bells ringing.

It wasn't until Zack lifted his head and listened that she realized he'd heard it, too. There it went again. Someone was ringing the doorbell.

Zack didn't move. "It could be Jessie, about Becca," Rowan whispered.

Zack shook his head. "Jessie would come to the back door." He sighed. "But I suppose it could be someone with a veterinary emergency."

"I'll get it. If they're selling magazines, I'll get rid of them." She gave Zack one more quick kiss. "Hold that thought. I'll be right back."

But when Rowan opened the door, Lauren was standing outside, waving an envelope. "Hi. Hope I'm not interrupting your dinner."

"We just finished. Come on in." Rowan led Lauren to the kitchen. What was she doing here? Not that having your sister-in-law drop in should be an unusual occurrence, but with all she had to do at the farm, Lauren wasn't prone to impromptu visits. "You're just in time to sample a new dessert."

Zack greeted Lauren while Rowan prepared a plate for her. Ordinarily when Rowan would give Lauren a new dish to taste, Lauren was all about the food, but today she hardly glanced at it before she handed over a thick envelope. "Here. This came for you today, but I couldn't bring it over until after the evening milking."

"You didn't have to drive over here. I could have picked it up tomorrow." Rowan didn't recognize the return address. Something about a food show. Probably selling kitchenware or something. But why would Lauren have come over to bring an ad? "You know what this is?"

"Yes. Maybe. Open it, already," Lauren ordered.

Rowan laughed. "Okay." She used a kitchen knife to slit the top of the envelope and pulled out a stack of papers. She skimmed the cover page.

"I don't understand. Something about a recipe and a liability waiver and a cooking show."

"Oh, my gosh." Lauren jumped up to read over her shoulder. "You won! I knew you would. This is great!"

"What did she win?" Zack asked.

"A recipe contest. Rowan, you remember when you made that chicken casserole and I said you should enter it in the contest advertised in *Cheesemaker* magazine?"

"Vaguely."

"Well, don't be mad, but I entered for you. Your recipe won five thousand dollars, plus the chance to compete in a television cook-off for the grand prize."

"Wow! Congratulations!" Zack got up and pulled Rowan into a hug. "I knew you made the best food I've ever tasted, but I didn't realize you were a prize-winning chef!"

"I'm not. I mean, I'm not even trained."

"It says here they had over three thousand entries, and only six were chosen," Lauren read. "Wow, the televised cook-off is in less than two weeks in Portland, Oregon. They sure don't give you a lot of time to make arrangements. I hope you can find a decent flight and don't end up taking a red-eye."

"Televised cook-off. How does that work?"

Zack asked, releasing Rowan from the hug but keeping an arm around her waist.

"Looks like it's one of those competitions where they give you some special ingredient and you're supposed to invent a recipe on the spot. Rowan is great at that."

"What's the prize?" Zack asked.

"Full tuition for a four-year degree from West Coast Culinary Institute," Lauren read.

Just for a moment, Rowan thought she saw a cloud pass over Zack's face, but it vanished so quickly she decided she'd imagined it. "Wow, that's huge."

"I can't compete in a televised cook-off," Rowan protested.

"Why not?" Zack and Lauren asked at the same time.

"Because I—" *Am a complete imposter and not nearly good enough to cook on television.* But how could she say that, after Lauren had demonstrated her faith by entering Rowan's recipe in the contest? "I need to be here to drive Becca and Charlotte to camp."

Zack shook his head. "Jessie and I can cover that."

"Last-minute airline tickets are bound to be expensive," Rowan told them.

Lauren pointed to the letter. "They're part of the prize. It says here they will reimburse your airfare. Your hotel and meals are covered, too. And it says you can't claim the five-thousand-dollar prize unless you agree to compete."

Zack touched her cheek to make her look at him. "What is it, Rowan? If it were me, it would be the cameras, but you're great at that sort of thing."

She let out a sigh. "I'm an amateur cook. I've never had formal culinary training, just what I've picked up from Gran and from cooking videos. I'd embarrass myself."

"But this is a contest for amateur cooks." Lauren flipped to the second page. "And it says here you're allowed to bring six signature ingredients of your choice. If you wanted, you could take some of the cheeses from Now and Forever Farms and use them in your dishes."

"That would be great marketing," Rowan admitted. "If the judges liked what I created anyway."

"Of course they will." Lauren tried a bite of the dessert. "If this is any indication of your creative powers, you'll be a shoe-in."

Was it possible? Not that she would win, but that she could hold her own in a national cook-off? Cooking had always been special to her, something she did independently of her mother. If she went on television and bombed, would that ruin cooking for her forever? But even if she bombed, five thousand dollars would buy a lot of rodent chow. "I don't know."

"You'd be great," Zack said, "but I'll support whatever you decide."

That did it. Zack had faith in her, and in her ability to decide for herself. If she bombed, so what? It wasn't as though she was planning a culinary career. "I'll do it. Thank you, Lauren, for sending in the recipe."

Lauren passed the letter back to Rowan. "I can't wait to call Patrick. Should I tell Bonnie, or do you want to?"

"I'll call Gran." Rowan glanced at the papers. "It says here I can take someone with me. I assume you wouldn't be able to get off work on such short notice?" she asked Zack.

He shook his head. "Christine is taking vacation then."

"Lauren?"

"I can't. I'm still short a farmhand right now."

"In that case, I'll get Gran to come with me. After all, she's the one who taught me to cook."

"Bonnie will be so proud," Lauren said.

"I just hope I can give her something to be proud of."

"Your recipe beat out three thousand others," Zack pointed out. "You should already be proud. I sure am."

CHAPTER TWENTY

"CHECK YOUR PANTRY and familiarize your-selves with the equipment. In one hour, report to makeup and preshow interviews. If you have any questions, Caro—" the producer pointed to-ward a college-aged woman with a red ponytail "—can help you. Good luck!"

As the other five contestants scrambled to their respective areas, Rowan stood, heart ham-mering, still not entirely sure this whole thing wasn't a dream. One of those dreams where she was trying to get somewhere, but her feet were stuck in quicksand.

"Nervous?" Caro asked her.

Rowan nodded and licked her dry lips.

"They may not look it, but they're just as ner-vous as you." Caro inclined her head toward the others. "You know that guy who threatened to quit because there was no pink salt on the pan-try list?"

"Yes?" He'd taken the role of temperamental chef to the extreme, yelling about the salt and storming outside. Twenty minutes later, he'd reappeared, and so had jars of pink salt for everyone.

"It was an excuse. He just didn't want to toss his cookies in front of you all."

"Oh." Another potential disaster Rowan hadn't considered. Maybe it was good she'd been too nervous to eat much breakfast.

"Go check out the ingredients. Touch the equipment. You'll find it calming."

Rowan pulled a chef's knife from the block and checked the blade. It had recently been sharpened, but she stroked it along the honing steel to align the edge. Caro was right; it did help to touch the familiar equipment. Rowan smiled. "Thanks for the tip."

"Anytime."

"Caro," one of the contestants called, "do you have the manual for this blast chiller?" Caro hurried away.

Blast chiller? Rowan wasn't even sure what that was, much less how to use one. What if they were expected to make something that required a blast chiller? What if—Rowan shook her head. She needed to focus. Remembering a technique someone had taught her, she sucked in a long breath and slowly exhaled while focusing on something in the distance: in this case, the empty bleachers in the back of the studio. Wait, the bleachers weren't completely empty. In the center of the top row, Gran waved wildly and blew a kiss. Rowan grinned and waved back.

Thank goodness for Gran. She'd spent the entire three-and-a-half-hour flight listening patiently to every disaster scenario Rowan could come up with and helping her brainstorm possible solutions. Finally, when Rowan had run out of possible calamities, Gran had laughed. "I swear, you could worry the horns off a billy goat. You've been cooking beside me since you were knee-high to a grasshopper. You know how to make good food."

Gran thought she could do it. So did Lauren, and Patrick, and Zack. Even Becca had solemnly assured her she was the "bestest cook in the whole world." Rowan pushed back her shoulders, waved once more to Gran and went to hear about blast chillers.

THREE HOURS LATER, the bleachers had filled with fans who cheered when the show's host, Etoile—a celebrity chef so popular she needed only one name—walked out onto the stage area. Etoile in turn introduced a panel of judges: a local restaurant owner, a food critic and a popular cookbook author.

"We have contestants here from across the United States, from Georgia to Alaska." Etoile dropped her voice to a mock whisper, like a golf announcer. "For the first round, our contestants will have forty-five minutes to produce an appetizer, using at least two of the signature ingredients they brought with them, plus the secret ingredient they're receiving now."

Caro set a covered plate in the center of each contestant's work area. Rowan, on the far left, received the last one. Caro whispered, "Good luck."

"Thanks." Rowan resisted the urge to wring her hands and instead tried for a zen-like smile as the camera panned past.

"At the end of this round, two contestants will be eliminated," Etoile continued. "Contestants, when the timer starts, you may reveal your secret ingredient." Rowan put her hand on the dome. "Get set. Go!"

Rowan lifted the lid to reveal a glass bowl filled with something crimson. Rose petals! Portland was known as the city of roses. She should have expected something like this. Okay. She'd brought six different cheeses from Now and Forever Farms as her signature ingredients. Too bad she didn't have time to make the rose petals into jam. She could bake it over Lauren's scrumptious double-cream brie. Hmm, maybe a rose petal syrup, instead. No time for puff pastry—ooh, but if she hurried, she could make a savory shortbread. The dough usually needed an hour of chilling time, but the blast chiller, which she'd learned was simply a superfast freezer, could save the day.

Working quickly, she created a dough of flour, butter, sharp cheddar and rosemary in the food processor, and then set it to chill while the oven preheated. Meanwhile, she chopped the rose petals and mixed them, along with some herbs and seasonings, with soft goat cheese, which she formed into a log and rolled in minced pine nuts. The shortbread dough was cool enough to work with, so she swapped out the cheese log for the dough, rolled it out, cut it into rounds and put it in to bake.

"Next we have Rowan Vogel, from Palmer, Alaska." Etoile spoke from over her shoulder, and Rowan jumped. For a moment, she'd forgotten all about the cameras. Funny, now that she was cooking, she wasn't nervous anymore.

She smiled but kept working, getting out a saucepan and bringing water to a boil. "Hello, Etoile. I'm so excited to be here."

"And what are you creating for us today with the rose petals?"

Rowan added sugar, rose petals and a curl of lemon zest to the water. "It's a syrup to go over a goat cheese spread on rosemary cheddar shortbread rounds." The timer sounded. Did she walk away in the middle of her interview? She couldn't very well let the shortbread burn just to be polite. "Excuse me, please." She hurried back to remove the baking sheet from the oven and the goat cheese from the cooler before returning to stir the syrup.

Etoile chuckled. "Looks like you have everything under control here. Have you cooked with rose petals before?"

"Mostly as a garnish in salads. Wild roses are common in Alaska, but my grandmother taught me to wait until August when the rose hips are ripe and use them along with raspberries to make jam."

"Sounds delicious. Contestants, ten minutes," she called out.

The syrup had thickened satisfactorily. Rowan would have liked to give the flavors more time to meld, but she didn't have that luxury. She strained out the rose petals and lemon rind, leaving a ruby-colored elixir to drizzle over the goat cheese slices stacked on top of the shortbread rounds. She'd just finished transferring six to a serving plate when Etoile called, "Time!"

In the fifteen minutes it took for the other five contestants to bring their offerings to the judges, answer questions and listen to comments, and move offstage, Rowan's emotions bobbed up and down like a cork in ocean swells.

The first contestant reminded Rowan of

a neighbor in Tokyo who practiced the art of *amezaiku*, sculpting rock candy into goldfish, dragons and other wondrous creatures. The contestant had created the most beautiful *onigiri*, the rose petals and Himalayan sea salt turning the rice balls a rich shade of pink. All three of the judges exclaimed over the color and two loved the flavor, although the cookbook author found them bland.

The second and third contestants had both created variations of rose petal chutney. The judges weren't particularly kind to the volatile guy who had stalked out earlier, finding his Greek yogurt and chutney dip too salty. Maybe after insisting on the Himalayan sea salt, he'd felt obligated to feature it. They were more complimentary of the other man's chutney although one judge complained the ginger overpowered the rose petals. He'd served the chutney alongside tiny sausages that were one of his signature items.

A white-haired gentleman whose vowels conjured up pictures of oak trees draped in Spanish moss was next. He'd added rose petals to an apple-based chicken salad and served it on tiny slider buns. The judges couldn't say enough good things about that combination. Rowan hoped there would be enough left that she could get a taste later.

The young woman just before Rowan served

up fresh arugula salads with rose petals and figs with a lime vinaigrette. All the judges rated it well, although the cookbook writer mentioned she had hoped for something more ambitious.

And then it was Rowan's turn. Drawing on years of practice smiling calmly no matter what might be going on inside, she carried her plate of canapés to the judges. They each took one and tasted a bite. The nods as they ate were encouraging.

The restaurant owner commented first. "Nice texture contrast with the crisp of the shortbread and the creamy cheese. It's easy to overdo rosemary, but you've got the right balance."

The cookbook writer finished chewing. "The rose petal syrup adds a nice floral note and sweetness." She wrote something on a pad.

"I want to know about the cheese," the food critic said. "It's extraordinary. There's a wonderful tanginess in the shortbread."

"Both the soft cheese and the cheddar are made from goat's milk," Rowan explained. "My sister-in-law is a master cheesemaker."

"She certainly is. Are these cheeses available commercially?"

"Yes. Now and Forever Farm cheeses are in stores in central Alaska and also available by mail order from the website."

"Will we be seeing more of this cheese in future rounds?" the restaurant owner asked.

Future rounds! That sounded encouraging. "These or others. I brought six different cheeses as my signature ingredients."

"Excellent. Thank you, Rowan."

"Thank you." Rowan gave a little bow and withdrew. Caro whisked her offstage to where the others were waiting, out of sight from the judges.

"They'll call us back in a few minutes," Caro told them. "The judges will announce the four who will move to the next round. The two who are eliminated will exit the stage this way. The rest of you, please wait at your stations until I get back." She touched the receiver in her ear. "They're ready for us. Everyone, please return to your cooking stations."

In a process that seemed unnecessarily long and dramatic, the judges announced the winners of the first round were the pink *onigiri* rice balls, the rose petal salad, the chicken salad sliders and, after an interminable wait, Rowan's shortbread and goat cheese. Rowan closed her eyes and let out a breath.

That meant the two chutneys were eliminated. The man who had demanded the pink salt turned and stalked off the stage without a word. The other cook nodded politely to judges before following. The judges went over the rules for the second round, which would be an entrée.

Caro returned and had them remove their aprons and exit the stage. "We'll break now to give us time to restock the cooking stations and set up for the next session. Be back at your stations in one hour," Caro told them. "In the meantime, relax. We've prepared a table of your leftovers for the studio audience to sample, and you can mingle with them if you like. Good job, everyone."

When Rowan arrived at the audience area, Gran was waiting with a hug. "You were brilliant!" She released Rowan and reached for a plate she'd set aside. "I got you samples. I knew you'd want to taste everything, and this mob," she said, waving her hand toward the crowd milling around the table, "they're like a swarm of locust. In five minutes, there won't be a bite left."

"Thanks!" Rowan tried the salad. "This is exceptionally good. Love the lime and rose together. Did you try it?"

"I liked it. I like those rice things, too. Origami or something?"

"Onigiri." Rowan bit into one just as she spotted their creator shyly watching her. Rowan waved her closer. "These are wonderful. Have you made them with rose petals before?"

"No, but I've used nasturtiums."

"Oh, that would be good, too, with that peppery taste, but I love how the rice absorbs the floral scent of the rose petals. And they're so pretty."

"Thank you." The woman's smile radiated joy. "I'm Sara."

"Rowan. And this is my grandmother, Bonnie."

"Hello. You're from Alaska, they said?"

"Yes."

"I live in Tacoma. My husband and I hope to visit Alaska someday."

"It's a beautiful place. I've lived there for more than sixty years," Gran told her. "If you like goats, you should drop by our farm in Palmer and try the cheese."

"I would enjoy that. Oh, there he is. I must go. It was good to meet you both."

"Nice lady," Gran commented.

"Yes, and a fabulous cook." Rowan finished the rice ball and tried the other items. The judges were right about the first chutney being too salty, but the one with the sausages had just the right blend of sweet and spicy. The mini chicken salad sandwich was wonderful. Rowan wasn't sure how the judges had made their final decision. It was all so tasty.

A familiar chime sounded from Gran's purse. She was holding Rowan's phone for her, since it wasn't allowed during the competition. She handed it to Rowan. "A text from Zack," Rowan told her.

Between getting ready for the trip and their usual activities, she and Zack hadn't found time to talk about her confession of love. At least that's what she told herself. The truth was, she'd avoided being alone with Zack since that evening. Yes, he'd kissed her, and yes, she'd taken that to mean the feeling was mutual, but what if the kiss was to comfort her before he broke the bad news that he didn't love her? She couldn't handle that possibility while already obsessing over making a fool of herself on television.

Still, Zack had been nothing but affectionate all week, touching her back whenever he passed by, lingering just a little when he kissed her goodbye in the morning. He'd taste-tested dozens of culinary experiments and insisted on driving Gran and her to the airport rather than having her leave a car in long-term parking. Surely all that meant something.

"I told him you made it through the first round," Gran whispered. "The audience all had to sign something saying we wouldn't tell anyone the results until the show airs week after next, but I figured that didn't apply to husbands. What did Zack say?"

"He's wishing me luck." Which was true, as

far as it went, but it was the rest of the message that made Rowan feel warm all over. I believe in you, followed by a little picture of a chef's hat. And a heart.

THE SECOND ROUND was trickier, with a secret ingredient of Dungeness crab. Rowan sorted through the pantry vegetables, carrots, celery, onions, sweet potatoes, leeks, both bell and po-blano peppers—peppers, maybe enchiladas? But her pantry didn't include tortillas and there wasn't time to make them from scratch and still bake the enchiladas. Next to the flour, she found a sack of cornmeal. Perhaps something like the tamale pie Gran used to make, but with a cheesy polenta base, and topped with crab, vegetables and Gouda. With a side of roasted sweet potatoes like the *yaki imo* trucks sold in Japan.

At the end of the round, the winners were Rowan's crab on polenta and Sara's elegant crab tempura on a bed of arugula, mushrooms and snow peas.

"We have our two finalists," Etoile stage-whispered. "The next round will determine the winner." But it wasn't until Rowan saw the excitement on Gran's face that it sunk in. She could actually win this!

For the final round, dessert, the secret ingredient was locally grown fresh pears. Rowan loved pears! Her favorite was pears with brie, but that wasn't so much a recipe as, well, pears with brie. And once again, no time to make a puff pastry and bake a brie en croute with roasted pears. But thanks to all her practice with Becca lately, she could stir up a drop sugar cookie dough in no time.

She shaped the dough into two ten-inch rounds. While it baked, she poached pear slices in a caramelized syrup and added in fresh raspberries for color. She blast-chilled the brie and then cut it into pieces and roughly chopped peppermint leaves. She glanced over at Sara, who appeared to be stirring together some sort of chocolate batter. It would be hard to beat pears and chocolate, but Rowan was committed now.

Once the giant cookies were done, she spread the red pear and berry mixture on top, arranged slices of brie, sprinkled them with mint and returned them to bake just until the brie began to melt. They came from the oven looking like classic Margherita pizzas. While the cookies cooled, she used fine sugar to glaze small clusters of mint leaves and whole raspberries, which she would use to garnish each serving.

Once the dessert pizzas were cool enough to hold their shape, she transferred them to a cutting board and was slicing them into wedges when she heard the crash of broken glass. She turned to see flames leap up and run across Sara's stovetop. Whatever Sara had spilled—rum, judging by the aroma—had caught fire. Sara turned off the burner and snatched a large skillet filled with rolled chocolate crepes off the stove. Rowan grabbed the box of baking soda from her countertop and threw it on the fire. The flames flickered, and then died.

Sara stood frozen, holding the pan of crepes.

Rowan looked around for Etoile. "How much time left?"

Etoile, seeing that the fire was out, set aside the fire extinguisher she'd grabbed and checked her stopwatch. "Four minutes."

"I'll clean up," Rowan told Sara. "Use my cooktop for your flambé."

"That was all my rum," Sara told her.

"You can use mine." Rowan ran to her pantry, sorted through the little bottles of flavorings and liquors until she found rum and returned it to her workspace. "Hurry!"

Sara poured the rum into the skillet to heat. Rowan used paper towels to wipe up the spilled rum and bits of glass from Sara's cooktop and the floor. When she looked back, Sara was lighting a piece of spaghetti from the gas burner. She turned off the burner, touched the flame to the warm rum and watched as blue flames began to dance around the crepes just as Etoile called, "Time. Contestants, stop where you are."

"Take Sara first, before her flame burns out," Rowan told her.

"But—" Sara protested.

"Come this way. Judges, we have a time-sensitive entry here." Etoile arranged a trivet on the judge's table so that Sara could set the skillet there.

"My apologies," Sara told them. "My intent was to serve in a chafing dish, but there was no time."

"It's still quite elegant," the cookbook author said as they watched the last of the flames die away. "Let's taste it."

The food critic spoke first. "Excellent. The pears are tender but not mushy. The chocolate of the crepes sets them off, and the caramel rum sauce is inspired. Really extraordinary."

Rowan, looking on, knew that her pear and brie dessert pizza could never match the elegance of Sara's crepe flambé. Especially since, in all the excitement, she'd forgotten to move it to a serving plate and add the garnish. She would have to serve it on the cutting board.

But the judges didn't mind, or if they did, they were kind about it. "Pear and raspberry pizzas on a cookie. How clever," the cookbook author exclaimed.

The restaurant owner tried a bite. "Lovely flavor blend. The mint brightens the deep flavor of the pears."

"It looks like the judges have their work cut out for them," Etoile spoke to the camera. "We'll be back with the winner after this."

Cara led Sara and Rowan offstage. "Wait here, and I'll bring your family members," she told them.

As soon as she'd gone, Sara turned to Rowan. "Why did you help me?"

"Why wouldn't I?"

"We're in competition. It wasn't your fault I dropped the bottle, and it could have given you the advantage."

"Your crepes deserved to be judged fairly, not with the final step undone. I wouldn't want to win that way."

Sara's husband arrived as Rowan was talking. He put an arm around his wife and offered a hand to Rowan. "Thank you for what you did. You don't know how much this means to us. Culinary school has been Sara's dream since she was a teenager, but it's never been possible. If she wins—"

"If she wins, it's because she deserves to win." Rowan had been so caught up in the idea of proving herself, she hadn't really considered what winning would mean. Or how much it might mean for the other contestants. "Sara is a wonderful cook."

"I'll say." Gran arrived in time to get in on the conversation. "I got a little bite of that crab you made, Sara. Best I ever tasted. Except yours, of course," she said to Rowan.

Rowan laughed. "Nice save, Gran."

"Do you think they'll let us have some of those flaming chocolate pancakes?" Gran asked. "I'm partial to chocolate."

"If we ever make it to Alaska," Sara said, "I will come to your farm and cook you all the chocolate crepes you can eat."

Gran beamed. "Now, that is something to look forward to."

Something squawked on Caro's headset. "They're ready for us."

"Okay." Rowan squeezed Gran's hand while Sara gave her husband a final hug. A camera panned with them as they crossed the stage to stand in front of the judge's table.

"It wasn't an easy choice," the restaurant owner told them. "We took all three rounds into consideration, but in the end, we all agreed that the winner is…"

Rowan reached for Sara's hand and held her breath, waiting.

Finally, the judge smiled. "Sara Arai."

Sara seemed stunned. Rowan hugged her and

then gave her a little push to propel her toward the judge's table. "Go on."

"But—"

"You deserve this. Go." Rowan smiled as the judges congratulated Sara.

Caro was signaling for her to leave the area. She crossed to the set to find Gran, waiting for her. "I'm sorry."

"I'm not. I just fell into this contest because Lauren liked my chicken and cheese casserole, but it's Sara's lifelong dream. She deserves to win." On the monitor, Rowan could see the tears of joy on Sara's cheeks. "I'm not sorry I came. I loved the challenge, and it was thrilling when the judges had good things to say about my food. But I don't want to go to cooking school in Portland. Zack and Becca need me in Alaska."

"No regrets?"

"None." Rowan hugged her grandmother, the woman who had started her down this path so many years ago, and then asked, "May I have my phone? I'd like to call Zack."

CHAPTER TWENTY-ONE

"HOW MUCH LONGER?" Becca asked, clutching the poster she and Charlotte had created.

Zack checked his watch. "It will be a while. The plane's not due to land for another fifteen minutes." He'd allowed extra time to drive to the Anchorage airport, in case of traffic or delays. After their long flight, he didn't want Rowan and her grandmother to have to wait.

Becca spotted a sign. "Frozen yogurt! Can we get some?"

"Why not." The shop was located right next to the security exit Rowan and her grandmother would have to pass through. He took the poster from Becca, leaving her free to wander the store and check out all the possible toppings. He glanced at his watch again. One more minute had gone by. The last three days without Rowan had been the longest of his life.

Rowan loved him! How amazing was that? This incredible woman, who had come into his and Becca's lives and made everything brighter, told him she loved him. But before he'd gathered his wits enough to respond to this declaration, to ask her to stay with them for the rest of their lives, Lauren had shown up waving that letter saying Rowan was in the running to win a four-year scholarship to a culinary school. So he'd tamped down his selfish instincts and encouraged her to try.

"I want strawberry yogurt with butterscotch syrup, chocolate chips and gummy bears," Becca decided.

"Gummy bears? Really?"

"They're good."

"Okay." Zack had his doubts, but then, he'd doubted some of the flavor combinations in Rowan's experiments, and he hadn't yet found a bad one. The server soon handed him a paper bowl piled with frozen goodies. He carried it outside the shop, got Becca settled at one of the café tables and checked his watch again. Still five minutes before the plane was due to land, plus however long it took them to get to the gate. Plenty of time for Becca to finish her yogurt and be in position to hold up her sparkly sign when Rowan came through security.

Rowan seemed to have no idea just how gifted she was, but in the end, she had done it—flown down to Portland and wowed the judges with her talent. And then, according to Bonnie, in the final round, Rowan had sacrificed time she could have spent perfecting her own dish to help her competition when she ran into trouble. So typical of Rowan, but it meant the other woman walked away with the four-year scholarship, and Rowan was returning home to him and Becca.

"Want a bite?" Becca asked, holding up a spoonful of pink yogurt with a gummy bear on top.

"Sure." Zack leaned forward and let her feed him.

"You're right," he told her. "Gummy bears are good with strawberry yogurt."

"I'll bet!" The familiar voice came from over his shoulder, and his heart did a double beat.

"Rowan!" He hugged her, and then for good measure, her grandmother.

"Our plane got in early."

"Me and Charlotte made you a sign!" Becca picked up the poster board from where Zack had left it leaning against the table.

"Let's see." Rowan stepped back to read the poster. It spelled out Congratulations, Rowan! in glitter paint, with each letter a different color. The letters started out with generous spaces in between, but got progressively more crowded, with the *i* obviously squeezed in after the fact. Flowers, along with pizza slices, doughnuts and something green that was probably a vegetable of some sort made a border down below. Zack thought it was perfect.

Apparently so did Rowan. She wiped away a tear before dropping to her knees to hug Becca. "It's beautiful! Thank you!"

"Wow." Bonnie picked up the sign from where Becca had dropped it. "Look at all these sparkles. What a great welcome home."

IN THE HOUR it took to drive from the Anchorage airport to Palmer, Becca had fallen asleep. Even when they parked at Bonnie's apartment building so that Zack could take her bag upstairs for her, Becca didn't stir. And yet, when Zack carried her upstairs and laid her on her own bed, her eyes flew open. "Aren't we going to read?"

Rowan sat down on the edge of the bed and smoothed Becca's hair back from her face. "You're tired. Maybe you should sleep now, and we'll read extra tomorrow."

"Just one story?" Becca yawned. "I like hearing your voice. I missed you."

"I missed you, too." Rowan gave the gentle smile that made Zack want to wrap them both in his arms and never let go. Instead, he chose one of Becca's favorite picture books and handed it to Rowan. It was meant for younger children, but he knew Becca found the rhymes and rhythms soothing.

While Rowan read, Zack adjusted the heavy curtains to block out the midnight sun and returned a few books to the shelf. "Good night, Becca," Rowan whispered, and kissed her cheek before slipping out into the hallway.

Zack added his own kiss to her forehead. "Good night."

"Night," Becca murmured. "I'm glad Rowan's home."

"I know," he answered. "I am, too."

He found Rowan in the kitchen, setting a kettle of water on the stove. "One of the sponsors gave us all gourmet gift baskets," she told him. "Thought I'd try this herbal tea blend. Want some?"

"Sure." Zack wasn't sure he'd ever tasted herbal tea, but Rowan was constantly expanding his horizons. He watched as her deft fingers made a small ceremony of filling a pierced metal ball with tea leaves and placing it in a teapot, pouring in boiling water and setting the pot on a tray along with two mugs.

"Shall we drink this on the deck?" she suggested.

"Let's." Zack picked up the tray and followed her outside. She moved a potted plant to make space for him to set the tray on a table in front of the bench. "Do you want to pour or—"

"Let's let it steep for a few minutes." Rowan

sat down. Zack set beside her and stretched an arm across the back of the bench. Rowan leaned in, as he'd hoped she would, resting her head against his shoulder. He let his arm drop and stroked the soft skin of her upper arm.

He'd been looking forward to this moment for days, but somehow, he couldn't find the words to start the conversation. Rowan didn't seem to be in any hurry. She snuggled closer and together they watched the dappled sunshine paint the edges of the forest floor. He caught a lock of her hair and rubbed it between his finger and thumb, soft and silky. He'd read once that pound for pound, silk was stronger than steel. Rowan was like that, soft and yielding, but with incredible strength.

He pressed a kiss to the top of her head. "I love you, too," he whispered.

She sat up and turned to him in surprise. "What did you say?"

"I said I love you, too. You know, building on that conversation from two weeks ago just before Lauren rang the doorbell. Remember?"

The dimple in her cheek appeared. "I do remember. But when you didn't bring it up again, I thought—"

"I didn't want to distract you from the competition. But now that it's behind us, I thought you should know. I love you, Rowan."

She touched his face and peered into his eyes as though testing the depths of them. She must have found what she was looking for there, because she smiled. "I love you, too."

"Yeah?"

"Yeah."

He leaned down to press a kiss upon her lips. She met him halfway and slid her fingers into the hair on the back of his head, pulling him closer. He shifted to take the kiss deeper, and she responded in kind. He heard the jingle of dog tags, but this time, without breaking the kiss, he pulled Rowan onto his lap so that there was no room for Ripley to push his way in between them. Rowan wrapped her arms around him and held him tight.

Ripley jumped onto the bench beside them and whimpered. When they ignored him, he jumped down, setting the table rocking. Rowan barely jumped up in time to steady it before it fell over and sent the teapot crashing to the ground. She laughed. "Well, the tea is ready anyway. Next time, maybe we should leave the d-o-g in the h-o-u-s-e."

"Good idea."

Rowan poured two mugs of tea and handed one to Zack. Having successfully interrupted their romantic interlude, Ripley moved on to the woods to investigate a magpie that was poking about. In a flash of black and white, the bird flew away while hurling insults at the dog. Zack concurred.

He sipped the tea. Not much taste, but it had a nice smell. "Your grandmother told me about how you helped out your competition during that last round in the cooking show. I'm sorry it cost you the win."

"I'm not," Rowan answered immediately. "Sara's pear-filled chocolate crepes were clearly a more difficult and elegant dessert than my fruit and cookie pizza, even if she'd been forced to skip the flambé stage. I didn't get the chance to add my garnish to my dessert, but it wouldn't have mattered. Hers was clearly better."

"If setting it on fire wasn't that important to her dish, why did you help her?"

"Honestly, I didn't think about it, I just acted." Rowan set her mug on the table and turned to face him. "I'm glad I did. After the filming, they showed us some of the footage, and I got to see Sara's preshow interview. Her father died when she was young, and she's been working since she was fifteen. Her younger brother and sister were both able to get partial college scholarships, but they wouldn't have been able to finish college without her financial support. The youngest graduated in May, and Sara and her husband married a week later. Her dream is to go to culinary school. If it wasn't for this contest, it might take years for the two of them to save up enough for her tuition."

"That's a nice story, but what about *your* dreams? If you'd won, wouldn't you have used the scholarship to go to culinary school?"

"If I'd wanted to go to culinary school, I could have. I thought about it briefly when I was a teenager, but my parents pointed out that most chefs don't make a lot of money and the hours are awful. They encouraged me to study business, instead."

"But it they hadn't steered you away, you would have gone to culinary school?"

"Possibly."

"And if you'd won this competition, would you have gone?"

She shrugged. "I believe things worked out the way they were supposed to." She traced a finger along his arm. "I missed you and Becca while I was in Portland."

"We missed you, too, more than you could imagine."

"I have a good imagination." She smiled. "I love you."

"I love you."

She leaned over his tea mug to kiss him lightly. "So where does that leave us?"

"Well, Mrs. Vogel, we're married, but we've

never dated. Maybe we should, you know, do that. Go to a movie or something. Spend some time alone together."

Ripley came trotting back and rested his head on Rowan's lap. She rubbed his ears. "Alone together? You mean like, just the two of us? No kids, no dogs, maybe a whole kiss without interruption?"

He laughed. "I think we can arrange that."

ROWAN SET A bowl of peonies from the farm on the embroidered tablecloth she'd borrowed from her grandmother's stash. The last two weeks had been wonderful. She'd never realized just what it meant to be in love. Everything, even something as mundane as setting the table, took on an extra sparkle of joy. Thank goodness she hadn't settled for "good enough" with Sutton. It seemed like every day she loved Zack and Becca a little more.

Last Friday, Charlotte had come for a sleepover, and Rowan had taught both girls to make miso soup. Saturday, she and Jessie took them shopping for school clothes. That night Becca had fallen asleep early, no doubt because she and Charlotte had stayed up giggling half the night before, allowing Zack and Rowan some quality time outside on the bench. And this time Ripley wasn't invited.

In between, Rowan had stayed busy helping with Now and Forever Farms, updating the website, printing new recipes and pitching in to fulfill mail orders when someone had called in sick. She'd also power-washed the deck at Zack's house, planning to apply a new coat of sealer on the first available sunny day.

The cooking competition had aired three days ago. They'd invited Rowan's family, the Mat Mates, all the wildlife center people and Zack's veterinarian partner, Christine, and her family to their house for a screening party. It made for a crowded but lively evening. Rowan had served all the dishes she made at the competition. Despite constant pressure, Gran had refused to divulge the results of the competition ahead of time. When the judges called Rowan and Sara in, everyone except Gran, Zack and Rowan had been on the edge of their seats, and even Zack looked a little shocked when the winner was announced.

Tonight, Becca was sleeping over with Charlotte. Rowan had created a three-course meal of Greek favorites. The back door opened, and Zack came in, carrying the day's mail. Without a word, he set it on the counter and reached for her, pulling her in for a long and satisfying kiss. When he lifted his head, she laughed. "Hello to you, too."

Zack grinned. "When the cat's away…"

"Are you implying we're the mice?" She picked up the mail and sorted through it, tossing the junk into the trash as she went.

"Something like that. What smells so good?"

"Moussaka. We also have dolmades, Greek salad and baklava for dessert." She paused as she came to a large envelope at the back of the pile. "Huh, something from the cooking competition."

"Maybe you forgot to sign something."

"Hard to imagine. I must have signed ten pounds of papers before I went on the show." She opened it up and read the cover letter. "Oh, my gosh."

"What?"

She looked up. "Apparently after the show aired, they must have gotten complaints about me giving Sara my rum and whether that was fair. They don't go into all the details, but the bottom line is that the sponsor, West Coast Culinary School, has decided to offer a full scholarship to me as well as the one they gave Sara."

Emotions flashed across his face too quickly to read. "That's great. I'm happy for you." But he didn't sound happy.

"This is so generous. I'll be sure to let them know I appreciate the gesture when I turn them down."

"You're turning them down?"

"Of course. That is, I thought—" She hesitated, suddenly unsure. "I thought you wanted me here, with you and Becca."

"I do. But…"

"But what?"

"It's an amazing opportunity. You should go."

"The custody hearing is in two weeks, and Clarissa hasn't agreed to give up parental rights," she pointed out. "You need me."

"No."

She sank into the chair by the kitchen desk. "You want me to leave?"

"No!" Zack knelt in front of her and took her hands in his. "I don't want you to leave any more than I would want Becca to. I love you, Rowan. That's why I can't be selfish about this. You need to do what's best for you. Becca and I were muddling along before you came. We can do it again."

"But what if I were to go and you lose custody?"

"There's no guarantee I'll win even if you stay."

"It improves your chances."

"Rowan, my family problems are not your problems." He squeezed her hands. "We committed to a year, not to a lifetime. This opportunity to pursue a career doing what you love is too good to pass up."

"I love being here with you. I love taking care of you and Becca and helping out at the wild-life center."

"Those are my responsibilities, not yours. You need to find your own dream."

She sat up straighter. "It's my decision."

"Yes."

"Then I want to stay here."

Zack paused before replying, "My mother met my father in Las Vegas. Did I ever tell you that?"

"You've never really talked about your mother."

"She lives in Florida now. Before she met my father, she was a dancer. When they married, she gave up her career and moved to Alaska. They divorced when I was four. Dad gave her custody, but only if she kept me here. So she stayed. She got a job in the credit union and worked her way up to senior loan officer, but a part of her was always bitter that she had sacrificed her career dreams for a man."

"So, what you're saying—"

"I can't say I love you, and then ask you to give up your dream."

"But what if—"

"I know you," he interrupted. "You always put everyone else's desires ahead of your own. You did it with your mother, you did it at the cooking competition, and you'll do it with me if I give

you the chance. You need to think about this ob-
jectively, and you can't do that here."

"But—"

"Go stay with your family at the farm. Think
about your future. Not just right now, but your
whole life."

"What about Becca?"

"I'll tell her your family needs you there right
now."

She studied his face, looking for any sign he
might back down, but his gaze was firm. "You
said you loved me, and now you're kicking me
out of your house?"

"If you're here, I'll be too tempted to kiss you
and hold you and try to make you want to stay.
That's not fair. Not until you've made your decision."

"Are you saying I have to choose between
school and you? I can't come back once I've
completed the degree?"

"Rowan." He shook his head slowly. "There
are no top-notch restaurants in Palmer. If we're
here, waiting, you won't be free to pursue your
new career. What if you're offered a job in a
Michelin-starred restaurant in San Francisco,
or New York, or Paris? I don't want to hold you
back. I'm sending you away because I love you."

"It doesn't feel like love." She wiped away

a tear before it could trickle down her cheek. "Love shouldn't hurt like this."

"I know." He pressed her hand against his chest. "But sometimes, it does."

CHAPTER TWENTY-TWO

CREAMY YELLOW SHREDS of Gouda fell from the grater. Rowan visually measured the size of the heap and decided she might as well grate the rest of the block. She already had a spinach, mushroom and egg strata waiting in the refrigerator to bake for Lauren and Patrick's breakfast, but she would use the Gouda in a selection of mini quiches for Gran and her friends. Any extras, she could pass out as free samples along with recipe cards to the people who came to the tasting room this afternoon.

The clock on the oven read five fifteen. No one else would be up for another hour or so, and Lauren would do the morning milking before breakfast, so Rowan didn't need to put the strata in the oven yet. Rowan should be in bed herself, but after staring at the ceiling for too many hours, she'd decided to cook. She'd long ago found problems that loomed large in the shadows of a bedroom would shrink to a reasonable size in the kitchen. At least most of them did, but not this one.

She missed Becca, and Ripley, and Fluff, but most of all, she missed Zack. The way he looked before his first cup of coffee, kind of befuddled and sweet. The way his eyes seemed to brighten when he came through the door each evening and saw her there to greet him. Snuggling beside him on the bench at the end of the day, watching the little dramas play out in the woods behind the house. She didn't want to give that up.

But Zack had a point. She needed to quit living life only to please other people. Lauren had her goats. Zack and Maggie had the wildlife center. Rowan loved to cook, but did she want to be a chef? Chefs worked when everyone else was home having dinner with their families at the end of the day.

She had called the culinary school to ask for more time to think it over. They were gracious, but they agreed to hold the spot for her for only two weeks, to give other prospective students time to enroll for the fall semester if the spot opened. People were lined up for the opportunity that had dropped into her lap. Would it be ungrateful to turn it down?

She set aside the cheese and pressed the button on the microwave to nuke the cup of tea she'd abandoned. While it warmed, she dug out the catalog the culinary school had enclosed with the letter and settled at the kitchen table to look through it once again.

The bachelor's degree included sixty credits of culinary classes but also liberal arts and quite a few business classes. Rowan already had a master's degree in business, but none of her credits would transfer since they were more than ten years old. Did she want to do it all again?

"Good morning." Patrick padded across the kitchen to the coffeemaker.

"What are you doing up so early?" Rowan would have made the coffee if she'd known he was awake.

"Thought I'd head over to the Little Susitna and see if I can catch my limit of reds. Want to come?"

Thoughts of salmon recipes immediately flitted through Rowan's mind. The dillweed in the vegetable garden was growing like, well, a weed. "I can't. I'm working the tasting room this afternoon. But if you catch 'em, I'll cook 'em." She got up and turned on the oven. "The breakfast casserole I put together last night will take forty-five minutes to bake, but if you're in a hurry I could scramble you some eggs or something."

He waved his hand. "Sit down. I can wait on myself. What's that you're looking at?"

"The degree requirements from the West Coast Culinary Institute." She flipped to the next page, which listed a degree in restaurant management. Nothing interesting there. If she wanted to be a manager, she'd have specialized in management instead of marketing.

Patrick poured a cup of coffee and sat down at the table next to her. "How many degrees do they offer?"

"Four bachelor-level degrees, several associate degrees and some specialty short courses—" she flipped to those pages "—like starting a catering business, for instance." She looked up from the book. "You like your career, right?"

"I like it a lot."

"How did you know you would? I mean, I know you've been tinkering with machines since you were a little kid." Patrick had always been the official fix-it person for the family, repairing ailing alarm clocks and kitchen appliances. "But when did you decide you wanted to be a professional electrician, rather than just do it as a hobby?"

"Well, you know Mom and Dad wanted me to study business, the same route you took, but that never appealed to me. I knew I wanted to live in Alaska, and I didn't want a desk job."

"You could have studied engineering."

"I could have, but it would still be mostly a desk job. I wanted something hands-on. The electrician apprentice program had openings."

"That's it? They had openings? Electrician wasn't a calling?"

"Working outside with my hands was a calling. I suppose I could have been a welder, or a carpenter, or a plumber. I probably would have been happy in any of those careers. But this one's good. I like working all out for two weeks on the slope, and then having two weeks off to help on the farm."

"Even when it's forty below zero on the slope?"

"We only work outside down to thirty below."

"Oh, thirty below. So, no problem, then."

He laughed. "Okay, still darn cold. Wire gets brittle and diesel engines revolt at those temperatures, so it's a challenge. I like it, keeping the lights on and everything running. It's a good job." He looked toward the refrigerator, where Lauren used magnets to post snapshots of family, friends and goats. "More importantly, it's a good life. It's all about balance." He drained the last of his coffee. "Guess I'd better get my fishing gear together. If the run holds, I'll probably go again in a couple days. Pencil it in on your calendar."

"I'll do that."

She opened the catalog again, flipping through the various offerings until a particular short course caught her eye. The germ of an idea formed, but she had no idea if it was feasible. If it was, this just might be the way to find that balance Patrick was talking about.

RIPLEY POUNCED ON a rolled-up sock that dropped from the basket Becca carried into the laundry room.

"Ew. What's that smell?"

"Your swimsuit." Zack tried not to breathe as he dumped it into the washer. Leaving it in a plastic bag for two days had allowed an aromatic colony of something to establish a foothold. "I forgot to get it out of your backpack." He took the basket of dirty clothes and dumped it in with the towels and swimsuit. He knew he was supposed to sort, but who had time? "Is this everything from your hamper?"

Becca nodded. "I'm hungry." She took the stray sock from Ripley's mouth and handed it to Zack, who unrolled it, tossed it in with the rest and set the washer to Run.

"I'm hungry, too. How about hot dogs for supper? They're quick."

"I guess." Becca dragged her foot along the floor. "When is Rowan coming home?"

He'd answered the question several times already, but Becca kept asking. "I told you, I'm not sure. She's got a lot going on right now."

He hated himself for sending her away, and

yet, what else could he have done? She deserved a chance to be her own person, to chart her own path. But he hadn't fully anticipated how much he would miss her. How empty it all seemed without her smiling face.

"Rowan is still coming to the campout on Tuesday, isn't she?" Becca asked. "She promised."

Oh, shoot. He'd forgotten all about the end-of-year campout. You'd think the camp would have sent a reminder—and then he noticed the soggy piece of paper that had been in the bag with the swimsuit. He unfolded it and managed to read enough of the blurred print to verify that it was, indeed, a reminder and suggested packing list.

Becca stared up at him, waiting for his answer. After his insistence that Rowan move out to have a neutral space to make her decision, was it fair to drag her back in? But Becca was counting on her. "After dinner, I'll call her and ask."

"Can you call her now?"

"I thought you wanted to eat."

"I want this more."

"All right. I'll call." He shooed Becca and the dog into the kitchen and followed them, closing the door behind him. He dialed and held his breath, waiting. Would she even answer? She hadn't been too happy with him when she drove away.

"Zack?"

"Hi. I hope I'm not disturbing anything."

"No, it's okay. How are you?"

Sad. Lonely. Miserable. "Fine," he managed. "You?" He wanted to ask if she'd come any closer to a decision, but the whole point was not to rush her.

"How about Becca? Anything new about the hearing?"

"No, but Becca is the reason I called. Her overnight—"

"That's day after tomorrow, right? I'm glad you called. What do I need to bring?"

"So, you are planning to come?"

"Of course. I promised."

If he hadn't already fallen in love with Rowan, he would have at hearing her say that. It didn't matter that she'd moved out. She'd made a promise to Becca, and it had never occurred to her that she wouldn't keep it. "They sent a packing list, but it's kind of hard to read."

"Ah, she put it in with her wet swimsuit, I'll bet. I'll see if they posted it on the camp's website. Tell Becca I can hardly wait."

MONDAY AFTERNOON, ROWAN got a call from Jessie. "Hi, you're doing the campout tomorrow night, right?"

"Yes. I've gathered my sleeping bag, my mosquito repellant and my appetite for s'mores."

Jessie laughed. "Sounds like you're all set. I just picked up the girls from camp, and Becca said she needs to ask you something."

"Okay." Rowan waited for Becca's voice.

"Rowan?" She must be in the back seat, because the speakerphone sounded as though she was calling from inside a tunnel.

"Hi, Becca. All set for the campout tomorrow?"

"Almost. I've got all my stuff together. I'm taking Zuma, but he needs his sleeping bag."

"Can't he share yours?"

"He has his own. Daddy got it. But it's at my other house."

"Oh."

"Zack can't take me to get it because somebody brought in a fox and he has to do surgery."

"And my daddy has a softball game we have to go to," Charlotte volunteered.

"Can you take me to get Zuma's sleeping bag?" Becca asked. "Please?"

"Sure. Where should I pick you up?"

"I was going to take her with us to the softball game," Jessie said, "but if you're coming now, I can drop her at the vet clinic on the way."

"Sounds good. Becca, I'll see you in about fifteen minutes."

Rowan was there in ten. When she stepped inside the clinic, she spotted Becca in the corner, watching the adoptable kittens through a window. When the bell rang to signal an opened door, Becca turned and launched herself in Rowan's direction. Rowan caught her and they shared a long hug.

"I missed you so much." Becca sniffed.

"I missed you, too." Rowan blinked back a tear. "Are you ready to go?"

Becca nodded and went to grab her backpack. Rowan exchanged greetings with the receptionist, Karen, who volunteered, "Zack just went into surgery. Someone hit a red fox with his car."

"That sounds bad. I hope the surgery is successful."

"It will be," she said with confidence. "Zack is a great surgeon."

"Yes." And a great brother, who deserved custody. The fact that he was risking that to give Rowan thinking space with this hearing looming next week...

"Rowan?" Becca was standing at the door with her backpack over one shoulder. "You ready?"

"Yes, let's go."

They stopped by Zack's house first so that Becca could drop off her backpack and Rowan could collect the keys to Zack's dad's house. Becca ran upstairs and returned with her precious stuffed animal. "Zuma is glad you're going to the campout tomorrow."

"I'm glad, too." If she took the scholarship, would Zack still allow her to contact Becca and spend time with her during breaks? The thought of never seeing Becca again made her stomach hurt.

During the drive over, Becca caught her up on everything that had happened at camp for the past several days. They parked in the circle drive in front of the big house. Rowan unlocked the door and dealt with the alarm system while Becca ran up the stairs. Rowan followed a moment later to find herself in a long hallway. "Becca, where are you?"

"In my room." The voice came from the end of the hall. Rowan followed it to find her crawling under a bed with a white footboard trimmed with gold curlicues. The matching headboard was partly masked by white netting hanging from the ceiling. Embroidered gold crowns embellished a pink bedspread.

The rest of the room carried out the theme, with pink walls glazed in subtle stripes of glossy and matte, a vanity table with an oval mirror and padded stool, and a pink satin slipper chair. Beautifully and professionally decorated, it reflected none of Becca's personality.

"I got it!" Becca dragged out a small suitcase

and carried it over to an alcove near the window. This was the only part of the room that looked like Becca, with a rocking chair, a pile of stuffed animals, three big floor pillows and a low bookcase with an ornate molding across the bottom that looked familiar. The shelves were half filled with books. Rowan suspected most of the collection in residence in Becca's room at Zack's house must have come from here.

Becca opened the suitcase and rummaged until she found what she was looking for. "See?" She pulled out a blue quilted miniature sleeping bag. "I told you Zuma had his own sleeping bag."

"How about that! What else do you have in there?"

"These are his costumes for holidays. Daddy got them. This one is for Halloween." She held up a cardboard rectangle displaying a mask and a cape with a tall collar. "And this one's for Christmas." A red-striped sweater and Santa hat. She picked up the next one: a red, white and blue sequined vest. "Oh, we missed the Fourth of July."

"I bet Zuma had fun watching the fireworks even without his costume," Rowan said. "These are all so fancy."

"Do you want to see his fancy collar? I'll show you." Becca crawled over to the bookshelf and pressed what looked like a knot in the wood on the side near the floor. The heavy molding that ran across the bottom of the lowest shelf lifted up.

"A secret compartment?" Rowan got down on her knees to look. "Wow."

Becca giggled. "You're the only one who knows about it. You and Daddy. He got me this bookshelf." She pulled out a flat box. Inside were a collection of childhood treasures, including pretty rocks, a feather, a Denali National Park quarter and a rhinestone bracelet. Becca fastened the bracelet around Zuma's neck.

"It used to be Mommy's, but she didn't like it," Becca explained. "So, Daddy gave it to me."

Hmm, maybe they weren't rhinestones. "It's very pretty. I can see why you keep it in your treasure box."

"Daddy said Zuma shouldn't wear it except at home, so it doesn't get lost." She removed the collar, returned it to the box and picked up the feather. "This feather is from an eagle that lived at the wildlife center while her wing healed. Wanna touch it?"

Rowan let Becca spend as much time as she wanted going through her things, but after a while, Becca returned the sleeping bag to the little suitcase and picked it up. "I'm ready to go home."

Home. She meant Zack's house, of course. That was home for her. This was just the place she used to live, with her daddy. Rowan couldn't let Becca get caught up as a pawn in a possible scheme of Clarissa's.

"Let's go, then." Rowan eased the molding closed over the secret compartment. "I need to pick up some sunscreen for camp tomorrow. Want to shop with me?"

"Yes!"

The local grocery was the most convenient place to buy sunscreen. Near the door, though, Rowan spotted some good-looking eggplant on sale. Tempting. Zack was always looking for ways to get more vegetables into Becca's diet. Why not? She collected the eggplant, an onion, plum tomatoes, and then, because she didn't want to take the time to swing by the farm, added a bunch of fresh basil and mozzarella and Parmesan cheeses.

They had just checked out and got into the car when Zack called. Rowan punched the speaker button. "Hi, Zack."

"Hi. I just got out of surgery and got Jessie's message you were taking Becca to the other house to get something. Sorry, I didn't tell Jessie about—"

"We're on the way home now. Buckle up, Becca."

After a brief hesitation, Zack asked, "Am I on speakerphone?"

"Yes," she said, relieved that he understood why she'd interrupted.

"Hi, Becca. Did you get everything you needed at the house?" he asked.

"We found Zuma's sleeping bag and I brought some more clothes for him, too. And some more books."

"You were in surgery for a long time," Rowan said. "Will the fox be okay?"

"She should recover. I'll need to stay here another hour or so. You can drop Becca at the clinic."

"Is it okay if I stay with Becca at the house?" Surely, she wasn't banned entirely.

"Are you sure you have time?"

"I'm sure," Rowan said.

"Then thanks. I will be there as soon as I can."

Once they got home, Rowan sliced and salted the eggplant and started cooking the tomatoes. With her help, Becca made a salad. Fluff walked into the kitchen and rubbed against Rowan's ankle.

"While you set the table, I'll be browning the eggplant," Rowan told Becca. Fluff yowled. "And feeding the cat."

Becca giggled. "Zack says—"

"I know. We'll tell him we already fed her. Otherwise, she'll meow our ears off." Rowan tossed out the last of the remaining kibble and replaced it with identical kibble, which Fluff immediately devoured. Rowan would never understand the workings of that cat's mind.

Once Rowan had arranged the breaded eggplant in the bottom of a casserole, she had Becca spread the tomato sauce and sprinkle basil leaves and cheeses over the top. "Doesn't that basil smell wonderful?" She slid the baking dish into the oven and went to wash the pans they'd used.

Zack walked in the back door and stopped when he saw Rowan standing at the sink. She met his eyes, suddenly feeling as though she was trespassing. "There's eggplant Parmesan in the oven. Just take it out when the timer rings and let it set for ten minutes before serving. Becca made a salad, too."

Becca grasped her hand. "Do you have to go?"

Rowan looked at Zack, but he didn't jump in to invite her to stay. "I'm afraid so, sweetie. I will be at your camp tomorrow morning for the overnight. We'll have a great time." She hugged Becca, picked up her bag and started toward the door. "Bye, Zack."

"You have to kiss goodbye," Becca insisted.

Rowan looked back, trying to come up with an excuse that would appease Becca without putting Zack on the spot. But he crossed the floor, put his arms around her waist and kissed her.

Not as drawn out and passionate as some of the ones they'd shared on the porch when Becca was asleep, but not just a peck, either. A real kiss.

Like he meant it.

CHAPTER TWENTY-THREE

THE DAY AT camp started with a trip to the pool. All the campers in Becca's group, including Charlotte, lined up at the end of the pool and waited for the signal. Rowan felt like her chest would burst with pride when Becca, wearing her otter swimsuit, dived into the deep end and swam the length of the pool with no assistance, only a few strokes behind Charlotte and three others.

"Wow, look at Becca go," Jessie commented. "You'd never know that she just started swimming a month ago."

"I know." Rowan beamed. "Charlotte's doing really well, too," she added quickly.

Jessie gave a knowing laugh, grabbed a towel and went to meet Charlotte. Rowan followed suit. When Becca climbed from the water, Rowan wrapped the towel around her and gave her a big hug. "You're amazing!"

The counselor came to them and handed over a blue ribbon. "Congratulations, Becca. You've earned your dolphin ribbon."

Becca couldn't have looked happier if she'd won the lottery. They ate sack lunches at the day camp area, and then loaded onto the bus that carried them to the reserved overnight campground.

It had been a long time since Rowan had been to camp, but she found it hadn't changed all that much. A hike around the small lake next to the campground, a game of kickball, a hot dog roast around the campfire. Camp songs and stories, although Rowan noticed none were ghost stories. Probably wise, if they expected a group of seven- to nine-year-olds to sleep tonight.

Now, in August, the days were getting shorter. While some counselors were leading the singalong, others set up the tents. Becca and Charlotte were assigned to tent number six, along with Rowan and Jessie. By ten, the four of them left the campfire, made a trip to the bathhouse and were heading to the tents when Jessie remembered she'd left her phone at the fire ring. "Go on ahead. Charlotte and I will be right there."

Rowan and Becca continued down the path and had just cleared the woods at the edge of the lake when the sun dropped behind the mountain. Huge orange and purple streaks painted the clouds and were reflected in the lake. Rowan stopped, spellbound.

Becca's small hand slipped into hers. "Pretty."

She squeezed Becca's hand. "It sure is." They stood there together until the colors began to fade. The distinctive cry of a loon carried across the water. Rowan had been all over the world, seen many beautiful sunsets, but there was something very special about this one. How many more Alaska sunsets would she see?

Jessie and Charlotte caught up and they found their way to their assigned tent. Becca tucked Zuma into his sleeping bag while Rowan and Jessie blew up the air mattresses. Finally, they all crawled into their bags and whispered their good-nights. After such an active day, it was no surprise when the two girls fell asleep almost immediately. Jessie and Rowan weren't far behind.

All was dark when Rowan was awakened by a nudge. "Rowan," Becca whispered. "What's that sound?"

"Shh, don't wake Charlotte and Jessie." Rowan lay still and listened until she heard the distinctive hoot. "It's an owl."

"Are you sure?" Becca inched closer. "It might be a ghost."

So much for Rowan's theory that skipping ghost stories would make the kids sleep better. "I'm sure," Rowan told her. "But if you want to come cuddle, you can."

Rowan didn't have to ask twice. Within less than a minute, Becca and Zuma were sharing the sleeping bag Rowan had borrowed from Patrick. She smoothed Becca's hair. "Feel better?" Becca didn't answer because she'd already fallen asleep.

After breakfast the next morning, the counselors announced an exercise where each girl and her adult partner would use a compass and map to look for a hidden prize.

"A treasure map," Becca whispered in wonder when the counselor handed her the paper. "Just like in that book Linda gave me."

"Do you know how to use a compass?" Charlotte asked Becca after she got her map.

"No, but Rowan does," Becca answered. Rowan was touched at Becca's faith in her skills. She just hoped she remembered how.

"Listen up, campers," a counselor called through a bullhorn. "Each map leads to a different cache. Inside you'll find a token with a number that matches the number on your map. Turn them in here to collect your prize. Make sure your token and your map match, because if you get someone else's token, it won't count. You have two hours. Go!"

Rowan read over the instructions. "First we need to find a double-crowned cottonwood tree." She pointed to the map. "It looks like it's next to a building."

"The bathhouse?" Becca suggested.

"That's the only building I've seen around here."

"Come on." Becca grabbed Rowan's hand and took off running toward the bathhouse. Rowan laughed and ran with her. All round them, pairs were scattering, looking for landmarks.

They reached the bathhouse. "Which tree is it?" Becca asked.

Rowan looked around. "Spruce, spruce, birch, don't know that one, pussy willow… This might be it."

Becca looked up. "Is it wearing a crown?"

"No, double crown means the top broke off and two tops grew back." Rowan backed up enough to see the top of the tree. "Yes, it has two crowns. Your turn. Read number two."

"Go north fifty paces. What are paces?"

"Steps. So, let's see. We'll start here against the trunk of the cottonwood and look at our compass. It points north. That direction." She gestured down a trail that led into the woods. "Let's count."

Rowan wasn't sure how long a pace should be, but hopefully the counselors took the children's shorter legs into account. She let Becca pace it off. "…forty-eight, forty-nine, fifty."

Rowan checked the instructions. "Look up at the blue."

"The sky?" White clouds floated in the spaces

between the trees, but that didn't give them any information.

Rowan eventually spotted a ditty bag hanging from a limb about ten feet in front of them, just past a junction in the trail. "Look!"

"It's blue!" They ran toward the bag. Inside was another note. "Return the way you came for three paces and then turn west for forty paces."

Becca looked at the compass. "West is that way. Let's go!"

Rowan watched Becca devour the clues as they led them all around the campground. Whoever had devised this hunt couldn't possibly have picked a better activity for Becca. Anything to do with clues, codes or hidden secrets was catnip to her. Her father must have shared her interests, since he gave her the bookshelf with the hidden compartment behind the fancy trick molding.

Rowan stopped short, suddenly remembering where she'd seen molding like that before. And if she was right—

"Rowan, come on." Becca tugged at her arm. "We have fifteen more paces to go."

"Just one minute." Rowan pulled out her phone. "I need to make a quick call to Zack. And then we'll find your treasure."

AFTER CAMP WAS dismissed a few hours later, Rowan pulled into the circular drive outside

Thomas Vogel's big house. The lawn looked freshly mown, and no weeds grew at the base of the twin dwarf Alberta spruce trees that flanked the front entryway. The landscape service must still be coming.

Rowan got out of the car and waited for Becca to join her on the porch. Orange hips were forming on the wild roses that separated the lawn from the forest behind. Funny that Clarissa would leave this house behind when people from all over the world flocked to Alaska for the summer.

"Why aren't we going in?" Becca asked.

"Zack is meeting us with the key. We're looking for some things Zack needs. Paperwork stuff." Becca had been thrilled with the wooden treasure box containing a roll of animal stickers she'd earned this morning, but the treasure hunt they were about to undertake might be worth much more. "I told Zack about the secret compartment in your bookcase. I hope that's okay."

"It's okay. Daddy wouldn't mind that you and Zack know about it."

"Oh, here he comes now."

Zack stopped his truck behind the jeep and got out. "How was the campout?"

"I got my dolphin ribbon," Becca told him, "and me and Rowan found treasure."

"Treasure, huh?" He exchanged amused

smiles with Rowan. "I want to hear all about that later." He unlocked the door, stepped inside and punched in the alarm code.

"Rowan said you want to see my secret hiding place." Becca followed him in.

"Yes, please."

"Come on." She led them up the stairs to her room and showed him the hidden button.

"I never would have recognized it," Zack admitted. "What happens when you push it?"

She pressed the button, and the molding lifted to expose the compartment underneath. "See?"

"That is so cool. I was trying to remember how long you've had this bookshelf."

"Daddy gave it to me for my birthday when I was five."

"So almost three years ago. That fits." He glanced at Rowan with barely contained excitement. "Dad had his first heart attack a little over three years ago."

"Do you want to see what I hid?" Becca asked.

"Of course."

Rowan could tell he was dying to get downstairs, but instead he admired each rock and feather as Becca explained where she found it and why she liked it. He raised his eyebrows over Zuma's "fancy" collar, reinforcing Rowan's suspicion that those weren't rhinestones, but his only comment was, "Zuma sure is a lucky puma."

It wasn't until she'd gone over every item, returned them to the box and closed the hidden compartment that he stood. "Why don't you pick out a couple more books to read tonight while Rowan and I go downstairs."

"Okay." Becca pulled a pillow to the bookshelf and began sorting through her collection.

Zack and Rowan hurried to the fishing room and examined the base molding. It matched! But the cabinets were built in and spanned the room, wall to wall, so there was no way to reach the same position where Becca's hidden button was located.

"See anything that looks like a button?" Zack asked.

"Not immediately."

"I suppose I could just try to pry it off," Zack said. "Although I hate to tear up such nice cabinets."

"Let's keep looking. Do you have the keys? Maybe the latch is inside."

Zack pulled out the small keys to unlock the glass doors. Together, they emptied all the rods, reels, nets and other fishing tackle to expose the shelf and brackets. Inch by inch, they ran their hands over the surfaces, looking for anything out of place.

"Let's try the next one," Zack suggested. "Maybe he only built it into one of the cabinets."

Rowan started to close the door and stopped. Was that screw head on the hinge inside the cabinet a slightly different color? "Wait." She touched the screw, and it seemed to give a little. She pressed harder, something clicked, and the molding popped up.

"It worked!" The flashlight Zack pulled from his pocket illuminated a stack of papers with a blue cover.

He lifted the first page and read aloud. "Last Will and Testament for Thomas James Vogel." He flipped to the end. "Signed and witnessed three years ago. I can't believe you found it!" He looked up at Rowan with an expression of wonder. "You really are a miracle worker."

ONCE AGAIN, ZACK sat at the same table in the same conference room at the lawyer's office, but this time he hadn't bothered with a tie. This time, thanks to Rowan, he had the cards. Which wasn't to say Clarissa's parental rights didn't carry weight, but the new documents they'd discovered should tip things in their favor. He hoped.

However, he also didn't have Rowan at his side. She'd wanted to come, but he knew at the first sign that Clarissa wasn't cooperating, Rowan would abandon her own interests to help him, and that wasn't fair. Instead, he'd asked if Rowan could take Becca and Charlotte for the day, now that camp was over and school not starting for another four days, and, of course, she'd agreed.

Clarissa was late. Zack shuffled his copies of the documents. The new will left Clarissa the amount specified in the prenup, the fishing collection to Zack and everything else to Becca in trust with Zack as trustee. In the hidden compartments in the other cabinets, he and Rowan had found the trust document and a copy of the prenuptial agreement that Clarissa had signed. They'd also found a note explaining that the will and trust were officially signed and witnessed, but they were duplicates of another set of original documents located in the office safe. Dad must have been afraid they might disappear, but as to why he'd never told Zack about the hiding place—he supposed he'd never know. Maybe that was what Dad had been trying to tell Zack in the hospital.

Clarissa and her lawyer whisked into the room at ten after the hour. "Sorry to keep you waiting," her lawyer said, as he opened his briefcase and removed some documents before sitting down. "I understand you have questions for us before the custody hearing tomorrow."

"First, we want to provide you with copies of

newly discovered documents." Teagarden picked up a stack of papers and handed them over.

"What documents?" the lawyer asked as he accepted the stack.

"A will and a trust agreement dated three years ago that revoke the previous will."

"But that's impossible," Clarissa burst out. "I—" She stopped talking when her lawyer put a hand on her arm.

He frowned as he glanced over the first page, and then flipped to the dated signature page. "Where did these come from?"

"They were in a secure location in Thomas's fishing collection room. A copy of the prenuptial agreement was also present."

"Where?" Clarissa demanded. "We looked through the cabinets there, and all we found was fishing equipment. Remember, Zack?"

"Yes. But it turns out those cabinets had a hidden compartment." Zack explained how they had found the papers. "I've got pictures if you need them."

The lawyer ignored him as he skimmed over the terms of the will in his photocopy, frowning. "May I see the signature page of that document?"

"Of course. We've already checked the signature and witnesses, and they appear to be in good order." Teagarden set the will Zack had recovered on the table between them and the lawyer flipped to the end to examine the inked signature.

"These aren't real," Clarissa declared. "They can't be." The look she gave Zack held more confusion than anger. "Why are you doing this, Zack?"

"The terms are clear," Teagarden said smoothly. "The corpus of the estate is to be held in trust for Becca, with Zack acting as trustee," Teagarden said. "Thomas obviously wanted to provide for Becca."

Clarissa's face crumpled. "But what about me?"

Zack had no answer. The prenup, invested wisely, would have yielded enough to support Clarissa in a modest lifestyle for the rest of her life, but she'd already spent a big chunk of it.

Clarissa turned on Zack. "You just want to keep all the money, and Becca, too. Well, you can't have her. I'm her mother. We'll see what the judge says at the hearing tomorrow." She flounced out of the room.

Her lawyer hastily began stuffing papers into his briefcase.

"We'll need that original will, please," Teagarden said, before it joined the copies.

Clarissa's lawyer handed it back. "You've certainly blindsided us here. We may need to re-schedule the hearing."

"Understandable," Teagarden agreed.

"I'll be in touch." With a nod to Zack, he left the room.

Zack blew out a breath. "That didn't go as well as I'd hoped."

"Oh?" Teagarden seemed amused. "I wouldn't worry. I suspect we'll be hearing from them shortly."

TWO LITTLE GIRLS romping with baby goats—did it get any cuter? Rowan had recruited Becca and Charlotte to tie ribbons on a few of the kids and play with them while she captured shots of the goats for the website, but she couldn't resist photographing the girls as well as they played and laughed.

Rowan laughed, too, but she wasn't able to keep her mind off of Zack and his conference today. Finding the documents that left the bulk of their father's estate to Becca with Zack as trustee would take away any financial motivation Clarissa might have to retain custody, but it wouldn't guarantee that Clarissa would allow Becca to stay in Alaska with Zack.

"Rowan, look!" A spotted kid with a red bow had jumped onto Becca's narrow shoulder and somehow balanced there, teetering but not falling.

"Love that!" Rowan snapped several shots before the goat jumped down. A surge of love warmed her heart. No matter what Zack said, Rowan was going to that custody hearing tomorrow. Becca was too important to leave anything to chance. Besides, Rowan had a plan. Now she just needed to sell it to Zack.

Hearing a vehicle, she looked up to see Zack's truck pull up near the farmhouse. She waved to let him know they were over by the tasting room. He waved back and walked toward them.

Halfway to the goats' pen, he pulled his phone from his pocket and stopped to answer it. He nodded and shifted his weight, nodded again, and then a slow grin spread across his face. He laughed—she couldn't hear the sound, but she could see it—and then he hung up.

The girls, still occupied with the goats, hadn't noticed his approach. Rowan met him a few steps away so they could talk privately. "Looks like good news."

"Teagarden just got a call from Clarissa's lawyer. They're not going to fight the current will, and Clarissa is willing to give me full custody."

"That's wonderful!" Rowan threw her arms around him.

He hugged her back. "It is, isn't it? They're drawing up the custody papers now."

"So, Clarissa gave up, just like that?"

"Not at first. When she saw the will, she stomped out of the meeting and I got the impression she was going to fight to her last breath. But her lawyer must have advised her differently, because thirty minutes later, we got the call."

"What changed her mind, do you think?"

"Teagarden said something about a document saying we don't intend to press charges against Clarissa."

"Charges for what?"

"Fraud. It is a felony to destroy a will. The letter we found makes it clear the will and trust should have been in the safe. It would be hard to prove she destroyed it, but I guess she doesn't want to take that chance."

"So, it's all over?"

"It's over," Zack agreed, but suddenly he didn't look as happy. "We need to talk. Can you come over tonight after I put Becca to bed?"

"I'll be there."

NATURALLY, BECCA WANTED an extra chapter that evening, but Zack eventually got her settled in. Fluff, curled up on her pillow, looked at Zack and winked, as though she knew all about his clandestine meeting with Rowan.

Downstairs, he put a kettle on. He was putting tea bags in mugs when the back door opened. "Okay if I come in?" Rowan asked softly.

"Hi. I was just making us some of that herbal tea you like." He poured water over the tea bags and handed her a mug. "Let's take this outside."

She smiled. "Let's."

They sat together on the bench, as they had so many times before, but tonight Zack made sure there was a space between them, even though what he really wanted was to pull her close and never let her go. Rowan took a sip of tea and set her mug on the table. "So, you wanted to talk?"

"Yes. My lawyer is drawing up custody papers. Once Clarissa has signed them, we're done. I mean, we still have to file and finish the estate and all that, but the decision is final." Zack set his tea down and turned the handle until it was parallel to hers while he gathered his courage. "I could ask him to draw up annulment papers, too."

A furrow formed between her eyebrows. "Is that what you want?"

No! But… "I think it's best. It leaves you free to get on with your life. I know we said a year, but I have custody, and you have this great opportunity."

Rowan fixed his eyes in a steady gaze. "What if I said I don't want an annulment, now or ever? What if, instead, I'd like to make this a real marriage? What would you say?"

He couldn't let her throw away her opportunity. "I don't—"

"You said you love me."

"I do. That's why I don't want you to sacrifice your career for me. My mother—"

She held up her hand. "Stop. I'm not your mother, and your logic is flawed. You can't protect me from making a sacrifice. That's how life works. You come to a Y in the road. If you go left, you sacrifice the right. Go right, you lose the left."

"But you can look down the road and try to decide which way leads to a better outcome. This is your opportunity—"

"Exactly. My opportunity. My decision." Her voice held conviction. "This last week while we've been apart, I've put in a lot of thought, I've done research, and I even called a special meeting of the Now and Forever Farms board." She gave a wry smile. "Granted, the board consists of Lauren, Patrick, Gran and me, so that wasn't hard to arrange. Anyway, I've come to that Y in the road, but instead of left or right, I believe I've figured out a way to make a new path. May I tell you my plan?"

"Please do."

"The four-year program West Coast Culinary offers is to prepare students for a career as chefs or restaurant managers. Chef is a highly competitive occupation, and the hours are brutal. I don't want that. But they also offer short courses, and there's a four-week intensive class in October on mobile food businesses."

"Mobile?"

"In Japan, they have *yaki imo*, like ice cream trucks, but they sell roasted sweet potatoes. Here, it's food trucks."

"Food trucks," Zack said thoughtfully.

"They're extremely popular right now, and the demand in Alaska far exceeds the supply. The board agrees with me that a Now and Forever Farms truck that specializes in cheese dishes could be great advertising for the farm's products as well as a profitable business on its own. I plan to develop a menu targeting the lunchtime working crowd. On weekends, I could offer mobile catering for outdoor parties and events."

He found himself nodding along. Her excitement was contagious. He'd pictured her in an upscale restaurant, but she didn't care about that. She just liked creating great food. "It sounds like an excellent plan."

"And the best part is it leaves late afternoon and evenings free to spend with my favorite people in the whole world." She reached for his hand.

"I sincerely hope you're not talking about your grandmother and her friends."

She laughed. "They're close seconds." She touched the wedding band on his finger. "I love you. I love your sister. Our agreement was for a year, but I want more. What would you say to a fifty-year contract with a renewal clause?"

He pretended to consider. "Nope, not good enough. I want the whole enchilada. Rowan, will you be my wife? For real? For a lifetime?"

She pressed her hand to his cheek and gave him the smile he loved so much. "I will."

He pulled her into his arms and tasted that sweet, sweet mouth. All his doubts and fears floated away as she responded, holding nothing back. She was his, and he was hers, and life was good.

The jingle of tags reminded him that he'd forgotten to lock the dog in the house again. But this time, Rowan was ready. She pulled a rawhide chew from her pocket and tossed it into the yard. Ripley dashed after it.

"My wife is as smart as she is beautiful," he whispered as he brushed a strand of silky hair back from her face.

Rowan's dimple flashed. "You're lucky to have her."

He brushed his lips over that adorable dimple. "Luckiest man alive."

EPILOGUE

ZACK HAD TO ADMIT, his mother-in-law threw a great party. Rowan had retained control of the menu, but she'd handed over all the other details of their six-month anniversary party-wedding reception into her mother's capable hands. Vases of tulips and pussy willow branches dotted the tables in the hotel ballroom, a band tuned up near the dance floor, and all the people Rowan and Zack loved mingled and laughed. A waiter stopped to offer Zack something from a tray of appetizers.

"Try the crab mac and cheese balls," Zack's mom advised, taking two from the tray and handing one over. "I can't get over how delicious they are."

"King crab macaroni and cheese is one of the best sellers on Rowan's food truck."

"I can see why." Mom finished the bite and straightened Zack's lapel. "It's almost time for the feature dance with your bride. Are you ready?"

"Ready as I'll ever be." Zack wasn't much of

a dancer, but after some tutoring from his mom, he was feeling guardedly confident. Besides, he never turned down an opportunity to hold Rowan in his arms. But where was she? Rowan had wandered off a few minutes ago, mumbling something about seeing what her grandmother was up to.

A sudden disturbance on the stage drew Zack's attention. A cymbal teetered and then fell over with a crash, as a familiar dachshund popped out from the middle of the band. Becca ran onto the stage and tried to grab him, but succeeded only in knocking over a microphone stand. The dog jumped from the stage and dashed across the dance floor with Becca and Charlotte in hot pursuit, shedding flowers from their hair as they ran.

Zack moved into position to head him off, but before he got close Rowan stepped out onto the floor, scooped up the dog and turned to face her grandmother. "Yours, I believe?" She was trying to look stern, but the dimple in her cheek revealed her amusement.

"I couldn't leave Wilson home alone," Bonnie protested, taking the dog. "He's been a nervous wreck ever since the New Year's fireworks. Zack, back me up on this."

The dog, wagging his tail at warp speed, looked more delighted than frightened, especially when Becca and Charlotte arrived to coo over him. The musicians, on the other hand, did look a little traumatized.

"Girls, why don't you go play with Wilson over there away from the band." Zack pointed to the quietest corner of the room.

"Wait." Rowan's mom, who had picked up the fallen flowers, tucked them back into the girls' braids. The corners of her mouth tugged upward as she took the dog from Bonnie and passed him to Becca. "Thanks, girls. Zack, do you remember the order of the dances?"

"Yes, ma'am." Renee had taken them through a rehearsal yesterday. Zack's mom had confided, with admiration, that most of the shows she'd performed in were less well choreographed than this party.

The band, once they'd righted their equipment, announced the first dance. "There's your cue." Renee gave Zack a nudge.

He swallowed, but when Rowan turned to smile at him, his nerves vanished. He took her into his arms and, as the music began, swept her onto the dance floor. Everyone applauded as they waltzed around the room, the skirt of her long velvet dress flaring around her.

"Thanks for being such a good sport about this whole ballroom dancing thing," Rowan whispered as they made their third pass. "It was important to Mom."

"As long as I don't have to make a speech, we're good."

Rowan laughed as the song came to an end and the second one began. Rowan's father stepped up for the next dance. "Ready, Rosebud?"

"Ready, Dad." They floated off, leaving Zack to claim his dance with his mother-in-law.

"Rowan looks radiant," Renee commented as she rested her hand on his shoulder and they took their first steps.

"Yes." Zack looked over to see Rowan's face alight with laughter over something her father had said. "But then, she's always smiling."

"That's true now, but before…" She trailed off as they executed a planned spin move. "My plans for Rowan never involved her living permanently in a small Alaska town and selling food from a truck, but this life suits her." He could see traces of Rowan's smile in her mother's. "You make my daughter happy, you and Becca, and even if I didn't like you, I'd love you for that."

"Um, thanks?"

Renee chuckled. "I said *if.* I do like you, Zack. Rowan chose well, better than I would have chosen for her. The way you look at her, it's obvious you adore her." As the music ended, she patted his cheek. "You're a good husband, Zack-ery Vogel."

A good husband. He'd laughed when Jessie had said it last summer, but now he knew he would give his life to make Rowan happy, and she would do the same for him. Together, they could face anything life might throw at them. Marriage—to the right person—was awesome.

Now that the feature dances were over, Zack was able to relax and enjoy the party. Maggie and her friend Tom twirled by. Zack's mom had paired up with Gordon Malee, the wildlife photographer, and judging from their fancy moves, this wasn't his first rodeo. Even the ladies from Bonnie's yoga class were bopping around, taking turns dancing with the one surviving husband, and having a great time. Rowan laughed as her brother swung her around, the sound sweeter than any music, at least to Zack's ears.

Later in the evening, Zack spotted Daphne whispering to the bandleader. A moment later, the Chicken Dance began to play. Daphne pulled Becca, Charlotte and Tony onto the dance floor and went back for more recruits. Soon Rowan, her mother, Bonnie and a dozen others were flapping their wings to the music. When Zack laughed, Rowan dragged him in, too. "Come on, shake those tail feathers."

The Chicken Dance wasn't one Zack's mom

had taught him, but he tried anyway, sending Becca into such a fit of giggles she could hardly stand up. When the song ended, the band segued into an old country waltz. Before Zack could claim Rowan for the dance, he spotted Wilson trying to climb up in a chair to reach a plate of appetizers someone had left on a table. Rowan stepped in to move the plate out of his reach.

"I'll take him," Charlotte volunteered.

"Thanks." Rowan chuckled as Charlotte and Becca whisked the disappointed dog away. "You know Gran only brought him to irk my mom."

"If so, it doesn't seem to be working." Zack nodded toward Rowan's parents, smiling into each other's eyes as they waltzed together. "She's been surprisingly mellow."

"I know," Rowan agreed. "It's like a miracle."

"Well, you are the miracle worker." Zack gazed at his beautiful bride. "You took in an insecure little girl and an overwhelmed veterinarian, and turned us into a happy family. And you do it again every single day." He slipped an arm around her waist. "I love you, Rowan."

That dimple appeared. "I love you, too."

Maggie and Tom stepped off the dance floor. "What a great party. You know, Zack," Maggie said with a twinkle in her eye, "proposing to Rowan may just be the smartest thing you've ever done."

"Actually," Rowan told her, "I proposed to him."

"Is that so?" Maggie smirked. "Maybe he's not as smart as I thought."

Zack grinned. "Maybe not. But even I was smart enough to figure out that when the most incredible woman in the world offers to spend the rest of her life with you—" Zack pressed a kiss to Rowan's temple "—the correct answer is 'yes.'"

* * * * *

For more great romances in
Beth Carpenter's Northern Lights series,
check out www.Harlequin.com today!